# THE HOMETOWN COP'S FOREVER FAMILY

TARA RANDEL

HEARTWARMING

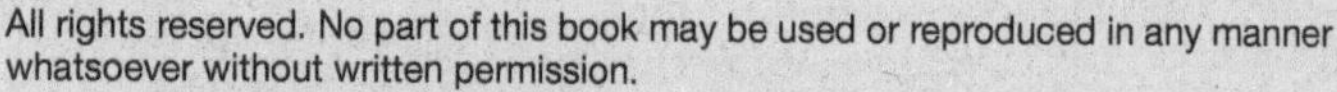

Recycling programs for this product may not exist in your area.

ISBN-13: 978-1-335-46044-8

The Hometown Cop's Forever Family



For questions and comments about the quality of this book, please contact us at CustomerService@Harlequin.com.

Harlequin Enterprises ULC
22 Adelaide St. West, 41st Floor
Toronto, Ontario M5H 4E3, Canada
www.Harlequin.com

HarperCollins Publishers
Macken House, 39/40 Mayor Street Upper,
Dublin 1, D01 C9W8, Ireland
www.HarperCollins.com

**Printed in U.S.A.**

**Cami flung herself at Jax.**

"Thank you," the little girl said, squeezing as hard as a four-year-old could manage. His heart melted, and he crouched down to envelop her. When Brie cleared her throat, he stood.

"It's time to get ready for bed," Brie announced.

"Oh, Mommy. Do I have to?"

Brie nodded. "You do. Go get in your jammies and I'll tell you a story."

"Can Jax read to me tonight?"

If his heart hadn't already been lost to this little girl, her invitation finished the job.

"Um...sure," Brie said. "I'll clean up in the kitchen while you're reading."

He watched Cami race from the room. Panic set in. "Brie, I've never read to a child. I don't..."

She laughed. "It's not rocket science."

"But it's important."

Brie slipped her hand in his and gave an affectionate squeeze. "Just use funny voices. And read the bunny book. It's her favorite."

He smiled.

"I'm ready!" Cami's muffled voice came from the other side of the house.

Brie pointed in the direction of her daughter's bedroom. "You can do this, hero."

Dear Reader,

I have always loved watching police procedural television shows. Whether it's seeing how criminals are apprehended or solving the mystery behind a crime, I'm glued to the screen until there are answers.

Now, in my favorite town of Golden, I've brought together two officers who are investigating a crime. It's always fun to decide what the offense will be and how the criminal will pull it off. But from the law enforcement angle, it's challenging to take all the information and figure out who did it.

Enter Briana Connelly and Jax Walker, who have been friends their entire lives. This is the first time they are working as partners. And while both are excited about the prospect of serving and protecting together, a pesky attraction starts to simmer between them. What will that do to their friendship? Will it affect how they work on the case? All reasonable questions that they must navigate while on the trail of the suspect.

Sit back, put your feet up, and join Briana and Jax as they work as a team, fighting crime in the mountain town I love, while juggling life, love and happiness.

Happy Reading!

*Tara*

**Tara Randel** is an award-winning, *USA TODAY* bestselling author. Family values, a bit of mystery and, of course, love and romance are her favorite themes because she believes love is the greatest gift of all. Tara lives on the west coast of Florida, where gorgeous sunsets inspire the creation of heartwarming stories. Tara has received the Heart of Excellence Readers' Choice Award and the National Excellence in Romance Fiction Award. For more information about her books, visit Tara at tararandel.com and like her on Facebook at tararandelbooks.

## Books by Tara Randel

### Harlequin Heartwarming

***A Golden, Georgia Romance***

*The Surprise Next Door*
*The Single Mom's Second Chance*

***The Golden Matchmakers Club***

*Stealing Her Best Friend's Heart*
*Her Christmastime Family*
*His Small Town Dream*
*Her Surprise Hometown Match*

Visit the Author Profile page at Harlequin.com for more titles.

To the men and woman in law enforcement
who serve and protect. Thank you for your sacrifice
and willingness to keep us safe.

# PROLOGUE

"COME ON, BRIE. It's a brilliant idea."

"I don't know, Jax."

The chilly midnight air swirled around them as they huddled together with their backs snug against the cement base of the bronze pickax and gold nugget monument in deserted Gold Dust Park. The damp grass seeped into the seat of Jax's jeans, but he ignored the discomfort. A few stars winked overhead in the hazy black sky, the moon fading in and out as thick clouds scuttled by. Both had snuck out of their respective homes, meeting up so Jax could pitch his plan.

"I'm leaving on Monday for boot camp."

She glowered at him, her long blond hair with blue streaks loose around her face, lifting from her cheeks as a gusty wind swept by. "You don't have to remind me."

They'd been friends since first grade. This was going to be the first real separation they'd experienced. The first time they couldn't walk down the street to each other's house to hang out. Jax would be in another state. He wasn't thrilled about being far from Briana, but he was excited to see what a military career in the Army would offer him. After all, Gramps had harped on the idea of duty and giving back for Jax's entire life.

"Come with me," he blurted.

She blinked in surprise.

"Look, I know going into the military means we won't see each other every day, but it's what I want."

"And I've never tried to talk you out of it."

She hadn't. And she hadn't been shocked when he'd initially come to his decision. It was no surprise that he wanted something bigger than life, bigger than Golden. It was the idea of being apart that threw them for a loop.

"Which I appreciate," he continued, placing clenched fists on his thighs. "You coming with me solves a lot of problems." He swiveled so that he was facing her head-on. "Ever since your dad left, you've been hurt and unsure of yourself. All you've talked about is how hard it is living in Golden and how your relationship with your sisters has unraveled. Coming with me once I get stationed will get you out of Golden, away from all the drama that's making you miserable."

She dropped her head. Picked at the hem of her sweater. "Jax, it's so sudden."

"Because I just thought of it." He sent her his most charming smile. "But you gotta admit, the idea has its merits."

Brie jumped up, pacing now. She still hadn't

given him an answer and it worried him. Usually, he could read her better.

"I don't know," she hedged. "We're only twenty. I don't know if I'm ready to leave Golden."

The darkness pressed upon him, but he couldn't give up on his pitch. They'd done everything together since they were six years old. How could all that change now?

"If you join me, it'll give you time away. You can get perspective about everything."

"I don't need any more perspective. My dad left us. For another woman." She let out a broken sigh. "And then to find out I have a half sister?"

Briana had been twelve when she discovered she had a sister six years younger than her. A sister her father hadn't mentioned until after he left the family.

"This is why I'm suggesting you come with me. You need a change of scenery."

She shook her head and spoke in a tone so quiet he strained to hear her. "My mom is trying to hang on for us, but she's not sure what to do next. She's a shell of the woman who has always been there for me and my sisters."

Jax rose, walking over to place a hand on Brie's shoulder to stop her frantic pace. His heart hurt for her, for her family. He might get lost in the shuffle with all his brothers and sisters, but his folks were there for each other and the siblings.

"Yeah, it stinks what he did." He hated that her dad made her so uncertain, so small. When Jax drew her into adventures and scrapes to satisfy her innate curiosity about life, Brie had been the first on the hiking paths in the woods to find undiscovered routes. They'd gotten into harmless mischief together, were side by side during life's struggles. After her dad left the family, it was like the candle flame had flickered out, leaving her with no inner light. "I know you two were close and how his betrayal affected you. I'm sorry your mom is taking it so hard." He placed his other hand on her shoulder, gazing into her eyes. "Don't you see? I'm trying to protect you, Brie."

She frowned. "I don't need your protection."

He recoiled. "Since when?"

"Since I found out the world can hurt you and I'm the only one who can control what happens to me," she snapped.

Shocked by her response, he dropped his hands. This wasn't Brie at all. With as much patience as possible, he gentled his tone. "I'm not telling you what to do. I'm looking out for you. I really think leaving is in your best interest, Brie."

Her shoulders slumped. Was he reaching her?

"I'm already halfway through this semester of college classes."

He hadn't expected Brie to be so stubborn. Okay, this was Brie so he should have known better, but… He tried another angle.

"You can finish somewhere else. Once I get settled and you join me, we'll take on the world like we always said we would."

Bitterness laced her tone. "It sounded better when we were full of ourselves and didn't think anything bad could touch us."

She wasn't wrong with that thinking. They thought they were invincible. Even with all the scrapes they'd gotten through together, the troublemaking and the good times, life had proven them wrong.

She faced him, her eyes clear. He recognized that dogged look and swallowed hard, waiting for what came next.

"Jax, I know this is coming from a good place. We've been friends our entire lives and I appreciate the offer, but my mom needs me. So do my sisters, even if they can't see the truth of it right now."

His heart sank. "I'm confused. Ever since that day we met at the school lunch table, it's been you and me. We've always been in agreement. Always had each other's back. Why would this time be different?"

She pulled her hair back and collected it in one hand. "You don't even know where you'll be stationed. It could be clear across the country." She dropped the handful of waves and shook her head. "No. I can't. I need to look out for my mom."

While he understood her loyalty to her mother, this was the first time she'd said no to him. To his dismay, her refusal changed everything he believed about them.

Another gust of wind swept by. He shivered, tugging the collar of his jacket closer to his neck. The chill went deeper than skin level.

He couldn't hide the tremor in his tone. "You're turning me down? You're not even going to consider it?"

"My family needs me, Jax. That's what is important right now."

For a moment he was at a loss for words. Brie's troubled expression pierced his soul. She wasn't wrong, but how did she expect to keep the family intact when her parents couldn't do it? She wasn't responsible for the mess they were in.

"You don't think I can do it," she challenged.

"I never said that."

"You didn't have to."

She clearly read the doubt on his face because she lifted her chin in a defiant angle. "That's my answer."

At her uncompromising tone, he knew he'd lost.

What would his world look like without Brie in it? She'd been there when his brother broke his ankle, and they dragged him home from the woods. When his father lost his job and Jax had worked at Linda's General Store because the family was worried about finances until his dad found another position. The myriad of secrets and dreams they'd shared. There was so much history between them. He hated having to find out what this new life would be like, but he was committed to the Army. He'd given his word and wouldn't back out now.

Pulling himself together, he managed to eke out a few words. "What am I going to do without my best friend?"

Her shiny gaze met his as she blinked back tears. "You'll be fine."

Would he? After his closest friend in the world had turned her back on his heartfelt request. What happened to the vow they'd made to always be there for each other?

Apparently, this time didn't count.

And with that she walked away, head held high, leaving Jax to wonder how he could have so poorly misjudged her reaction and why it felt like their strong connection was in jeopardy. His heart ached as Brie disappeared under the stone archway of the park, leaving him alone for the first time in their long friendship.

# CHAPTER ONE

BRIANA CONNELLY STROLLED into the Golden, Georgia, police department at 9:00 a.m., ready for her shift to begin. The office was brimming with activity: multiple phones ringing, officers on duty typing reports or speaking to citizens, typical for a midweek morning.

It was a small force, consisting of the chief and six officers. Briana loved the bond between the officers and residents. Assisting the people of Golden was more than a calling, it fulfilled a longing deep in her soul.

"Right on time," her boss, Police Chief Brady Davis, said as he exited his office with a file folder in hand. "Follow me to the conference room."

His request could only mean one thing. The identity of the newest addition to the PD was about to be revealed.

After Briana's partner had left to work with fire and rescue as a paramedic, it had been a hush-hush process to find a replacement, which was over the top for Brady. But he explained that he wanted to be sure the new hire would be a good fit for the department before introducing him or her to the others.

"I still don't understand why you haven't told me who it is," Briana griped.

"I didn't want to get ahead of myself. It took a lot of back-and-forth negotiations to get him to uproot his life and move here."

So, it was a guy.

Brady pointed in the direction of the conference room. "Besides, you were off for a few days when I confirmed the hire."

True. She'd taken a long weekend to spend quality time with her daughter. Most days she juggled a hectic schedule and from time to time took a long weekend to focus on Cami. They slept late, made their favorite meals and took lots of hikes in the surrounding woods of their community. The fall weather had tourists and locals alike enjoying the outdoors and the annual Octoberfest activities. The cooler temperatures and changing foliage were a major draw to Golden and one of the reasons why she had never left.

Since her daughter was only four, Briana didn't want to miss any milestones, a worry that came with working long hours and being a single mom. Brady did his best to accommodate her schedule, instilling his philosophy that a happy home life made for more productive officers.

Briana dropped her bag by her desk and hurried to catch up with Brady who was striding across the room. "He's finally here?"

"Yes," Brady said over his shoulder. "That's why I want you to join me."

More curious than ever, a trait that made her good at her job but often got her into trouble, Briana caught up and followed Brady into the room. She stopped short when a tall, dark-haired man rose from the chair. His piercing blue eyes, so very familiar to Briana, shone with an intensity she'd never admit she missed.

"Briana."

Her mouth dropped open, but she quickly regrouped to save face.

"Jackson?" she asked, trying to moderate her tone so the higher pitch didn't reach into the frequency only dogs heard.

"This isn't going to be awkward, is it?" Brady asked in a serious tone, a tone he rarely used unless he meant business. His gaze moved between the two.

She'd answer if she could find her voice.

When Brady told her he'd hired a new recruit for the department she'd been nervous but excited about meeting her new co-worker. She'd trained hard for her place on the PD so she could serve her town. Of all the people in the world she imagined would be her future colleague, Jax Walker, her best friend when they were growing up, was not it.

She didn't even know he'd come back to town. Which pinched her heart. The last time they'd crossed paths was this past summer when he'd visited for a brief period after his grandfather needed a medical procedure.

"No, um, we'll be fine," she mumbled, still trying to cover her shock.

"Good, because I'm making you partners."

She blinked at Jax, then at Brady. "So soon?"

"There's no time to waste. You're minus a partner since Evan left, so Jax will fill the slot. Besides, you already know each other."

That was an understatement. From first grade until Jax left to join the military, they'd been cohorts in all sorts of adventures. But their relationship had changed when she'd made the firm decision not to leave Golden to join him on a new quest.

"Yes," she challenged, "but we haven't been together in years."

"Are you questioning me, Officer Connelly?"

She stood straight. "No, sir."

"That's what I thought." Brady's serious expression vanished, and his small grin lifted the mood. "Everyone, please take a seat."

Briana pulled out a chair and dropped down as Jax lowered himself back into his seat. She couldn't help peeking out of the corner of her eye to assess her old friend. A million questions plagued her. Why hadn't he called to tell her he was taking the job? Why had he left his position with the security firm he'd worked for after leaving the military? What did this mean for them, working together when they'd never quite recovered from the separation they'd endured after he left for boot camp all those years ago? Sure, they'd glossed over her refusal to join him and had maintained a long-distance pseudo-friendship for all these years, but they'd never dealt with the issue that had created lasting doubt between them.

When Brady cleared his throat, she knew those answers would have to wait.

"I'm not going to give you much time to get used to things around here, Jax. In light of the movie prop collection tour arriving in only a few days, plus the crowds in town for Oktoberfest, we need to dive right in."

Jax nodded. "No problem. I adapt quickly."

"That's another reason I partnered you with Briana. She can show you the ropes as we jump into this new detail. Also, you've had experience with big-picture missions, and she's detail oriented. I think your strengths will mesh well."

Jax rested his elbows on the table and leaned forward, the sleeves of his navy shirt rolled to mid-forearm, revealing tan arms. The shirt brought out the deep blue of his eyes. She'd forgotten how mesmerizing his gaze could be.

"You said something about guarding props made of real gold when we spoke on the phone."

"Correct," Brady answered. "As Briana already knows, the town has been preparing to host a traveling display from the award-winning movie, *Riches of the Past*, which used gold mined in the mountains around Golden to create the jewelry used in the original film. With a remake of the movie soon to be released in theaters, the owners of the collection planned a major tour to stir up excitement for the brand-new production prior to returning the collection to Los Angeles in time for the red-carpet event. The final week of the nationwide tour ends here in Golden."

"So, not your usual props," Jax said.

"That's right," Briana said, now finding the wherewithal to join in the conversation. "The jewelry presents a problem in that it needs to be properly secured during the last leg of the tour in Golden."

Jax frowned. "Don't they have traveling security?"

"They do." Brady opened a file and removed some papers to slide toward Jax. "Which worked fine for the short stops along the tour, but the collection will stay in Golden for a week. We want extra eyes on the display to make sure nothing happens."

"Do you expect trouble?" Jax asked as he scanned the reports.

"There have been no specific problems as the tour has moved from city to city, but we currently have a larger than usual tourist population for Oktoberfest to take into consideration. The representative from the consortium that owns the collection wants extra security, which means the PD fills in where needed."

Jax looked up. "So we're already short on help?"

"Oktoberfest started a week ago," Briana went on to explain. They were halfway through October and Halloween was two weeks away. "I was working on that detail, but Brady wants me…us, to focus on keeping the gold collection safe."

"I've assigned my other officers to cover day-to-day duties along with Oktoberfest crowd control," Brady concurred. "I've contracted with the county for additional deputies to take the night shifts."

Jax continued reading then asked, "Why have two major events happening at the same time?"

"Two reasons," Briana explained. "The company bringing the movie collection picked the tour dates in Golden to coincide with the end of the nationwide tour. The Chamber of Commerce loves that the dates coincide with Oktoberfest. They want to make Golden a tourist destination by publicizing popular events. Having two back-to-back events fulfills that strategy."

"But in light of the value of the collection, we aren't taking any chances," the chief added.

Jax nodded. "Agreed."

Briana could almost imagine the wheels turning in Jax's head. He'd always been able to tackle a problem and find solutions. Considering his work in military intelligence, she expected that he'd grown even sharper over the years.

"There are all kinds of events planned in Golden during the week of the tour," Brady went on, "in honor of Golden's contribution to the original movie and to boast our town history. Throw Oktoberfest in and it's a logistical nightmare."

Golden had been established after the gold rush of 1835 when a vein of gold had been discovered in the surrounding mountains. Once the earth had been picked over, many moved to California, chasing after the lure of new gold deposits, but the few who stayed behind created the hometown Briana loved.

Jax flipped a page. "I see that the collection will be displayed at Mountain Spa Center."

"That's right. The resort and day spa has the largest multipurpose room to accommodate the crowd we're expecting. We like the fact that it's a bit of a drive since the resort is located on the outskirts of town. We're hoping to control crowd size which would have been overwhelming if the collection was featured downtown along with Oktoberfest and easily reached by foot traffic. After we're finished here, I need you and Briana to head over to the resort and speak to the manager to confirm the collection arrival, familiarize Jax with the layout of the building and grounds, arrange daily bank transport, etc."

"Wait." A frown marred Jax's forehead. "We're to transfer the gold from the resort to and from the bank every day. That doesn't make sense."

Brady emitted a long-suffering sigh as he rubbed his temples.

"The resort doesn't have a safe on the premises

big enough to store the collection each night," Briana clarified.

"And the rep for the consortium who owns the collection, Mason Franklin, is a stickler for being in the loop of our procedures." Brady dug through the file and slid another page Jax's way. "The insurance policy covering the collection states that the collection must be kept in a secure location like a bank, or its equivalent, with a vault. The resort can't accommodate that provision."

Jax held up the paper. "A one-page policy?"

"He only gave me a copy of that page to back his assertion that we need the transfer each night. To counter, I told him we'd follow the policy mandate, but the collection would only be displayed until 6:00 p.m. each evening. I don't want you driving through town with the collection late into the night."

"Except for the black-tie party for special donors on the second night of the tour," Briana reminded him.

"Correct. I'll have two officers deliver the collection each morning. You and Briana will take the later shift."

"Even though I'm catching up?" Jax asked.

"The collection will be here in two days. You'll need to get up to speed fast."

Jax sent him an incredulous look.

"Part of the reason it'll work is that you're familiar with Golden."

"I haven't lived here for fourteen years."

"True, but you still know the back roads and with your military experience, you'll figure things out quickly."

"Besides," Briana chimed in, "not much has changed in Golden."

Jax's frown countered that claim but he said, "I don't like the distance between the resort and the bank. Anything out of our control can happen."

A muscle ticked in Brady's jaw. "Franklin won't budge, and we need to do all we can to cooperate until the gold safely leaves town."

"It's not ideal but we'll make it work." Jax scanned the report. "There is a three-person staff traveling with Franklin?"

"Plus a small security team. They're all staying in resort guest rooms so they can be present during the visiting hours of the collection. You and Briana will arrive late in the afternoon and remain on the premises until the transfer. Each night we'll leave at a different time, no later than 7:00 p.m., giving the staff time to pack up the pieces, so there is no discernable pattern. Any would-be perp wouldn't know the schedule."

"Heather, the resort general manger," Briana said, "called to tell me that one member of the staff, Robert Long, has arrived before the rest of them to oversee the display particulars."

Jax nodded and kept reading.

Briana watched him, waiting for a spark of the old Jax to emerge. A reassuring smile. A wink. Anything that made the idea of partnering with him less daunting. Because it would be. She could feel it in her bones.

But that didn't happen. He was all business, with a seriousness she didn't recognize.

"Franklin was concerned about the size of the department, but I flat-out told him that the officers who serve on this PD are above reproach and competent to handle the job." Brady made a scoffing sound. "Like I would hire anyone without those qualities. We may be a small town, but we aren't clueless like this Franklin guy implies."

"Is he from LA?" Jax asked.

"Yeah. Guess that explains his big-city attitude."

Briana locked eyes with Jax. "All the officers have worked together for a long time, Jax. We're good at what we do."

He met her gaze, but she still couldn't read him. "Doesn't mean things can't go sideways."

"We're prepared," she insisted.

They stared for a drawn-out moment before he said, "That's why I agreed to sign on. Move back home."

"And we're happy to have you," Brady said as he rose and slapped Jax on the back. "You two need to get to work. Briana has been studying up on the collection pieces, how many there are and the value. She can fill you in on the way to the resort."

As soon as Brady left the room, Briana rose from her chair.

"Jackson? Why didn't you give me a heads-up?"

When he rolled his eyes, Briana wondered how

things could get more awkward or be more familiar at the same time. This was the Jax she was used to.

"Guess we really have been out of touch for too long if you're calling me Jackson. You only did that when you were mad at me."

"Or caught off guard, which I totally was."

He shrugged. "This was a last-minute decision. I can only guess that Brady didn't want to jump the gun until I was one hundred percent onboard."

"That sounds about right," she allowed, her hands gripping the back of the chair in front of her so tightly that her knuckles were white. "But you could have called me."

"Like you did before you adopted Cami?"

She grimaced and her shoulders dropped.

He ran a hand over his short black hair. "I'm sorry. That was harsh."

"But true."

He collected the papers on the desk and placed them in a pile. "I could have called, but this move was sudden. I was busy leaving a job, packing up my life and making sure that I had a place to stay once I got here."

She shifted her feet. "I never thought you'd come home."

Jax stood. "Gramps needs me."

Right. He'd come back for his beloved grandfather. Why did it bother her that he hadn't come home for her?

She shook off the selfish thought.

When Alvin Walker had been ill, Jax returned

for a brief time, but Briana hadn't seen him much. He'd been busy and she had Cami and the job. Excuses? Probably, much to her chagrin. The longer time went on, the more the distance grew between them.

"My mom told me that since Gramps got the pacemaker he's been going overboard, doing too much. He thinks this gives him a license to do what he wants at the expense of his health." Jax pushed his chair under the table. "The man is close to his eighties, for Pete's sake. I thought this was a good time to come home and ride herd on him."

Briana envisioned Mr. Walker's reaction. "Oh, he's going to love that."

"No, he won't, but he'll just have to deal."

She shook her head. "You two are so similar, like you came from the same mold. I'd love to be a fly on the wall during the conversation when you tell him he needs to slow down."

He shrugged. "I'm back whether he likes it or not."

"Is that the same for me?"

NOT SURPRISED BY her question, Jax tempered his response. Seeing Brie here, in the station where they would work together, delivered more of an emotional punch than he expected. "I get it. You would have liked advance notice."

It wasn't like he hadn't thought about it. In fact, the first call he'd planned to make was directly to Brie. But then he thought about the years that had stretched between, how their lives had become separate from one another, and decided to wait and see her when he got to town. Easier to decipher her reaction in person than over the phone.

"I need to finish filling out my employment papers. We can go to the resort afterward if that's okay with you."

She nodded. A slight frown marred her forehead.

Picking up the papers, he walked to the door.

"Are we going to discuss this?" she asked.

His back to her, he closed his eyes. There was a lot to say, but he wasn't ready. Yes, they'd stayed in touch over the years, but their interaction wasn't like before she'd turned him down. That night in the park had been a defining moment for him. Since then, they made important decisions exclusive of each other. Showing up in Golden, unannounced to her, added to the strain between them. But he was home. Now they were partners. Was that enough to establish what they'd lost?

Opening his eyes, he turned and caught a hint of jasmine. The exotic scent was new to him. "Let's get settled in this partnership first. The rest will follow."

She didn't seem convinced. If he was honest, he felt the same way.

Before they left the room he blurted, "You cut your hair."

Her hand flew to the short hairstyle.

"It's a short bob," she explained, her tone defensive. "Easy to manage."

She'd always worn her hair long, sporting different colors as fancy took her. The long bangs and shorter style flattered her high cheekbones and blue-green eyes that changed shade depending on her mood. It suited her but was another reminder of what he'd missed by not living in Golden.

She didn't respond after her brief answer. He opened the door and let her exit the room before him, out of sorts again.

They made their way back to the busy duty station, an open room with individual desks for each officer. Brady's office, his door closed, was located on the far side of the room. A visitor's foyer was situated just inside the main doors, with a reception area that separated the public from the staff. Mrs. Paxton, who had worked at the PD forever, manned the front desk with patience and a no-nonsense attitude that either set people straight or conveyed sympathy before even talking to an officer. She answered the phone and handled people with the same aplomb he remembered from his youth.

An officer rose to shake Jax's hand. "Roan Donovan. Glad to have you onboard." He pointed to an empty desk. "You're here."

"Thanks."

Before he had a chance to sit, a middle-aged woman approached and placed what seemed to be a ream of papers on his desk. "I'm Becky Holder. These are the forms you need to fill out and return to me."

"She's a cross between HR and office administrator," Roan informed him.

"That's my job," she told Jax then turned to Roan. "And you haven't handed in your latest arrest log."

"I'll get right on that, ma'am," Roan saluted before returning to his chair.

Becky pointed in the direction of Jax's desk. "I'd like them back before you leave for the day."

"I'll have it finished," he said, squelching an inward sigh over the paperwork.

Becky walked away as Jax sat to start the task at hand.

"A word of warning," Roan said in a loud stage whisper. "Becky is a stickler for reports returned in a timely fashion."

Jax found a pen and started on the first page. "Used to it. Seems like that's all we did in the military."

"Yeah. Heard you did three tours."

"I did. Recently worked in the private sector." He laughed. "Even they require paperwork."

"Probably the worst part of the job." Roan grinned. "Unless you're Briana," he said in a loud voice.

"I can hear you perfectly fine," she said, gaze glued to her computer screen.

Brady had assured him he'd fit in fine with his officers, despite the low-key tension between him and Brie. He'd worked with enough capable men and women during his time in the military to realize that while paperwork was dreaded, people in this profession knew it was part of the drill.

"As far as the department goes, there's Briana and me," Roan went on to say. "Wes and Kelli are out on a call. You'll meet them soon enough. Hank Jones normally works overnight, but with so much going on, Brady moved him to days until next month. A deputy sheriff will cover nights for now."

After that the conversation tapered off as the officers got busy. Roan eventually left on a call. Brady remained holed up in his office. Finally, Jax delivered the intake papers to Becky and returned to Brie's desk with a tan shirt in hand.

She looked over at him. "Becky gave you a uniform?"

"She did. I'll go change and we can leave."

First, he went outside to the back seat of his truck cab to rummage through the boxes of personal belongings he hadn't yet unpacked. There were some particular items he liked to carry while on duty. "I really need to get moved in," he muttered to himself, then went inside, changed and stopped at Brie's desk.

"Ready to head out?"

She held up a finger to signal one sec, then signed off of her computer and stuffed a folder in her bag before shouldering it. "All set." She tossed him a ring with keys. "You might as well drive. Prove that you remember the back roads."

He caught the ring, his competitive streak ramping up. Brie always knew how to provoke that side of him, whether it was a real dare or if she was just giving him a hard time.

"Squad cars are out back." She motioned to a door and headed that way. Before long they stepped into a prefect autumn day. He inhaled deeply. No matter where in the country he'd been stationed, no place had that distinctive scent he always associated with Golden. Fresh air, damp earth and pine. He slipped on his sunglasses against the sunny glare.

Once they reached a white SUV, they both got in and Jax started the engine.

"We have this one unmarked vehicle," Brie told him. "It'll serve our purposes when we transfer the gold each night. There's a locker bolted down in the back cargo area where we will store the collection en route."

As he pulled out of the lot, Jax glimpsed the local pub as they passed by. "Smitty's still the place to hang out?"

"It is. The food has really improved since Jamey's girlfriend joined him in the kitchen."

He checked the rearview mirror for traffic. "That's saying a lot since it was pretty good to begin with."

"You'll have to check it out."

He noticed she didn't invite him to go with her.

Golden's greater downtown consisted of six blocks of wide sidewalks built on an increasing incline. There were gift shops, restaurants, lodging, professional offices and the all-important, centrally located coffee shop. The buildings were painted in vivid colors. Old-fashioned lampposts lined the main street, supporting large planters overflowing with seasonal flowers. This month, gold and maroon zinnias burst from the planters.

As they drove down Main Street, she pointed out a few of the shops they'd frequented as kids and gave him a rundown of new merchants. As they passed Gold Dust Park, he could just make out the tents and tables set up for the Oktoberfest festivities that would be in full swing later in the day, which included food and music.

"Any trouble at the park?" he asked.

"There have been pickpocketing incidents which Roan is monitoring."

"Is that usual?"

"Not until this year. There are always minor infractions when you have this many people partying, but nothing serious."

Soon he made a turn to drive to the resort. Downtown gave way to residential streets which turned into swaths of wooded area with leaves that had a golden hue. He rolled down the window, inhaling the faint scene of woodsmoke.

He'd lived in Texas for the last couple of years, but as he steered the winding mountain roads, he realized how much he'd missed Golden. The small town, untouched woods and waterfalls, tall pine trees and scenic mountain overlooks were imprinted on his mind. Memories resurfaced at every turn, most of them including Brie. Growing up in this small town had molded Jax into the man he was today. Leaving Brie behind taught him that friendship was a bond one shouldn't let dissolve so easily.

If only he'd realized that before it was too late.

Well on their way to the spa resort, neither spoke about the job or Jax's return to Golden. He figured Brie would stay stubbornly mute, so he broke the awkward silence. "Tell me more about what is going to be displayed."

"It's quite something," she said, pulling a file from her bag. "The collection is a mishmash of styles from different time periods. The movie, *Riches of the Past*, was about a team of archaeologists who discover a major find in Egypt during the 1930s and then bring the artifacts back to New York City after enduring all sorts of upsets along the way. There's a mixture of styles in the film—the Egyptian jewelry the actors find on their quest and the art deco pieces the actors wear in the movie to reflect the period." She tapped the folder. "I have another folder with pictures and background of the entire collection for you to peruse."

"Thanks. I'll take a look later."

"Although the original film came out in the sixties, the collection has been in safekeeping ever since."

"What's included in the collection?"

Brie checked her file. "A collar necklace embroidered with beads to resemble Cleopatra's jewelry. It's spectacular." She shuffled some papers. "A gold choker with an amulet scarab. Scarabs were a popular symbol in ancient Egypt. The amulet was thought to give protection against evil, danger and disease. The gold is molded into a beetle design.

"There are multiple rings in varied designs, some with gemstones, mostly art deco worn by the actors on-screen. Five necklaces, various earrings, oh and the pièce de resistance, a solid gold tiara. While the gemstones on the tiara are fake, added during the filming of the movie, the diamonds are real."

"You've really done your homework."

Out of the corner of his eye he could see her tilt her head.

"Are you surprised?"

"Not really. You always were a wiz in school."

"My mom said it was because I was curious."

"Also true. But you've managed to turn that trait into a necessary quality for a police officer."

Her voice oozed confidence when she said, "It's really my niche, research and details."

"I recall hours spent studying with you."

She was silent, turning to stare out the window. Maybe he should limit references to their past.

After a brief moment, she returned to the conversation. "Throw in a glamorous gold lamé dress shot through with real gold thread, and the collection is complete." She closed her file. "That's why they need a bigger security vault than what the resort could offer."

"Worth?"

"If you have to ask, you can't afford it."

A small smile curved his lips. Typical Brie response.

"Does your answer have anything to do with the time we drove to Atlanta after graduation to have dinner at that fancy restaurant?"

Brie laughed, the first carefree expression that came off as real. "I thought you were going to fall out of the chair when the check came."

"No one told me that no prices listed on the menu meant the restaurant was out of my range," he groused.

"Thankfully your grandfather knew the restaurant and sent you with his credit card."

"Which took me a couple of paychecks to work off."

She poked his arm. "It was worth it."

He turned his head. Their gazes met and held. "So worth it."

After a moment, she cleared her throat. "Anyway, the value is significant." She paused, for effect, Jax figured. "The gold itself comes in at about fifty grand, give or take because of daily fluctuating values. Add in the diamonds and the number goes up."

Jax blew out a long whistle.

"Puts a new perspective on the job, doesn't it."

"You'd think there'd be more security traveling with the display."

Brie closed the file. "Since the other stops on the tour were shorter and they're working with local police, Mr. Franklin might not have thought it was necessary."

"He's in charge. Gotta hope he knows what he's doing."

Silence filled the vehicle as Jax's mind ran over every possible scenario, good or bad. He stopped on one question his mind kept returning to.

"Why did they make all these props out of real gold? Wouldn't it have been easier and safer to make copies of the original designs? A moviegoer wouldn't know the difference."

"There's a story behind it." She shifted in the seat. "Do you remember the Forsythe name?"

"Yeah. They were instrumental in establishing Golden's beginning years."

"They had a large stake in the gold recovery in the mountains. Became super wealthy. Mrs. Forsythe had an interest in the movie industry and dreamed of becoming a star. They moved to LA so she could indulge her passion but from what I could uncover, she didn't make much of a splash in the film world. When they were casting for *Riches of the Past*, she offered to have the pieces made of actual gold to bring authenticity to the movie."

Jax came to a stop sign. He braked, glanced left and right, then eased the accelerator. "And?"

"You think there's more?"

"I doubt she offered out of the goodness of her heart. That's a lot of gold."

Brie chuckled. "You'd be right. She offered it in exchange for a part in the movie. The producers jumped at the idea because they could promote the movie and the gold, and she was in. Sadly, it was her only notable role."

"Risky."

"More like she used her wealth to impress. Either way, the pieces made quite a stir back then, especially after the movie won an award for most popular movie."

"Does the family own any of the collection?"

"No. They sold the contents to the consortium years ago."

Jax met her gaze for a quick moment. "The one we'll be dealing with?"

"Yes. Heirloom Assets. Been in business for twenty years. They buy and sell a lot of valuable keepsakes from production companies and private owners."

"But they didn't sell this collection."

"No. It's one of the original collections the consortium has hung onto over the years. Good call, since the remake of the movie is bringing attention to the collection."

"I'm clearly not an expert on anything Hollywood, but you seem to have a good handle on the matter."

"When the request came in, Brady had me research the consortium, the staff traveling with Mr. Franklin, the collection and the security team. My sister has worked on movie sets. I've got her on standby in case we need an experienced eye when it comes to the collection."

This was news to him. "Which sister?"

She hesitated. "Taylor."

Her answer surprised him. He wasn't sure if he wanted to wade into those waters but had to ask. "She lives in Golden?"

"Yes. Once her mom and my father divorced, she moved away. Worked in the movie industry in Atlanta for a while. Staging or costumes, I think."

"And you're okay calling her?"

Tone wry, she said, "My mom has all the sisters coming to dinner at her house every week, so yeah, I can handle it. If my mom can insist that Taylor be included, I can certainly put aside my issues for the sake of the job."

"That's pretty big of your mom."

"You know her. She loves everyone."

True. Jax had been on that list once. He doubted he'd make the cut now. Linda Connelly loved her daughters and his leaving Brie at a low point probably didn't sit well with her.

They reached the long driveway leading to the main building of the resort. The incline made the arrival more dramatic when the building came into view over the rise. A modern take on a lodge, there were large windows in front, the structure made of heavy timber and brick. Pines surrounded the lodge and two-story hotel that branched off from the main building. Jax pulled into the parking lot and found a space near the entrance. As he shut off the engine, he asked, "Have you seen the movie?"

"I did. The original film came out in the sixties and was a big hit. In fact, it was one of my mother's favorite movies. We watched it all the time when we were kids. When the Chamber of Commerce announced the tour, she made us have a girls' night to watch it again so we'd be ready when the tour arrived." She glanced his way, a slow smile forming. "Did I mention that the award statue is traveling with the display? Which brings the value of the collection up considerably."

With one hand on the wheel, he used the other to press his thumb and middle finger against his eyes. "This just keeps getting better and better."

Brie opened the car door. "Let's get inside and I'll give you a rundown of the place."

Jax joined her, his gaze sweeping the manicured grounds and the woods beyond. Then his gaze halted on Brie. Her step was sure and steady as she headed toward the main entrance.

He allowed a small smile. No matter what phase Brie had gone through when they were growing up—black Goth, rainbow-colored hair or funky clothing choices—she had a flair. Being an officer didn't change a thing about her. Instead of the tan uniform shirt being boxy or unflattering, her inherent femininity lessened the severity of the professional attire. Add the fact that her long honey-blond bangs brushed her thick eyelashes, and he couldn't look away.

*No staring at your friend.*

She stopped before they went inside, her expression serious as he caught up to her. "Look, Jax, this assignment is important. We can't let the way we left each other get in the way of doing our job. We're going to be working long hours together. Maybe it's best if we let it go for now."

He knew what she was referring to but asked anyway. "It?"

She frowned. "The argument over me choosing to stay in Golden. It caused a wedge in our relationship."

"It did."

"The years we let go by without seeing each other didn't help matters. Trying to catch up on fourteen years isn't going to be done in a day."

She was right. He'd be in town for the long haul and they could figure out what to do about their strained friendship then.

"I agree. But at some point, we need to hash things out. Especially since we'll both be living in Golden."

She opened her mouth to say something, then closed it just as quickly, turning on her heel to head inside.

Had she intended to argue with him? He hoped not. He wanted to set things straight, tricky when there was a lot of suppressed emotion involved. They had time to wade through it all, if they could get on the same page.

But as he followed Brie, Jax couldn't help wondering: how did you fix a lifelong friendship and protect a priceless gold collection at the same time?

## *CHAPTER TWO*

BRIANA TURNED WHEN she realized Jax wasn't right behind her. Weird that after all this time she was still attuned to him. Would that be a positive step forward as they worked together?

Before he followed her inside, Jax took another passing sweep of the parking lot, surveilling the area surrounding the spa building and the guest wing from a new angle. Sunshine gleamed in his black hair. She imagined the intensity shining in his blue eyes hidden behind the sunglasses. Even his cologne, woodsmoke with a hint of spice—which she'd discreetly sniffed—was an adult scent. The scrawny twenty-year-old boy who'd left Golden all those years ago was gone. Before her stood a man, all six feet of muscle and strength.

His face had matured with lines that added character. It had been five, no, six years since she'd last visited with him in person. When she'd decided to adopt a baby and then had taken Cami home, their interactions were less frequent. By this time Jax had taken a security job instead of returning to town after he left the military, establishing his life elsewhere. When Briana thought about Jax, it was still from the childhood years, not the man standing in front of her now.

The surprise at finding him in the conference room at the station didn't allow time to study him. She'd been trying to contain her roller-coaster emotions and remain competent while discussing the collection with him. But now, his unexpected appearance and adjusting to the situation caught up to her. Did he think of the old Briana when he looked at her? Did he notice any differences? That she'd also matured? Did he still see his old friend or the woman she'd become? Maybe it didn't matter since they had a job to do, not catalog the changes in each other. But she had to admit, Jax cut quite a figure. Did other women think so?

Annoyed with her line of thinking, she called, "You coming?"

He picked up his pace to join her.

"Nice of you to catch up."

"If memory serves, I was always catching up when it came to you."

She shot a sharp glance his way. Did he mean that as a compliment?

"The general manager's office is this way," she said, leading Jax across a spacious lobby that was meant to impress guests. They passed the rustic reception desk with one employee speaking on the phone, another checking in a middle-aged couple. Tasteful couches and chairs were angled in groups, an invitation to sit and visit or wait for an appointment for the amenities the spa offered. A huge stone fireplace, with logs stacked inside, took up the bulk of one wall. Fresh flower arrangements were scattered about, and the high ceilings gave an impression of airiness. A long table stood along one wall with a dispenser filled with water and lemon slices with glasses available for the guests.

They moved into a short hallway heading toward the back of the building, their footsteps echoing on the hardwood flooring. Halfway down, an office door was open. Briana stopped to knock on the frame.

"Come in," beckoned a female voice.

Briana strolled in as the resort manager, Heather Baine, stood behind her desk, a smoked glass top with wrought iron legs. The woman was stylishly dressed in a cranberry-colored sheath dress paired with high heels. Her dark hair was swept into a trendy style. Briana raised a hand to pat at her normally unruly hair she wrangled straight with a flat iron that morning.

From the corner of the room a man rose, his light blond hair brushed back from his broad forehead. Briana momentarily halted, quickly taking inventory of her surroundings as she'd been trained to do. When Heather spoke in a normal voice, not one that would signal trouble, Briana relaxed.

Heather waved her arm in welcome. "Briana, Jax, please come in." The manager rounded her desk. "Good timing. I'd like you to meet Robert

Long, part of the advance team with Heirloom Assets."

Robert stepped forward and they shook hands.

"I'm glad you're here," Robert said, getting right to business. "With the collection arriving in days, I wanted to walk through the staging area with some officers."

"That's why we're here," Briana confirmed.

Heather smiled at Jax. "Heard you were back in town."

"I am."

"For good?"

Jax's gaze lit on Briana before quickly shifting back to Heather. "Looks that way."

What was with that eye movement? Surely he wasn't basing any future plans on her opinion. Look how well that had worked out the last time he tried.

"Why don't we head to the event room now?" Heather suggested.

The foursome left the office, following Heather to the spacious multipurpose room. "We're excited to host the movie display," she said as they passed through the lobby and into another part of the building that housed a dining room, kitchen and event rooms.

"You'll see that we've been getting ready," Robert added.

Briana strode alongside Robert. "I'm hoping you have an official list of all the pieces, just in case anything has changed."

"Absolutely," Robert replied. "The list is still the same as the original sent to the PD. Nothing has changed from that end."

"But something has changed?" Jax asked from behind, his deep voice taking on an uncompromising air of authority.

"Only the display setup. Some of the locations we've used on the tour have been small, but with this room, we can spread out the pieces, allowing more space for tourists and locals to linger as they view the collection." When they arrived at the double doors, Robert opened one. "Please," he said, and waved to allow Heather and Briana access to the room before him.

The thick carpet muted their footsteps once they entered. The wall was an off-white shade, the perfect backdrop for several colorful paintings hung around the room. Large windows ushered in plenty of natural lighting. The display tables had already been set up in various locations around the large room.

"Since this is the longest stop of the trip," Robert went on to say, "we wanted to make sure that the viewing process would flow well."

Briana walked the length of the room, noticing that the tables were positioned for easy access. Placards identifying the pieces were already placed on the tables. Before taking a second sweep, Jax joined her.

"Your take?" he asked in a low tone.

Pleased that he would ask, she answered, "We'll

have to do a better job securing the doors that lead into the kitchen, and the one outside door." She turned to Heather. "Will refreshments be served?"

"Only the night of the black-tie donor party. There will be food and drinks, but that is going to be catered. The kitchen will only be used by the caterers for setup and to get ice for drinks."

"After that event we can make sure the kitchen doors are more secure?" Jax asked Heather.

"Yes. As for the egress door, we can't block it, but it will be locked. It can only open from the inside."

"One of the consortium staff and a security guard will be in the room whenever the collection is displayed. All of us will be on the premises during viewing hours," Robert told them.

Jax nodded, his eyes skimming each section of the room. "What about security cameras? I see two in opposite corners of the room. They're operational?"

"Of course," Heather said, her tone clearly taking umbrage with his question.

"Had to ask. You'd be surprised how many businesses mount cameras just for show."

"Not here," Heather insisted.

Briana nodded to the door. "What about outside cameras?"

"In order for the insurance company to agree to showing the collection here," Heather said, "we added cameras by the door."

"We'll walk the perimeter before we leave," Briana told them.

Robert's phone rang. He checked the device and said, "My boss. I need to take this."

"If we have any additional questions, we'll let you know," Jax told the man.

With a nod Robert tapped the screen and placed the phone beside his ear as he exited the room.

Heather puffed out a breath.

"Are you okay?" Briana asked.

"Yes. Sorry for coming off dramatic. Getting ready to host the collection has been a bit more stressful than I anticipated."

"In what way?" Jax asked.

"Mr. Franklin, the consortium representative, hasn't arrived yet, but I've talked to him enough times on the phone to know he's a stickler for protocol. I had to submit multiple suggestions on how to display the collection before he finally agreed. Then Robert showed up with his own expectations. He's nice enough, but a little on edge."

Briana recalled that the chief had fielded plenty of calls from Mr. Franklin, asking about procedures and trying to micromanage from a distance. What would he be like in person? After those conversations, Brady would rub his temples to relieve the tension.

"I suppose traveling with a valuable gold collection brings out the nerves," Briana said. "For everyone."

Heather gave a half-hearted shrug. "I suppose, but it seems like more."

Jax frowned. "Have there been problems?"

Heather shook her head. "No, that's the point. We've provided everything they've asked for. Carrie with the Chamber of Commerce has done a wonderful job with promotion and we're ready for the collection to arrive."

"Yet he's still finding places you can improve," Jax surmised.

"That's a good way to put it. Mr. Franklin is definitely a Type A personality." Heather smiled weakly. "My concerns are probably just last-minute jitters."

Briana placed a hand on Heather's arm. "That's why we're here. To assure everyone that we'll be diligent and hopefully tensions will ease."

"Thanks."

Briana and Jax asked a few more questions until Heather's assistant came into the room.

"Ms. Baine, we need you at reception."

Heather smiled at them. "Duty calls. If you need anything..."

"We know where to find you." Briana finished her sentence as Heather left the room.

Once they were alone, Briana asked, "Security wise, is this room okay?"

"It is. The windows don't open. The cameras will cover the entire room. Before we leave, let's walk through the lobby."

They spent the next fifteen minutes making notes and discussing security. Then they walked outside and checked the area around the door leading from the event room where they would transfer the collection each night to deliver it to the bank vault. A short driveway ran to the door, most likely for deliveries.

"I think Heather has made sure we have access where needed," Briana summed up. "Knowing the cameras are mounted out here should dissuade anyone who thinks they can stop us from protecting the collection."

"I've worked on cases where the property stays in one place. It's carrying out the transfer that can cause problems."

"We might not have the private security experience you have, but the PD takes this seriously."

He removed his sunglasses and met her gaze point-blank. His eyes were as blue as a cloudless day. "I didn't say you aren't serious. I just want to be certain that until the collection is on its way back to LA, we don't let our guard down."

"I have no intention of letting that happen. I won't disappoint the PD."

He replaced his sunglasses. "Now that we've gotten the layout of the resort, we should drive the route we'll follow to the bank."

"Routes," she said with a smile.

His lips quivered. "Touché."

IT WAS STRANGE to see Brie in police mode. Not that he didn't think she was capable. No, it reminded Jax that Brie was smart, prepared and had insights he never saw coming. He'd do well to remember that.

Her lively blue-green eyes held a twinkle of mischief. Yeah, she'd one-upped him by intimating that there was more than one route they could follow. How many times had her eyes sparkled with a secret they shared? More times than he could count. At least some things stayed the same.

"Why don't you drive," he offered as they returned to the squad vehicle.

She stopped short. "Giving up control?"

"No. You made it clear you've mapped the routes. I want to observe the surroundings as we travel." He tossed her the key ring just as she had done with him earlier. "And for the record, I know you take this job seriously."

A flash of relief came and went. "Thanks."

They got inside and Brie drove out of the lot. When she reached the main road, she braked and pointed. "This is the straight shot to town. Obvious, but the fastest."

"And if anyone is studying what we do, this would make an easy target."

"Exactly. That's why we'll take a different route every night."

"What are the alternatives?"

"I thought you'd never ask."

He held in a smile. Flashes of camaraderie were still there. Was it enough to rebuild on?

Just after she'd accelerated onto the road to town, Brie made another quick turn onto a street on the right. "This road curves through a residential neighborhood. There are two stop signs before connecting with Main Street. The bank is right at that intersection."

He kept silent as she drove, committing the side streets to memory. At the second stop sign he asked, "Is this a new neighborhood?"

"Kind of."

He raised an eyebrow.

"The houses off Main were here when we were kids, but as the population started to grow, housing expanded toward the resort."

"Things have changed," he said quietly. Logically he knew that when he came home he'd have to catch up, catalog all the places and people he hadn't seen in years in order to navigate life in Golden. Being thrown right into work was probably the best way to get acclimated, especially with Brie as his guide.

She quickly turned her head at the comment, then focused back on the road. "It's not a huge difference."

"Just a reminder that I've missed out on a lot."

*Like years of our friendship.*

She slowed down and pointed to a Cape Cod style house on the passenger side of the SUV.

"Do you remember Mark and Gina?"

"Sure. We all went to prom together."

"They're married now. Have two kids."

"Makes sense. Even in high school it was obvious they were destined to be together." He pulled his gaze from the house back to her. "I got you a corsage that night. White roses. My mom helped me pick it out so it would go with your blue dress."

"You remember that?"

"It was a memorable night."

She tilted her head.

"We didn't get into mischief," he said, a grin tugging at his lips.

"One of the few times," she said as she picked up speed to continue down the street.

They were quiet. Jax's mind flipped like a movie picture reel, continuous scenes of their life together.

Brie broke the silence. "Jax, you seemed happy living in Texas."

Had he been? He thought so until Gramps needed him. Now he'd returned to find new houses or new streets leading to who knew where, he didn't know. But yes. It had been his choice to stay away.

"I'm sure your grandfather keeps you up to date."

He shifted in the seat. "He has, but seeing it in person? It's a lot."

"Which we'll remedy in no time. This will be like the times we drove all over Golden after we got our driver's licenses."

He chuckled. "Dad wasn't thrilled with the mileage I racked up on his car."

"Did he ever find out that you let me behind the wheel?"

How many times had he teased her about the tight grip she kept on the wheel of his father's sedan, the way she bit her lower lip in concentration. She'd always been so serious when tackling something new, just as adamant when she disagreed over a topic. Like not leaving Golden with him.

He shook off the vision. "If he did, he never said."

"If it wasn't for you, I don't think I would have learned to drive."

He turned his head. "I forgot, why were you so chicken?"

"Excuse me?" she huffed.

"Make that apprehensive."

He noticed her fingers tightened on the wheel just like old times.

"After that near-miss accident when I was with my dad on the highway down to Atlanta, I think the idea of driving made me nervous."

"Until your dad offered to buy you a car."

"Which never happened, by the way."

"Yeah. He didn't…"

Her tone wavered. "Keep his word?"

Jax regretted bringing up her father. "Something like that."

"He didn't, so I chauffeured my sisters around in Mom's minivan."

They reached Main Street.

"Route one." She sent him a big grin before steering into the bank parking lot.

Time to abandon memory lane and focus on the task at hand. "You have another?"

"I think the way we just came works the best,

but in a pinch, we can take a different road to and from the resort."

She pulled out of the lot and drove down the main thoroughfare, waving to the folks she knew.

"This part of town looks the same."

"It is." Pride laced her tone. "The heart of Golden."

As they drove a few blocks south, the businesses began to spread out. She slowed to a crawl and pointed to a building. "That's the place Dad left us."

Jax moved forward in the seat, glancing through the windshield. "The Sinclair Building." He read the name carved in the stone lintel above the main entrance.

"Yep." She wrinkled her nose. "Although I think we need to change the name."

"All In Fitness," he said as he read a sign.

"My sister Addie's fitness center."

"I'll need to check it out."

"If you don't, Brady will insist on it. He's all about his officers being in tip-top shape."

He angled his head. "What are you doing with the upper floors?"

"The second floor has office space. Nicole is using one for her event planning business."

"A real family affair."

"Except for Taylor. Her shop is across the street and up a few blocks."

He twisted in the seat to look out the back window. "What kind of shop?"

"She bought the clothing store when Tessa retired."

Repositioning himself, he said, "So you're the only one who doesn't need the space."

"The PD is good enough for me."

"And what about the third floor?"

"Offices were never built, even though it's framed out. If we get interest in renting out the other offices, we'll expand."

"Sounds like your dad set you up for the future."

"Yep."

At her one-word answer, and the fact that the car sped up, he knew the conversation about her father was over.

"Okay, this is Oak Street." She turned left. "We'll take it a few blocks, then the road curves until we meet the main route back to the resort."

He studied their environment as she drove, taking in milestones and anything that would make a possible trap. As they passed familiar houses, he asked about old friends, if they were still living in Golden and what they did now. Brie had the 411 on everyone.

Once back at the resort, she said, "Thoughts?"

"We have three options. I agree, the first is probably the best, so we'll leave the straight shot for emergencies. Driving through a neighborhood will seem less conspicuous and anyone trying to stop us won't want to do so with neighborhood eyes on them. The road we just took would be my last choice. It's less traveled. We passed dense forest and isolated areas where we could possibly be run off the road. Too many risks this way."

"It's available if we need it. And I still think rotating is the way to go."

"I agree."

She circled around the parking lot. "Should we go back to the station and write out our plan? I'm sure Mr. Franklin will want a detailed report."

"I think we're ready."

About halfway back, Jax's cell phone rang. He read the screen and frowned. "It's Gramps."

"Take it."

He answered. "Gramps? Are you okay?"

"Why is everyone's first words to ask if I'm okay? What ever happened to a civil hello?"

He bit back a sigh. "Hello, Grandfather."

"Wise guy."

"I'm working, Gramps. Did you need something?"

"No, but you need to get to Smitty's. There's a big bruhaha going on."

"Describe it."

"Yelling. Fists in the air. No contact yet but it's coming."

Jax's fingers tightened on the device. "Gramps, you know that's not how this works. You need to call the station with a formal complaint. They'll send an officer."

"Don't want any old officer. We want you."

Massaging his forehead with his free hand, Jax said, "Gramps…"

"Fine. I'll call it in."

The line went dead.

Brie glanced at him, eyebrows angled over her blue-green eyes. “Trouble?”

“It appears that my grandfather had decided he can bypass official regulations and just call me to take care of problems.”

“He was a cop. He knows procedure.”

“He does.” Jax expelled a frustrated breath, feeling a headache coming on. “Now that he’s retired, he doesn’t think the rules apply to him.”

Just then static signaled a call from dispatch. “Car Five. We have a disturbance at Smitty’s Pub.”

Jax dropped his head with a groan.

Brie reached for the car radio and responded, “Ten-four. En route.”

Without turning on the lights, Brie picked up speed. Soon they were at the location. Jamey, the owner of the pub, stood outside the door, a dish towel slung over his shoulder and hands on his hips.

“What, no siren?” he asked as they stepped from the car.

“Did you want a siren?” Brie asked.

“And add to the excitement? No way. What I want is for the old dudes in there to calm down.” He glanced at Jax. “Glad to see you onboard.”

“Please tell me my grandfather isn’t the ringleader.”

“No, but he is the instigator.”

The headache had arrived, pounding on Jax’s skull.

Jamey opened the door. Jax held him back. "You need to stay out here for the time being."

The bear of a man didn't look happy. "Fine but make this quick. It's lunch hour and I need to get back to the kitchen."

Jax followed Brie into the pub. When he removed his sunglasses, it took a few seconds for his eyes to adjust from the bright sunlight to the dimmer setting. Loud voices carried their way until they walked right into the middle of a group of gray-haired men screaming at the televisions mounted on the wall.

Jamey came up behind Jax. "World Series. Game two."

"I told you to stay outside."

Jamey shrugged, clearly ignoring his command. "I won't even mention the betting."

Jax was going to have words with his grandfather, who at that moment was slinking off, making his way to the door.

"Freeze," Jax called out in his best cop tone.

Alvin Walker turned, hands in the air. "I didn't do anything, Officer."

"Yeah, he did," came a yell. "He said Nyss was pitching. He lied."

"He was in the original lineup," Gramps defended himself. "I can't help it they changed the roster prior to the game."

"We lost," came another yell.

"Don't blame me," Gramps yelled back, "I wasn't pitching."

"Gramps, let's go outside." Trying to get ahold of the situation, he took his grandfather by the arm and steered him to the door.

"Don't need an escort, son."

Jax ground his teeth together.

Once outside, Gramps squinted at Jax. "Well?"

"Well, what? You called in the disturbance."

"It wasn't so much a disturbance as it was a difference of opinion."

Jax ran a hand though his hair.

His grandfather held up a hand. "Hey, I didn't need to make it official. I just needed you to come by and calm things down."

"Couldn't Jamey do that?"

Gramps shrugged. "I suppose."

Yeah, that's what Jax figured.

The door opened and Brie strode out. "I called in that the situation is resolved." She grinned at his grandfather. "Hey, Mr. Walker."

"Come here and give me a hug."

She walked over and he enveloped her.

"And call me Al."

"Don't think I can."

He pulled back. "Gramps?"

She smiled at him. "Can't do that either."

"Alvin?"

She shrugged.

"I'll take that as a maybe." He winked at Jax. "Aren't you glad to be back in Golden?"

Between reestablishing his friendship with Brie

and Gramps's antics, Jax was beginning to have second thoughts about his decision.

Gramps placed his arm around Brie's shoulder and squeezed. "Now, can you give me a ride home?"

# *CHAPTER THREE*

A FEW HOURS LATER, Jax came through the back door of his grandfather's house and tossed his keys and the file he'd brought home from the station onto the counter. He needed to read the contents tonight to get up to speed on the assignment he shared with Brie, but not until he dealt with Gramps. And after dinner. The scents filling the kitchen had his stomach growling.

Even though he'd only taken a cursory glance, he saw that Brie had compiled a comprehensive outline of the prop collection, the people who were traveling with the tour and a history lesson on Heirloom Assets. When they'd finally gotten back to the station, she outlined the routes they'd follow when taking the collection to the bank vault each night and added it to the file. Tomorrow they would go to the bank so Jax could meet the branch manager.

On the surface, everything seemed under control. But Jax knew from experience that even the most airtight plans could erupt into chaos at any moment. He'd keep an eye out on all avenues, including Brie. She may be a great cop, but she was still his best friend, and he'd always protect her, just like when they were kids. He also knew she immersed herself in a project to the exclusion of all else and he'd be there to remind her to take a break. He didn't imagine that aspect of her character had changed much. Curiosity was good, so long as it didn't become obsession.

She wouldn't appreciate him being overprotective, not with that deep sense of responsibility that was an integral part of her. They'd probably argue over it, but he couldn't help it. That was the way he was wired. And now she had a daughter so that upped the ante. He wouldn't let anything happen to Brie, her daughter, or the folks of Golden.

His life had been relatively peaceful in Texas. Now he wondered what he'd signed up for.

"Gramps. You here?"

His grandfather strolled into the kitchen, mug in hand.

Jax nodded his way. "That better be decaf."

The older man shuddered. "Why would I drink that? That's no fun."

Jax rubbed his forehead.

"Oh, and just so you know, son, I found the saltshakers you hid in the back of the cabinet."

Reining in his frustration, Jax folded his arms over his chest and rested his lower back against the counter. "When did we switch places? In high school I was a troublemaker, and you always preached the straight and narrow. Now I feel like I'm going to be wrangling you in that direction."

Gramps shrugged. "Time gives people new perspectives. We evolve."

"You may have a pacemaker now, but your doctor still wants you to be vigilant about your health."

"You think I don't know that?" he muttered under his breath. "You need to lighten up."

"I can't. I have a big detail coming up and I need to be focused. I don't need any of your shenanigans to get me sidetracked."

Gramps rolled his eyes.

His eyes trained on Gramps, Jax demanded, "Want to explain what happened today?"

"Just some good old-fashioned fun."

"A fight almost broke out."

"Son, for years I was on your side of the law. Now I get to experience the other half."

"I don't believe this."

Gramps set his mug on the counter a little too roughly. The stoneware clanked. "I need something to do. Can't say I'm a fan of retirement."

Jax pushed away from the counter. "Hold that thought. I need to take a shower before we dive into that conversation."

His grandfather nodded. "Dinner will be ready when you're finished."

Jax sniffed the air. "Baked chicken?"

"Your favorite," Gramps replied. "Thought I'd make a good meal after your first day on the job. Just like your grandma did for me."

Jax caught a glimpse of sadness creeping across his grandfather's craggy features. Since he'd been home, Jax noticed that the crow's-feet extending from Gramps's eyes were deeper. He knew his grandfather missed his wife of fifty-something years. She'd been gone for five. Everyone felt the void.

"I'll be down soon." Jax pointed at the man. "Don't do anything you shouldn't."

At Gramps's innocent expression, Jax realized that he was asking a lot. He thought returning to Golden for a new job and getting to know Brie again was going to be the biggest hurdle. Living with his grandfather was going to test every bit of his patience.

Fifteen minutes later he was back in the kitchen, hair damp, wearing a long-sleeved T-shirt and worn jeans. His grandfather had already set the table, placing a platter at the center. Jax almost expected his grandmother to rush in from the living room, fussing at Gramps. He swallowed hard and took a seat at the table.

"Thanks for this," he said.

Gramps shrugged.

They ate in silence for the first couple of minutes then Jax placed his fork down. "Gramps, what's going on?"

"I told you." He poked at the food on his plate. "Just some harmless fun."

"Fun that you called into the station as a disturbance. What if we'd been needed elsewhere?"

"Yeah, I do regret that."

His grandfather seemed truly repentant. If Jax

had ever pulled that stunt, he'd have been grounded for a century.

Jax picked up his fork and knife and sliced a piece of chicken. "What are you doing now that you're retired?"

"Not much. Me and the boys have coffee every morning."

"That's it?"

His eyes grew dark. "What more is there to do?"

"I don't know. Get a hobby. Work as a bagboy at Linda's General Store."

"Can't. She kicked us out last week."

Jax nearly dropped his fork. "Come again?"

"She got tired of us loitering."

Which didn't sound right. The owner, Brie's mom, was the nicest person Jax knew and loved when people hung out at the store.

"Define loitering."

"Taking up all the rocking chairs on the front porch of the store so tourists can't sit."

Why hadn't his family told Jax how serious this had become?

"But I think I have a solution," Gramps said.

While Jax was relieved by the positive note in Gramps's voice, he was also wary. "I'm all ears."

"With all that's going on with Oktoberfest and this valuable collection coming to town, you're going to need an extra pair of eyes. Six officers from the PD ain't gonna cut it with all the people in town."

He wasn't wrong, but Jax said, "Gramps, we don't need you butting in."

"Nothing like that. Me and the boys are just gonna keep an eye out." He paused. "We've formed an unofficial watch group."

"Watch? As in?"

"Keeping guard over Golden."

When Jax didn't shoot him down, because it was a good idea, Gramps's face suddenly looked younger. "I can text you if I see something shady going on. Or if I see a sketchy character hanging around where they don't belong."

Bottom line? His grandfather needed to be useful. After his years as a police officer, serving right here in Golden, stepping away was costing him more than Jax realized. Besides, his grandfather had made a career in law enforcement. He knew what kind of unusual behavior to look out for. He could be an asset.

Plus, Gramps was right. With all the activities going on in town at one time, things would be hectic.

He might regret this, but said, "I'll agree as long as this is off the books."

"I promise," Gramps answered quickly.

"And in the meantime, you'll stay out of trouble?"

Gramps pointed his fork at Jax. "Can't make that promise, but I will rein it in some."

At this point, that's all Jax could ask for.

Satisfied, Gramps went back to his meal. He'd

taken a few bites before asking, "Now tell me what's going on with Briana."

Jax pushed his plate away. "For starters, we're partners."

Gramps shook his head. "That Brady's got a sense of humor."

"No, he knew which officers to pair together. Brie and I know each other well."

"*Did* know each other well. You two haven't spent real time together in years."

Which was evident. They'd spent the day together, but it hadn't felt like the old days. There were still barriers, on both sides. "I'm aware. We'll ease back into our friendship the longer I'm home."

"Okay, I'll give you that but what else?"

"There is nothing else. We're just two old friends working together and living in the same town."

Gramps leveled a skeptical gaze at him. "You don't see that as a problem?"

"Why would I?"

"It seems to me that when that gal turned you down and you went off to the military with your tail tucked between your legs, it left a big chip on your shoulder."

It annoyed him that his grandfather read him that clearly.

"Use enough clichés there, Gramps?"

"Just saying that you never did get over her refusal."

Jax thought he'd put what happened that night aside, but after spending time with Brie, a tiny part of him could admit that his grandfather was right. Her refusal to join him still stung, which was ridiculous after all these years. They'd stayed in touch for the most part and he still considered her his friend.

But she had an entire life without him. Despite his efforts to ignore it, the tiny kernel of doubt that she could so easily choose something else over him again, remained.

Even with the strain between them, he'd trust her with his deepest, darkest secrets. Or drop everything if she found herself in trouble. He'd wager she felt the same way. But the fact was that there was an underlying distance between them, and he wasn't sure how to overcome it.

His grandfather eyed him, then said, "You two will figure it out."

Gramps spoke with a surety Jax didn't feel.

"But on the other hand, you got a problem with your mama."

Concern rushed through Jax. "What are you talking about?"

"Jax, you've been out of town long enough to evade a group of bossy matchmakers who have decided it is their mission to romantically match the young, single people in town."

Jax's eyes went wide. "What has that got to do with me?"

Gramps sat back in his chair. "Really? Didn't think you were that obtuse."

When Jax didn't reply, his grandfather continued.

"From the minute your mama found out you were headed home she's been talking to them. And the last time I saw Mrs. M., the ringleader of this little club, she had a gleam in her eye like she's plotting and planning to find the right woman for you."

Surprise rendered Jax speechless for about a minute. Mrs. Masterson. A matchmaker?

"When did this start?"

"Couple of years ago. Mrs. M.'s grandson, Logan, was the test subject. Then they got to his brother Reid. Since they were successful, they branched out and some other unwitting couples followed. Even your co-worker Roan got hoodwinked, although I don't think he'd cop to that." Gramps scratched his chin. "He and Faith are pretty happy so I suppose the matchmakers are performing a public service."

Jax ran a hand over his chin.

"They did a pretty good job since all those couples are together, either married or on the way to the altar." Gramps rested his elbows on the table. "I think your mama just wants to see you happy."

Either that or she was disappointed that he was the only one of his siblings not married and with children, still living in Golden. He was going to have to seek out his old childhood buddies to get the details on this matchmaking business and how to avoid it.

"I'm not going to deny that I want to find a special woman and settle down," he admitted. "I just don't want outside help."

"They're sneaky and you won't see them coming."

"I beg to differ. I'm a professional and I'll know."

His grandfather sent him a look filled with pity. "No, you won't."

Jax rose and carried his plate to the sink. "That's all well and good. If they want to interfere, they can have at it, but not until next month when things slow down."

"This is Golden, son." Gramps's smile was enigmatic. "Things don't slow down."

Jax rubbed the pain lingering in his right temple. "There's enough going on to keep me busy. I don't need a woman thrown into the mix to add fuel to the fire."

Gramps followed, plate in hand. He placed his free hand firmly on Jax's shoulder.

"You're working with Briana. There's already enough firewood to turn that flame into a blaze."

BRIGHT AND EARLY Thursday morning, Briana let loose a long breath, fell back onto the workout mat and threw a damp arm over her eyes. "I thought this was supposed to be fun."

"Hey, no one forced you into yoga," her sister, Addie, admonished.

Lifting her arm, Briana peered at her sister through a squinted eye. "Really? I seem to remember that you made us promise to take your classes when you opened the fitness center."

"Yes, but I didn't specify which one."

"She got you there," her other sister, Nicole said, legs crossed, totally unfazed by the workout.

Sitting up, Briana pulled her knees up and rested her arms atop them, her workout pants stretching with the move. The matching top clung to her torso. "It was either yoga or high-intensity intervals. I've seen the women who sweat their way through that workout." She shuddered. "That's not for me."

"Yoga is good for you," Addie announced as she crouched to roll up her mat before standing. "Besides, you've only been doing it for a month." She tilted her head. "You're all lean muscle anyway."

"You're saying I don't have to go through this torture anymore?"

"Chief Davis wants everyone on the PD to work out in some fashion," Addie reminded her.

"Yeah, my boss is really into fitness." Briana wrinkled her nose. "I'd rather eat a bag of chips or better yet, French fries, with a big mound of ketchup to slide them through."

Addie pointed at her. "That diet of yours is going to do you in."

"Potatoes are vegetables," Briana countered. "I don't see the problem."

Nicole rolled her eyes. "You wouldn't."

Briana rose just as Addie yelled, "Incoming."

Bracing her legs, Briana readied for her four-year-old daughter, Cami, to launch herself and wrap her little arms around Briana's calves.

"Mommy. I did some of the pretzel moves."

Addie slammed a hand on her hips. "Pretzel?"

Cami giggled. "That's what Mommy calls yoga."

Briana met her sister's gaze. "Well, that's what it feels like."

"Aunt Addie said it's good for dancing," Cami told her with all the seriousness of a young child.

Briana reached down to pick Cami up and twirl her around. Silky straight brown hair flew around her child's head. "I don't dance."

Over her peals of laughter, Cami said, "I want you to, Mommy."

The momentum slowed and Briana tightly hugged Cami. Her daughter loved to twirl around their house, singing a made-up song as she moved. "That's your department."

Cami pushed back against Briana to peer into her eyes. "Grammy says you don't dance because you don't have anyone to dance with."

Setting her daughter on the floor, Briana frowned. It intensified when she heard Nicole chuckle. She sent her sister a warning glare.

Nicole held up a hand. "Hey, it's true."

"Just because I'm single is not the reason I don't dance."

She used to, when she was little. Her father would turn on the radio and they'd frolic to the music in the living room while her sisters sat on the sidelines and clapped. But that was a long time ago, and years later, her father had betrayed them and now he was gone. There was no fixing the past.

Addie and Nicole exchanged a glance that made

the heat rise in Briana's face. "What?" she demanded.

Nicole bit her lip then asked, "You still haven't read your letter from Dad, have you?"

Briana bent over to roll up her mat. Her sisters knew this was a sore subject with her and they usually didn't bring it up. It was painful, messy and she didn't want to deal with it. Once she stood and gained her composure, she said, "Not yet."

Wisely, neither sister said a word.

"So how is your new office working out?" she redirected Nicole.

"I see what you did there." Nicole deftly shook off the change of subject. "It's been great. I decided to name the business Events by Nicole."

"That has a nice ring to it."

"Oh, did Addie tell you that we rented two other spaces?"

"No."

"We now have an accounting firm and a vacation home management company."

Keeping her eye on Cami, Briana watched her daughter dance around the large gym floor. At nine in the morning, the fitness center wasn't as busy as when Addie opened at 6:00 a.m. or after four in the afternoon, prime time for local working folks to schedule a day's workout. With a sigh, Briana had to admit, their father's inheritance had worked out well for her sisters.

Well, two of them anyway.

After Kenneth Connelly's passing, he bequeathed

the four sisters the building they were currently standing in. Briana was never quite sure why he'd purchased the run-down-looking place, but after an inspection it was determined to have good bones. Taking the sisters' encouragement, Addie had claimed the entire downstairs and opened All In Fitness, once a dream, now a reality of hers. After some paint and sprucing up inside and out, they'd decided to lease the offices upstairs. Nicole was the first tenant, needing a place to meet with clients for her event planning business. Their half sister, Taylor, owned a vintage clothing boutique on the other side of Main Street. All four Connelly sisters now resided in town, which had its ups and downs. Like when they pressed Briana about the letter she stubbornly refused to read. It had been part of the inheritance, the building and a letter for each sister. So far, Nicole and Addie had read theirs. Taylor had never mentioned if she'd opened her envelope.

"Before long we'll have to frame out the third floor for additional tenants," Briana remarked.

"Who knew this place would come in handy," Nicole said as they moved to the other side of the room. Addie ducked inside her office and returned with bottles of water she handed out.

Twisting off the cap on her bottle, Addie said, "Especially if the Oktoberfest traffic draws potential renters. Business is up all around town."

Briana took a long swig, then shook her head. "Between the festival and the movie collection, it's going to be a hectic week."

"You'll be working a lot?" Nicole asked.

"We all will."

"Are you on the collection detail?" Addie asked.

"Yes. The delivery is tomorrow. I'll be swamped with prep details. That's why I came in this morning for class. I needed a stress reliever." Briana searched around her to find the bag she'd dropped against the wall when she came in. "And thanks for letting Cami hang out in your office. I hate to be away from her any more than necessary. I'm so glad Mom steps in when my usual sitter can't accommodate a sudden change in my work schedule."

"My pleasure. And I understand the feeling, although Mom loves having Cami visit."

"Same with Jacob," Briana said, returning the sentiment. The cousins were the apple of their grandmother's eye. "As much as the hours are not ideal right now, my work schedule is going to be hectic the week the collection is in town."

"Are you kidding? It's what Mom lives for," Addie said. "Before I started dating Nolan, I swear that Jacob preferred her house to ours."

"Since he's a baseball fan, and adores Nolan, life sure has changed for the two of you."

Addie smiled. "Life certainly caught us all by surprise."

Briana couldn't dispute that claim. Nicole had moved back to town and fallen in love with the town vet, Ethan Price, and his delightful daughter Holly. Addie and retired pro pitcher Nolan Travers had a summer romance and were settling into a relationship. And since she'd adopted Cami, things were never boring at Briana's house. She couldn't really speak for Taylor, as she mostly kept to herself. Finding out their father had an affair, remarried and had another daughter had shattered the sisters' world, but they were slowly coming to terms with the past.

But forgiving her father? Briana still hadn't gotten into that headspace. Didn't think she ever would.

The door opened. In walked a few officers from the PD. She couldn't help but notice that Jax had already become one of the guys as they strolled in.

"Jax," Cami yelled and streaked across the floor to the man in question.

His piercing blue eyes lit up as he dropped his gym bag and scooped Cami up like she weighed nothing. Well, after the weight he probably lifted, the little girl wouldn't even register.

When Cami had become old enough, Briana organized a few video calls with Jax so the two could get to know each other. He'd been miffed at first because she hadn't told him her plans to adopt, and having them meet, even over a computer screen, was a concession on her part for her not including him in that decision.

Cami had immediately fallen in love with Jax, during a brief visit this summer when he came to town to see his grandfather. The meeting at the town park had been a treat for both Jax and Cami while Briana had mostly stayed on the sidelines. But Cami still talked about him often.

Jax met her gaze, his expression hooded as usual. She sighed.

Adopting Cami had been an in-the-moment decision, and she couldn't come up with a good reason for keeping the news from him. Had she been afraid he'd tell her she couldn't do it on her own? That she always took on too much responsibility, like she had for her mom and sisters after their dad left? She wouldn't have taken well to those reasons because she already loved the baby. And given the distance that had formed between them after her refusal to join him following boot camp, she couldn't risk it. Or could it have been that she didn't want the one person whose opinion mattered most to disagree with her choice? Making Cami a part of his life had been her way of apologizing. After his comment at the police station, it must not have been enough.

He walked over and she forced a smile. Now that reality had settled in, she was still coming to terms with having her friend home and working at the PD with him.

His gaze met hers. "Finish your workout already?"

"We did."

"One of these days you're gonna have to work out with us."

"Today is not that day," she said, taking Cami from him. "But you strong manly men have at it."

"Before you go, I wanted to run something by you."

*Oh boy.* "Shoot."

"Since we haven't had a proper sit-down since I've been home, I was thinking we could meet up at Smitty's Pub after the collection tour leaves town. Nothing fancy, just time to catch up."

Her heartbeat picked up at the idea of spending quality time with her friend but also filled her with dread. Was she being silly, looking for problems that might not arise? "I'd like that."

"Great. We can look at the work schedule when we're in the office next." Jax nodded and picked up his bag to disappear into the men's locker room.

"Why don't you work out with Brady and the guys?" Addie asked. "I never see you in here when they come in."

Briana shrugged. "I don't really want to bulk up and they like to lift weights. I just want to make sure I can run after bad guys and meet the chief's department guidelines."

"Since I gave Brady a discount so the PD could work out here, you all come in on a regular basis."

"Thanks for that, by the way. It's so much easier to come here than drive out to the resort."

"That's why I wanted to open this place." Addie beamed with pride. "So the locals could take advantage of the proximity to downtown."

Voices sounded from the other side of the room as Chief Davis, Jax and Roan moved to the weight bench. Dressed in department T-shirts and shorts, they made quite a trio. All built, all business and not the type you'd want to mess with.

Nicole pointed her bottle toward the guys. "How is it having Jax back in town?"

How to answer that question? She'd never told them about their parting argument. And since their father's affair had caused disarray in their home, her sisters never noticed how much Jax's leaving had affected her. How second-guessing herself had made her touchy and sad. Eventually she'd found out from Jax's mom where he was stationed, and she'd begged him to let her visit. He agreed, but the weekend had been stilted, her decision hanging over them. After that, they still talked, but not every day like they had when he lived in Golden.

At some point Jax had lightened up about the past and they spoke more regularly, until his career took off. Then she joined the PD, Cami came along and their communication petered out.

It was great to have her buddy back. But at the same time, things felt…off between them. He wasn't the same guy who'd left Golden all those years ago to join the military. Now, he was a grown man, handsome and confident, in ways he'd never been before. It threw her off, but she was determined that they could adjust and get back to the old camaraderie she'd missed when he was gone. "It's been good. I mean, we've only worked together one day to get up to speed before the collection arrives. We haven't had time to hang out yet, but I'm glad he's home."

"You two used to be inseparable."

Briana shrugged. He'd been the most important person in her life, once upon a time. "Well, we live adult lives now. He's staying with his grandfather since Mr. Walker has the room. Plus, I like to maintain a steady schedule for Cami, so it might take some work to reconnect as we'd like to."

After getting over the shock of her friend returning to Golden, Briana hoped their lives would easily meld, as if he'd never left. She wasn't entirely sure if that would happen.

"Is it strange working with him?" Addie asked.

"Not really. We got to catch up a little during our shift yesterday, but like I said, we just became partners."

"I always thought you guys would end up together," Nicole said.

Briana's stomach twisted at the idea of falling for her best friend. "Why? Jax left town. We sort of grew apart."

"Apart?" Addie laughed. "Anytime he came home to visit you were at his house."

For a while. She'd wanted them to fix what was broken, but Jax grew distant, and she didn't push the issue. Her sisters eventually left town and didn't realize that Briana wasn't close to Jax any longer. Her mom noticed but never made an issue out of it, for which Briana was grateful.

"We still keep in touch but it's not like when we were kids."

"Why'd he come home anyway?" Nicole asked.

"Brady needed to fill the position Evan left behind when he decided to become a paramedic. And after Mr. Walker had his health issues, Jax decided that he was needed here."

"I'm sure Alvin is thrilled to have him home." Addie laughed. "Probably not so thrilled to have someone monitoring his every move."

"Jax tries not to make it obvious."

"Still, Alvin can't like his limitations."

Briana pictured Mr. Walker's grumpy expression if anyone told him to slow down. The man had always done his own thing. "No, but he's happy to have Jax home so I guess it all evens out."

Cami raced out of Addie's office. "Mommy. I'm hungry."

"Right. We need to go home and get changed, then get you to Grammy so I can run a few errands before going to work."

"I'll draw you a picture while you're running," her daughter promised.

Briana laughed. "One more to add to the scrapbook," she said as she gathered her belongings and took Cami's hand. "And thanks for class, Addie. I might complain, but I do feel a difference."

"That's all I care about." Addie bent down to kiss Cami's cheek. "Make sure your mother practices her pretzel moves at home."

"I will." Cami tugged on Briana's hand. "C'mon."

"Okay, Miss Impatience." She grinned at her sisters. "See you at Mom's for our weekly meal? Breakfast this week since I'm on a later shift."

"We'll be there," her sisters echoed in unison. Before leaving, Briana glanced over at the men. Jax nodded at her and a sense of longing swept over her. She wished they were as close as they'd once been. Don't get her wrong, she was glad they made the effort to see each other over the years after he left town, even as spotty as it was, but there was something missing. She couldn't put her finger on it, probably shouldn't worry so much, but it was there just the same.

## *CHAPTER FOUR*

"Do you think Grammy will let me draw at her desk?" Cami asked as she zigzagged along the sidewalk beside Briana before entering Linda's General Store. The movie collection was arriving tomorrow morning and not letting any opportunities go to waste, the opening day event was scheduled for Friday afternoon. The official opening of the display to the public was on Saturday. With the town all abuzz, Briana needed her head in the game.

Inhaling deeply, she took pleasure in the beautiful October day. The changing leaf colors from green to deep browns, vibrant yellows and bright reds, brought her joy. The temperatures were chilly at night and in the mornings, requiring warm, comfy sweaters, but the days warmed up enough to get out and enjoy the sunshine and all the outdoor activities the Golden area offered. She couldn't wait for her next day off to go hiking in the woods.

"I think Grammy has a space ready for you," Briana assured her daughter as she shifted the sparkly backpack over her shoulder, containing everything Cami might need for the hours away from home.

Dressed in her uniform of a tan Golden PD button-down shirt, jeans and boots, her bangs pulled back from her forehead, Briana was prepared for her shift at the station. But not before the fun part of getting Cami all dolled up for an afternoon with her grandmother.

Briana loved dressing her daughter in colorful outfits and pulling her silky hair up in two high pigtails. It reminded Briana of the years she'd dyed her hair different colors, wore funky clothing, and even went through a cringey black phase. Through it all her mother left her alone, aware that Briana was trying to find herself. Their father's betrayal had thrown Briana off-kilter, and it had taken a lot of time to settle into herself afterward. The end result was that she'd become more wary in her relationships. The walls were sturdy and because of that she wanted her daughter to have a happy, carefree childhood and did everything in her power to deliver on the promise she'd made the day Cami officially became a Connelly.

"Will you be home at dinner or am I going to Grammy's?"

"I'll pick you up after dinner."

"Okay." Her agreeable daughter skipped across the street from where Briana had parked. When they reached the large homey building with big windows and a wide front porch, Cami dropped Briana's hand and climbed the steps on her own, showing a little streak of independence. As she held the door open, Briana wasn't sure how she felt about her daughter quickly growing up.

"Grammy!" her daughter yelled when she glimpsed the store owner standing beside the bakery display case.

"Are you ready to work?" Briana's mother asked as she scooped up her granddaughter.

"Grammy, I'm little."

"But you're the best store greeter I've ever had."

Cami's brown eyes lit up. "Really?"

Her grandmother bopped her nose. "Really."

She swiveled. "Did you hear that, Mommy?"

"I did and I'm not surprised."

Alyssa, the store manager, joined them. "But you can't get to work until you've had a good breakfast."

"We had breakfast before going to the gym," Briana told her.

"Not from the bakery."

Briana opened her mouth to say that Cami didn't need a sugary treat, until she saw the excited gleam in her daughter's eyes. As her mother put Cami down, Alyssa took her hand.

"No sticky buns," Briana instructed.

"I was thinking an egg sandwich and orange juice," Alyssa told Cami.

Cami jumped up and down. "I love egg samiches." Then she got a sly expression on her face. "I didn't eat the oatmeal, Mommy. I let Mr. Darcy lick it."

Briana gasped. "He's a cat. He can't eat our food."

"But he likes it."

So much for reasoning with a four-year-old. Or protecting her cat. Now that she thought about it, both daughter and cat were strong-willed.

"We'll talk about Mr. Darcy's diet later."

"K. Can I have a samich?"

Briana nodded at Alyssa and the two took off.

"She reminds me of someone," her mother sing-songed.

"I'll take that as a compliment."

Her mother pulled Briana into a warm embrace. She hugged back, love for her mother gushing through her. Linda Connelly had been through her share of emotional turmoil, but she'd always been there for her daughters. She was the role model Briana aspired to be as a mother.

"So," her mom asked as she pulled back, "busy today?"

"Final prep before the collection arrives."

"How is that going?"

"We're ready for any situation."

"And partnering with Jax?" her mother asked in a much too innocent tone.

Briana shrugged. "It's work."

"And the personal side of your relationship?"

She frowned at her mother.

"Honey, I was there the night you came home in tears after you snuck out to meet Jax. You raced right past me when you ran up to your room. Stayed locked up for days after Jax left."

"And here I thought I was so stealthy sneaking out that night."

"After the phone call you'd had with Jax earlier in the evening, I knew something was up. Call it mom radar. I listened and heard you leave the house."

"I didn't know what to expect myself."

Certainly not Jax asking her to leave with him when her mother needed Briana. That sense of responsibility still lingered but was less prominent now that her mom had made a success of the store and found new love.

"You never did confide in me, but once Jax left, you were quiet and kept to yourself. I put two and two together."

"And what would that be?"

"That he asked you to go with him."

Briana's jaw dropped. "How did you figure that out?"

"Because I knew Jax. He was always protective of you, whether you wanted him to be or not. And you were so upset with your father it made sense."

If only it had made sense to her at the time.

"Were there other times you knew I'd snuck out?"

Her mom laughed. "The after-prom party. The graduation bash you insisted you didn't want to attend, just to name a few."

All instigated by Jax. She'd always been his willing partner.

"Thankfully I outgrew that phase."

"And look at you now. An upstanding officer in Golden."

She transferred Cami's backpack to her mother. "Who needs to get going."

"I'll walk with you," her mother said as she took the bag and they moved through the store.

What a difference from the day her mother bought the existing business from an older couple who'd allowed the store to become dilapidated. There'd been a lot of elbow grease, painting sessions and decorating opinions as her mother got the place in tip-top shape. She also recalled that her sisters had shied away from working with Briana since she'd been on their father's side before the divorce. Everyone had suspected something was wrong at home, but she'd looked the other way. Wouldn't believe that the hushed rumors could be true. Not her father. But that was before she learned all the facts, and still, she and her siblings couldn't work side by side. Being in the store always dredged up conflicting memories, even when she tried to shut them down.

*The lunch crowd had slowed, leaving Briana time to clean up behind the deli counter. Out of the corner of her eye she noticed a customer approaching and pasted on a welcoming smile, which slipped the moment she realized it was her father.*

*"What are you doing here?" he demanded.*

*"I work here."*

*"I went to the high school, but you weren't there. Why aren't you at debate practice?"*

*"I quit the team."*

*Surprise crossed his face. "Why would you do that? You have a competition coming up."*

*"Because someone has to help Mom. Clearly that's not you."*

*His face slowly grew red. "It's not your responsibility."*

*"You made it my responsibility when you left."*

*"Where is your mother? I'm going to insist she find someone else to take your place here so you can go to practice."*

*"No, you won't. This is my decision and I'm not going to change it just because you say so." Her anger welled into dangerous territory, but Briana couldn't stop the onslaught. "You did what you wanted when you left and look where it got us." She pointed to the door. "Please leave."*

*He stared at her for a beat, then turned on his heel and stomped to the door. Once the door closed behind him, she started to shake. She blinked away the tears in her eyes, not giving him the satisfaction of making her upset.*

"We are so excited for the opening event," her mother was saying, dragging Briana from the past.

Briana smiled so her mother wouldn't suspect she'd been thinking about her dad.

"I even got a costume."

The marketing director at the Golden Chamber of Commerce had come up with all kinds of events to promote the collection. The first day was a soft opening and anyone who had worked on one of the committees for the event was invited. Costumes were optional, but it seemed like everyone was onboard.

"Let me guess," Briana said, cocking her head. "Mrs. Palmer, the wealthy museum patron in the movie?"

They'd watched the film enough times for Briana to know her mom's favorite character.

"I've always loved the fashion from that era. And Mrs. Palmer's suits were so sophisticated, just like the woman." Her mom ran her hand through her hair. "I booked an appointment at the salon to get a special style."

"I'm glad you're excited, Mom."

"It'll be fun after the hours of work we've accrued. As a member of the liaison committee, I've been in constant contact with Heather at the resort. Since Robert is the first of the staff to arrive, I've been there to assist in any way I can. The opening day will give us a good idea of how to attract the crowds to see the exhibit."

"See, thinking like a museum patron already."

"In another life, maybe. Mostly I'm a happy store owner."

"And I'm proud of you."

After her parents' divorce, it took her mom time to decide what she wanted to do with her life. The settlement had allowed her mother to buy the old general store and in the ensuing years, she'd turned it not only into a go-to for locals, but a tourist destination as well.

One side of the store was dedicated to grocery items, with a deli and stellar bakery, the other featured all sorts of products made by local artisans. Colorful candles, soaps, handmade jewelry and pottery adorned the shelves.

"Thanks. And now this store owner needs to get to work." She glanced at Briana. "Do you want anything to eat before you go?"

"No, I actually ate my oatmeal."

"Well, you'd better be checking to see what Mr. Darcy is being fed behind your back."

Briana knew that presented a challenge. "Maybe you can get Cami to fess up about what she's been doing."

"Oh no. That's your job." Her mother chuckled. "I get to be the fun gramma who has a great time with Cami and then send her home for a serious conversation with her mother."

Briana couldn't argue that point. Since becoming a mom, she'd learned that while sometimes it was a messy job, the rewards were well worth the rough patches.

With a wave, Briana left the store and got into her car to run a few errands. An hour later, she arrived at the police station. Once inside, she checked her computer for any internal department memos and caught up on paperwork before Jax strolled in, looking ready for a day on duty after his workout. When he stopped at her desk, her stomach dipped. Would today be the day they fell back into their easy friendship?

"Ready to go to the bank?"

"Ready," she replied.

"Am I driving?"

"Do I have a choice?"

"You always have a choice."

Briana frowned. He'd given her a choice years ago and she'd turned him down, creating a rift in their relationship.

Not wanting to let his words affect her, she forced a smile. "I know you like to drive, so have at it."

Something shifted in his expression. "Sorry. I shouldn't have said that."

"No, but obviously it's still an issue."

"One I need to deal with if we're to be successful partners." He met her gaze. "But I will."

She hoped so.

After retrieving the keys, they arrived at the bank to go over the storage details with the manager. The vault was more than enough for their needs and the manager, a middle-aged man, who Briana remembered working as a teller when she and Jax opened their first savings accounts, was thrilled to be an integral part of the collection event. They went over the transfer steps and Jax made sure the manager understood the gravity of the coming week. When they finished, the next stop was the Chamber of Commerce.

Carrie Mitchell, the marketing director of the chamber, ushered them into her office.

"Thanks for stopping by. Things are sooo busy

today, but I wanted to meet with you. Kelli and Wes should be here soon."

They'd already been on patrol when Briana arrived at the station.

"Are you ready for all the festivities?" Briana asked Carrie.

"Hopefully things will go smoothly. Mr. Franklin is very involved with the planning of the events so we're both on the same page. And the volunteers have been amazing, so I have no complaints."

Minutes later, the other officers arrived.

"Good, you're all here." Carrie searched through the paperwork on her desk. "Let's start with the chamber's expectations and then we'll review the lineup of opening day through the final event."

Briana found herself impressed by everything the director had accomplished since arranging the final stop of the movie collection tour. The big-city girl who had taken to small-town life certainly had a way of publicizing Golden's advantages for the business community. She'd made sure local merchants were featured in the publicity and their place of business used to host special events. Now it was Briana's job to make sure that all of Carrie's hard work would be remembered positively after the collection traveled back to LA.

"How did she manage to finagle this tour to begin with?" Jax asked as they returned to the squad car.

"Her background is in marketing. According to my mother, who is on one of the committees, the consortium reached out to her, and Carrie took the event to the next level."

The remainder of the day flew by. When they finally parked the patrol car, Briana was more than ready to go home.

"Any plans?" Jax asked as they exited the car.

"I need to pick up Cami at my mom's house and take her home." She paused, not wanting to let her curiosity show. "Why do you ask?"

He shrugged but she sensed it was anything but casual. "Thought maybe you'd want to get a bite at Smitty's Pub."

"Sorry. I go from police duty to mom duty."

His shoulders went stiff. "Of course. I should have realized."

She thought about it for a minute then asked, "Do you want to come over? I'm not sure what I plan to throw together for dinner, but you're welcome."

"Thanks, but I don't want to impose."

"How is that possible? We were always at each other's houses growing up."

And while that was true, their life had taken different paths, leaving them in an awkward moment.

"You sound like you have a routine with your daughter." Jax's voice was hesitant, which bothered Briana.

"I do, but she'd be happy to have you join us." Briana shifted. "Especially since I need to have a heart-to-heart with Cami tonight. Seems she's been feeding our cat table food."

"How is Mr. Darcy?"

"Still crotchety."

"You mean spoiled?"

"Hey!" She playfully smacked his arm. "You came up with that impression after meeting him only once."

"Once was enough." He chuckled, but to Briana's ears, it sounded sad. "Maybe another time. I don't want to interfere with that mother daughter talk."

"Another night when there isn't so much going on."

"Right." He held up the keys. "I'll drop these off, then I'm going to review my notes one more time."

"We're ready, Jax."

"Yeah, but it doesn't hurt to go over the procedures again."

She wanted to say more but was at a loss. Her wish for easy camaraderie with Jax wasn't panning out. Briana was afraid it would continue that way until they hashed out the past. And even that wasn't a guarantee.

JAX WALKED INTO the station, drinking in a few minutes of quiet since most of the officers had gone home for the night. He nodded at Deputy Thompson who was covering the evening shift until the collection left town, then made his way to his desk.

Could the parting conversation with Brie when their shift ended have been any more uncomfortable? For a moment he'd forgotten that she had responsibilities. All he wanted was to spend time with his old friend. He wasn't sure if that would be an option going forward.

It was evident that Brie had moved on with her life. If he hadn't come back to town and observed the change firsthand, he never would have recognized it with the few and far between conversations they'd been reduced to. He'd been too cautious with his feelings, and it made him realize how foolish it had been to stay away from Golden.

Straightening his desk, he thought about jumping straight into work with the PD. On top of that, settling in with Gramps took up most of his time and energy. He'd unpacked the belongings he'd need until he found his own place. The days had been a whirlwind since arriving back in Golden.

On the one hand, Golden seemed the same, a small town of busybodies who claimed they needed to be in your business in order to keep the integrity of the town. Right. After many years serving in military intelligence, he knew the difference between gossip and actual tactics to secure a mission, or in this case, to keep a town safe. But on the other hand, the town had grown. There were many new businesses. His grandfather had kept him informed about how the local folks were onboard in making Golden a vacation destination. Looks like they'd reached their objective.

There were new faces, along with plenty of familiar people welcoming him home. He knew that in short order, his personal life would become public fodder. If he allowed it. Which he wouldn't. He'd been fortunate to secure a job with the PD when one of the officers wanted to make a career switch and Jax intended on focusing on the new opportunity, his family and maybe finding the right woman to settle down with. So far, his luck in the dating department hadn't been great.

He stood beside his desk, mentally reviewing today's meetings, when Brady and Roan came in through the back door.

"I'm just saying that you can use me at the resort too," Roan was saying.

"If it's warranted, but right now I need you in the park until Oktoberfest is over."

"You're the boss," Roan grumbled.

"Nice of you to remember."

Jax hid a grin. He'd learned that Brady and Roan were good friends outside of the job, with Brady often hanging out at the Donovan home. It appeared to Jax that they maintained a good work balance but apparently Roan sometimes forgot that the chief was in charge.

Brady continued. "You seem to have a handle on the pickpocket episodes affecting the crowd."

Roan nodded. "Initially three wallets were lifted, but last night was quiet."

"Then I suggest we put this to a stop permanently."

When Brady walked away, Jax turned to Roan. "Whoever he or she is, they're slippery."

Roan blew out a breath. "I need a little more time, and I'll get him."

Jax recognized the frustration.

Roan continued. "From what I've observed, I get the feeling it's an organized group. Maybe two or three people at the most involved."

"Brady must trust you if he's asked you to continue on that detail."

"You'd think that would be enough excitement for me what with all we've got going on in town." Roan's face grew serious. "Whoever it is, they're going to mess up and I'll be right there to stop them."

As Roan got ready to head to the park, his words repeated in Jax's head. *He's gonna mess up.* Just like Jax had years ago.

It wasn't a time Jax liked to dwell on, but if it hadn't been for his short-lived youthful rebellion, he never would have turned the corner and walked the straight and narrow. Being the middle kid in a large family, Jax had been overlooked and resentful. He'd become mixed up with a rough crowd, almost made a huge mistake that would have impacted his future differently.

Brie and Gramps had finally gotten him to take a good long look at his life. He didn't like what he saw. Once he'd adjusted his attitude, his grades improved in school, family life became more tolerable, and he and Gramps formed an unbreakable bond. Brie had been going through her own family drama, but at least they'd had each other to lean on. He'd hated leaving her to join the Army, but he had to continue proving his worth, to his grandfather, and mostly to himself.

"Brady said you and Briana go way back?" Roan said as he donned his tactical vest.

"Yeah. We grew up together."

He remembered the day they'd become friends like it was yesterday.

*It was the first day of first grade. Jax scooted his chair over when a girl dropped down next to him at the lunch table. Her honey-blond hair stuck out in different directions, like she'd just come in from a storm and hadn't taken the time to find a brush. Her blue-green eyes sparkled like she had a secret she couldn't contain any longer.*

*"What's your name?" the girl asked.*

*"Jax."*

*"The teacher called you Jackson."*

*"That's my real name, but my family calls me Jax."*

*"I will too." She tilted her head. "I'm Briana. We're both in Mrs. Fischer's class."*

*"So."*

*"So that means we gotta stick together."*

*Jax wasn't sure how she came to that conclusion, but he nodded anyway.*

*"I have two sisters," she announced.*

*"I have four brothers and two sisters."*

*Her eyes went wide. "Wow."*

*Jax shrugged. "It's not so bad."*

*Even though it was. His mom nearly forgot to make his lunch this morning.*

*His new friend unrolled the neatly folded top of her insulated bag. Jax grabbed his paper bag, which was now wrinkly. Smoothing it out, he carefully removed the contents.*

*Briana craned her neck to get a look. "Hey, are you gonna eat those potato chips?"*

*He looked at the chip bag, then at her. "You want to trade?"*

*Briana dumped her lunch on the table. "Yeah, but all I got is an orange." She eyed his chips. "I really love chips but Mom says I gotta eat good food."*

*He stared at the bag. "Chips aren't good?"*

*"I guess not."*

*Jax considered it and said, "Orange for chips? Sure."*

*She held out her hand to shake. He stared at it. "What are you doing?"*

*"My dad says you gotta shake when you make a deal. Makes it official and all."*

*Jax shrugged then shook her hand.*

*"This makes us friends now," Briana said as she passed over the orange then grabbed the chip bag and proceeded to unwrap her sandwich. "And we get to trade at every lunch."*

*Jax considered that then agreed. "Deal."*

*They ate in silence until it was time to return to the classroom.*

*"Hey," Briana said as they walked in line. "Maybe we can sit next to each other in class."*

*"The teacher already gave us our seats."*

*A grin spread over her face. "Bet I can get her to switch so we're near each other."*

*"You can do that?"*

*"I can do anything."*

*He wasn't so sure about her powers, until they got back to the room. Sure enough, Briana talked Mrs. Fischer into seating them side by side. He was impressed. And decided he needed to stick by this girl for the long haul.*

After that they were inseparable. Sitting near each other in class, even though his last name began with *W* and hers with a *C*, Brie finagled the teachers into relenting to her request. Sometime along the way he started calling her Brie. They played at recess, walked home together. All through elementary, middle and high school. Through family ups and downs. Through breakups, prom dates and SAT scores. Until he left Golden and Brie behind to prove he could be a good man.

"I've known her since we were six," he told Roan.

"Wow. You're what, you're both thirty-four now?"

"Yep."

"Good for you guys."

"I couldn't imagine life without her in one fashion or another."

Even with the distance and awkwardness they were working through.

"Good thing you came home. Now you get to team up again."

Jax liked that idea. There was still so much catching up to do, but if they were partners, spending a good chunk of time together might help them get their relationship back on track.

"Were you around when Briana adopted Cami?"

It hurt that she hadn't discussed her decision with him. Then he had to remind himself that he'd left Golden. She could do whatever suited her without his input. He didn't call Brie every time he made a major decision, did he?

"No. I was stationed on the West Coast at the time. I'm not surprised though."

Roan checked the equipment in the pouches of his vest. "Why is that?"

"Brie always had a soft spot for underdogs, people in need and animals."

"But to do it on her own? Not that she isn't capable," Roan rushed to say. "I raised my daughters alone for a few years before Faith and I got married. Gotta say, there's something special when you have a partner involved."

"Brie is responsible enough to do it solo."

To a fault. Had to be the oldest child syndrome. That side of her had dimmed for a short period after her family had imploded, but then her strong spirit and dedicated attitude returned, showing up when going after what she wanted, making sure everyone she cared about was okay.

Roan checked the radio. "Maybe she'll meet someone she wants to settle down with."

The possibility threw Jax for a loop. Neither had

been in a serious relationship. What would it look like if Brie found a guy to share her life with? She had only grown prettier with age and since becoming a mother, there was a certain glow about her that just added to the lovely package. She kept in shape, as evidenced by her time at the gym, and she was still scary smart. Becoming a police officer had turned out to be a great job for a woman who posed questions about everything and didn't rest until she found the answers.

Still, was she looking for a guy to spend the rest of her life with?

"Hasn't happened yet," he said, mostly to reassure himself.

"What about you?"

Jax reared back. "Me? We're talking about Brie."

Roan chuckled. "You aren't looking?"

"I could find the right woman," Jax protested.

*Then why haven't you?* a pesky voice questioned in his head.

Roan snorted. "Yeah. What does that look like? You've been solo since you got here."

"It's been all of two days."

Roan sent him a wily smile. "I could put a bug in the Golden Matchmakers' ears. They'd find you someone in no time."

"Yeah, I heard about them." He winced. "And no thanks. When I find the right woman, I'll do it on my own."

"Okay. But if you change your mind..."

In a firm tone he said, "I won't."

"Won't what?" Brady asked as he rejoined them.

The corners of Roan's eyes crinkled. "Just offering to let the Matchmakers know that Jax is single and ready to mingle."

Jax held up both hands in a stop motion. "Hold on. I'm not looking. My life is full right now."

Brady shivered. "The idea of that group searching for a woman for any of us is scary."

Roan puffed out this chest. "Hey, it worked with Faith and me."

"I'd wager that once you two spent time together, you'd have fallen in love anyway."

"True. But the way Mrs. M. masterminded the whole thing? Impressive. And worth it."

Jax shook his head. "No thanks."

"Ditto," Brady said.

"At least I'm not home alone at night," Roan bragged.

"I could change that," Brady said. "Put you on nights permanently after Oktoberfest."

Roan paled.

"But then I'd have to explain why to Faith, and I like your wife."

Roan made a gesture of locking his lips.

"Good call," Jax teased.

"I'm headed to the park," Roan said after making sure he was set for duty. "What're you guys up to?"

"I'm going to take a final sweep of town," Brady said.

"Getting some sleep," Jax replied.

The opening events were tomorrow. He wanted

to be sharp. And he hoped to come up with ways to improve his relationship with Brie.

Why was picking up where they left off so difficult?

# CHAPTER FIVE

AFTER THE PREVIOUS day of endless meetings followed by a sleepless night, Jax drove the unmarked SUV to the resort. The Friday morning meeting with the Heirloom Assets team was mandatory before the festivities began. His mind had spun with details about protecting the collection; car routes, the spa and resort layout and working with Brie. She was seated in the passenger seat, staring out the window. Had her night been as restless as his?

The valuable items had arrived early this morning, just in time for the soft opening to view the collection later on that afternoon, sponsored by the Chamber of Commerce. The Golden Merchants Association and the Professional Businessowners Alliance had also worked together to make the events featuring the collection possible. As a thank-you, the volunteers were invited to a sneak preview of the movie props, while the Chamber of Commerce threw an outdoor party with food and live music. Folks were encouraged to dress up as characters from *Riches of the Past*. But before the crowd arrived, Jax and Brie were here for a meeting with

Mason Franklin, the lead representative of the consortium.

They walked into the multipurpose room to find a group of people gathered, including Robert Long, removing the jewelry and other items from metal cases and placing them at the corresponding display tables.

Wes and Kelli, who were tasked with delivering the cases of gold from the bank each morning, were exiting the room.

"Just had our briefing with the rep," Wes said as the four stopped at the doorway.

"How'd it go?" Brie asked.

Wes shrugged. "A bit intense, but then if I had to be responsible for that valuable collection, I'd be pretty hands-on too."

Kelli held up a paper. "Instructions for delivery and drop-off. I'm sure you'll get a copy too."

"Good to know." Since they were scheduled to talk to Mr. Franklin next, Jax was raring to get started. This was why they all wore tactical vests with pockets filled with an assortment of equipment over T-shirts today and would wear them whenever on duty to transfer the collection.

"Next officers, please," came an authoritative voice.

Wes's grin was tight as they passed by. "Your turn."

As the officers left, Jax and Brie took their places.

Without exchanging pleasantries, Franklin barked,

"Are you the officers who will transfer the collection to the bank each night?"

Brie walked forward and held out her hand. "I'm Officer Connelly." She hitched her thumb toward Jax. "Officer Walker."

The rep squinted to read the nameplates and badges affixed to the front of their vests as if confirming her claim. A tall man, with graying hair and trendy glasses over dark brown eyes, he wore a suit and tie and held an air of one in charge. Satisfied, he nodded and took her hand. "Mason Franklin." He then shook Jax's hand.

"Nice to meet you, sir."

"Let's get right to it." He handed each of them a paper. "These are the requirements for your handling of the collection."

Jax scanned the list. Pretty much everything they had taken into consideration was listed, with a few more added details.

"We're to call you after dropping the collection off at the bank to confirm it is safely stored?" Jax queried. This was not one of the original requests, but not unexpected.

"Yes. I've listed my contact information which I'd like you to add to your phone. If I don't hear from you in a reasonable amount of time after the drop-off, I'll call your chief."

Brady was going to love that.

"And you want us to take pictures of the collection in the cases before we leave the resort and after we make the deposit at the bank," Jax went on.

"As per our insurance policy. I know you understand the chain of custody."

This, too, wasn't an unreasonable request and Jax could understand their concern for their property.

"If you have any issues whatsoever, you are to call me or my associate Robert."

Robert heard his name and waved in their direction.

"My other colleagues, Jill Hastings and Kat Bevins," Mr. Franklin said. "And our security guards, Gil and Alec." He nodded to two men.

Both women appeared to be mid-twenties, dressed professionally, Jill's blond hair pulled back, Kat's short dark hair spiky. The security guards were also young but built. Their appearance alone would discourage anyone who might be thinking about touching the collection.

"I believe you were told we are all staying at the resort hotel," Franklin continued.

"Correct," Jax answered.

"Now," Franklin said, "the collection. As you can see, we've placed the dress displayed on the mannequin in the center with four tables on the perimeter."

Jax followed as they stopped by each table. Franklin explained why certain pieces were grouped together, like the art deco jewelry or the Egyptian necklaces. Blue velvet had been draped over each table, falling to the floor, so that the pieces were beautifully displayed. "As you can see, on each placard we've given a synopsis of scenes from the movie where the jewelry would have been featured. This gives the viewer a connection to the original film."

"And the pieces will be in the same location each day?" Jax asked.

"Yes." Franklin stopped short. "We haven't brought it out yet, but the award statue will be displayed on a pedestal beside the gold dress." He pointed in that direction. "The tiara will rest on another pedestal on the opposite side."

"And you'll limit the amount of people who are allowed in the room?"

"Yes, there will be groups of twenty on the half hour."

If the man had forgotten anything, Jax couldn't find what that would be.

Franklin steered them toward the egress door. "May I see the vehicle you and the other officers are using to transport the collection?"

"It's parked just outside the door," Brie said.

Franklin led the way, opened the egress door and propped it open as they filed outside. Jax popped the back hatch and Frankin leaned over to view the rear cargo space and large rectangle box inside.

"The locker is bolted to the vehicle," Jax explained. "There is more than enough room to place the cases inside, along with the larger ones containing the tiara and award. We normally use the locker to transport evidence or firearms, so it's secure."

"Acceptable." Franklin placed his hands on his

hips. "I don't have to stress the importance of your vigilance when it comes to handling the collection."

"No, sir," Brie answered. "We understand how valuable the contents are."

Franklin nodded. "Very well. We're still getting up to speed for today's tour, but you will be on the grounds during the viewing hours?"

"We will," Jax answered.

"Then I will see you tonight at the preestablished time." Franklin walked inside and closed the door behind him with a slam.

"Guess that's the end of our meeting," Jax said.

"I get that Franklin has a lot to deal with, but he sure is…"

"Rude?"

"I was going to say short with us, but your description is more on the nose."

"Since we're dealing with him in a limited capacity, I don't really care how he acts as long as we have no barriers to keeping the collection safe."

"I agree." Brie shifted the vest over her shoulders. "Let's go out front and see if Carrie is here. She's in charge of the shindig this afternoon."

Once they rounded the building, Jax registered all the activity. While they'd been inside, two food trucks had parked on either side of the blocked-off parking lot, with generators running. Additional parking was routed to the side of the hotel. A local band was setting up equipment in a corner of the lot.

Jax watched as excited volunteers, many of them

in costume, mingled in the specified space. "Looks like we dodged a bullet with those outfits."

"I don't know," Brie countered in a wistful tone. "It would have been fun to dress up."

"Really?" He considered that for a moment. "What character would you have picked?"

Brie's eyes widened. "You watched the movie?"

"First night home."

"Hmm, okay." It didn't take her long to reveal, "I'd be the suave Manhattan historian who worked with the archaeology team, has a killer wardrobe and beautiful jewelry. You?"

"The Fed working the case after the antiques are stolen."

She rolled her eyes. "Kind of one-dimensional, don't you think?"

"Hey, you go with what you know." He paused, then a slow grin curved his lips. "Like the time you dyed your hair red, but it came out bright orange."

She grimaced. "You have to admit, the look did raise eyebrows." Then her eyes went wide. "Wait. I remember that you would tell anyone who listened that I was signed up for clown school."

"It was the only explanation that made sense."

She puffed out a laugh. "It was a terrible idea, wasn't it."

"At least you went back to your natural color for prom."

"Which, as I recall, was the year you decided to go all seventies on me and wear a powder blue tux."

He cringed. "I forgot about that."

"Trust me, I didn't, but it made us even."

They both laughed, caught up in the good memories they'd made when they were kids.

A blonde woman headed their way, a sense of purpose etched on her face.

"There's Carrie," Brie informed him. "And look at that dress."

Carrie looked like she'd walked right off the set of a movie, in a green dress with a rounded neck and a flared skirt that swirled around her legs, covered by a short striped green-and-black bolero jacket with wide shoulders. A diamond flashed on her left hand in the bright sunshine.

"Oh my gosh," Brie gushed. "Take a look at those chunky black lace-up Oxford heels and the green-and-black velvet cloche hat. I'm so jealous."

Jax had little interest in fashion but remembered that Brie had enjoyed many different clothing styles while they were growing up. This outfit, like all the rest, would have been perfect for her.

Hands resting on his utility belt, Jax waited for the woman to arrive.

"Sorry we didn't get a chance to chat beyond business yesterday," Carrie said right away. "I had a tight schedule, but now that I have a little breather, I wanted to tell you I'm glad to meet you, Jax. I've heard all about you."

He frowned at the disadvantage.

He glanced at Brie, but she just shrugged. "It wasn't me."

Another voice added, "I'm the guilty party."

Jax turned to see a man decked out like a costumer would depict an archaeologist in a movie, tan pants and shirt, brown fedora hat and worn boots. "Just so you know, the only way I'd dress up like this is because Carrie asked."

Jax grinned as he took the hand of one of his high school friends. "Good to see you, Adam."

They shook.

"Long time," Adam said.

"And let me say, Carrie, you look amazing," Brie piped in.

She fluffed out the sides of her skirt and curtsied. "I love vintage styles."

Adam groaned.

Carrie slipped her arm around his waist. "It's for a good cause."

Tugging at the shirt collar, Adam muttered, "So you keep telling me."

"Gotta say, wearing this vest isn't so bad right now," Jax said as he hitched his thumbs under the vest at his shoulders.

"Don't rub it in," Adam said, then his expression lightened. "Welcome back."

"Glad to be back."

"And just in time," Carrie said. "This entire process has been planned with a fine-tooth comb. We need a strong PD."

Jax nodded. "We'll be patrolling the event perimeter if you need us."

"Thanks." Carrie's phone dinged. She glanced at the screen. "I need to put out a fire."

Adam's smile widened as his gaze followed his departing girlfriend.

"Heard you're getting married," Jax said.

"Hopefully next year. I proposed before this event was on the radar and ever since, Carrie has been busy. Once the collection is on the way back to LA, we're setting a date."

"Are you and Colin still running Deep North Adventures?"

"My brother and I share the duties, but we each have side interests, so my folks fill in for us from time to time."

"I'll have to stop by after this detail is over."

"Colin and I will get the gang together."

Carrie called Adam's name. "I need to pitch in today. See you later."

"Sure," Jax said, trying to ignore the little pinch of jealousy that Adam had found a woman to share his life with.

After a quiet moment Brie asked, "How has it been running into old friends?"

Even though it had only been a couple of days, running into a few buddies had been like sliding into his old life with a few more years of wisdom under his belt. People had been friendly and inquisitive and oddly curious about him being partnered with Brie. Why? He couldn't fathom. He'd always been protective of her, for one. And two, had people guessed about the way things ended between them when he left town?

Back to Brie's question. "Everyone's lives are moving in positive directions."

"As opposed to yours?"

He frowned. "I didn't say that."

"Sorry, didn't mean to read anything into that comment," she said, voice tight.

"But you did."

She stared at him.

"No. I… I'm happy to be home, Brie."

"I'm glad you feel that way because Cami wants you to stop by and visit."

A little wave of panic welled up in him. He'd barely had time to pick up the pieces with Brie. He thought he was ready, but…not with the past hanging between them. "The three of us?"

"Yes. She's heard so many stories about us from when we were growing up, she thinks you're a part of the family."

"Then how can I say no?"

Before she could say more, Brie's mother called Jax's name.

"Watch out," Brie warned under her breath when Linda Connelly hurried over to give Jax a big hug. Her perfume reminded him of home, since he'd spent so many hours at the Connelly house when he was a kid. She pulled back, a huge smile on her face. "I couldn't believe my ears when Alvin told me the news. It's been far too long, Jackson."

He tried not to wince when she used his full name. It reminded him of when he and Brie would get caught creating mischief. Her use of his full name never ended well.

"Stop by for dinner anytime," she said, less an invitation and more of a command.

Apparently, she didn't hold his leaving and upsetting Brie against him, which was a relief. He was glad Brie had her family close, even if he had moved out of the ranks of the inner circle.

"Yes ma'am."

Linda turned to Brie. "I'm meeting Royce at the ticket table. I'll bring him over later."

"Love your outfit, by the way," Brie said. "With that suit, you look like you stepped out of the movie."

"Really?" Linda smiled as she smoothed the straight checkered skirt, a match to the belted jacket that fell below her waist. "I feel pretty special."

Brie chuckled. "Get to work now," she teased her mom.

Linda hugged Jax again. "So happy to see you."

"Same here, Mrs. Connelly."

As she hurried off, Jax glanced at Brie. "Royce?"

"New boyfriend."

"Huh."

Brie laughed. "Uh-huh, that's how we all felt."

Around 1:00 p.m., the band started to play a musical set, and the lot filled up with curious volunteers. Jax suggested they separate to walk either side of the festivities, meeting at the other end. He didn't notice any problems, just folks having a good time while they waited to be ushered inside to see the collection.

"Anything suspicious?" Jax asked when they both reached the end of the lot.

"No. Everyone here is a local. Once the tourists start coming to see the collection we'll really be on guard."

Out of the corner of his eye, Jax noticed Mr. Franklin exiting the resort. Carrie walked up to him, they exchanged a few words, and then she moved to the lead singer of the band to take one of their microphones.

She thumped on the live mic to get everyone's attention. "Welcome, Golden." She turned toward Franklin. "I'm honored to introduce you to Mr. Mason Franklin, traveling with the collection. Please give him a warm Golden welcome."

He waved at the crowd's applause, but Jax noticed that his smile didn't reach his eyes.

"Today you'll get a sneak preview of the collection from *Riches of the Past*," Carrie told the crowd. "You'll see a table set up just over here to my right. Volunteers will hand out tickets and we'll have small groups, one at a time, go inside for the viewing."

As people headed to the table, Jax said, "One of us should be stationed at the front door."

"I'll do it since my mom is the volunteer there. She'll keep me in the loop."

He nodded, watching Franklin stride back inside, his gait stiff. Was the man always uptight?

Before Brie could walk away, Gramps strolled up. "I got the boys with me," he said.

Brie frowned. "Boys?"

"You don't want to know," Jax told her.

Gramps winked at her and sauntered off.

"That wasn't the least bit cryptic," Brie said in a dry tone.

"I'll tell you later."

"You're right you will," she said, then left to go to her post by the front door.

In the next hours, Jax patrolled the grounds, but all was calm. Everyone seemed to be enjoying themselves. Groups had been in and out of the collection room. He heard snatches of conversations about how the pieces didn't fail to impress. The display was everything it was hyped to be.

As the sun started to sink in the sky, the band finished their last set, the food trucks shut down and folks started heading home. He caught up with Brie after speaking to Carrie one final time, then they walked to the event room.

"What was up with your grandfather?" Brie asked.

"He's recruited his buddies to keep an eye out around town because both Oktoberfest and the collection are big highlights." He rattled off the names of the men. "They call themselves the Golden Watch Network."

"Does Brady know?"

"I told him."

Her eyebrows rose. "And he's okay with it?"

"Apparently Gramps consults with Brady from time to time, so yes. And Brady can't stop concerned citizens from guarding the town as long as they don't interfere with any ongoing investigations."

"There is an investigation involving Oktoberfest."

"Gramps's friends know better than to insert themselves, but it's good to have additional expertise on scene."

Just before they reached the doors to the multipurpose room, Jax's phone dinged. He read the screen then shook his head.

"Let me guess. Your grandfather?"

"Checking in from the park. He confirms that there are only a few sketchy characters to report."

Brie laughed. "Sketchy, huh?"

"And only a few." Jax texted back then said, "Let's get moving."

Once they were inside the room, Robert closed the doors to the public.

Franklin marched over to them, relief written on his face. "The first day is always the most stressful."

Finally, the man had relaxed. He rolled his neck and loosened his tie a fraction. "Let us show you our closing protocol."

Jax watched as the staff loaded the jewelry into four silver fireproof lock cases with sturdy handles. Each item had a specific place in a specific case.

Once the boxes were full, they were locked and set on a rolling cart to move outside.

"We use the cart to get everything to the doorway." Franklin glanced around. "Oh, one small change."

Jax stiffened.

"Since the mannequin with the dress is too large to transport, we'll roll it to Heather's office and lock it up for the night."

"That's okay with the insurance company?"

Annoyance flashed in Franklin's eyes. "Yes. I received confirmation when we arrived on-site and I explained the setup."

Jax never liked last-minute modifications, especially when the people he was dealing with were wound as tight as Franklin, but he wasn't going to argue the point. If he had any ongoing concerns, he'd call the insurance company himself.

Once loaded, Robert pushed the cart across the room. Franklin opened the door. The man's tension had returned and rolled off him in waves. "Gil and Alec will remain outside with you."

"We've got this, sir." Jax wasn't positive if his assurance helped. He got the distinct impression that Franklin wanted to load the cases himself.

Franklin nodded but stood in the doorway as Brie started loading the cases safely into the locker. Jax scanned the surrounding area. Long shadows formed in the murky light that shifted during the transition from evening to night. It was eerily quiet, except for Brie loading the collection. As he took another scan of the area, he noticed movement in a row of bushes about twenty feet away. He placed a hand near his holster. Not moving a muscle, he waited. Nothing stirred again. Deciding it was the wind, Jax faced Franklin.

"We'll call you after drop-off."

"Thank you."

Franklin turned and stepped inside.

"Let's move," Brie said.

Jax nodded to the guards who hovered by the door.

Just as Brie turned to walk to the passenger side of the SUV, Jax noticed movement again in his peripheral vision. He grabbed her arm and pulled her to the rear of the vehicle, placing their bodies between a possible threat and the valuables in the cargo area. Sensing trouble, the guards joined them.

"Jax, what's wrong?" Brie asked, voice taut.

"I thought I saw movement in the woods."

Her hand moved to her service weapon at the same time he rested his free hand on the grip of his. For a long moment they both searched, but nothing moved again.

"False alarm," he said.

Brie relaxed.

The guards moved away.

Jax locked gazes with Brie. In the hazy light from the outdoor fixture, Brie's eyes had turned a deep blue-green. Neither spoke, the hush punctuated by the loudness of his beating heart. Finally, she blinked. That's when he realized he still had his hand curled around her upper arm. They stared at each other again before he dropped his hand.

"Sorry about that."

She stepped back.

"You know me. Protective streak."

She cleared her throat. "Let's go."

As she hurried to the passenger door, he closed his eyes for a moment.

*Protective streak.*

Right. That was the only excuse he could come up with for holding on to her for so long.

# CHAPTER SIX

EARLY SATURDAY MORNING, Briana sat on a bench in Gold Dust Park watching Cami scamper about the playground while waiting for her sisters. The sun shone upon the jungle gyms, painted in vivid colors. Cami raced around the swing set, her sneakers kicking up the wood chips scattered around the area. Squirrels chattered as they jumped from branch to branch in the pine trees above her. The rich scent of autumn perfumed the air. She should be enjoying the morning, but her mind was elsewhere.

The transfer from the night before had gone off without a hitch. They'd gotten the collection to the vault, sent a picture to Franklin along with a call, and ended their shift. It was the other events of the evening that lingered in Briana's mind.

She'd tried not to dwell on Jax's touch when he warned of a possible threat. Like he said, he was being protective. Not that she couldn't take care of herself. And she did appreciate his concern for her as his partner. But the look on his face? His piercing blue eyes had been intense when he gazed at her. Enough that she almost shivered. Thankfully she hadn't, which would have been hard to explain. But it kept her awake for hours, wondering what was going on between them.

Cami called out "Mommy" and waved from the top of the slide. Briana waved back, wishing she could be as carefree as her four-year-old.

When she and Jax were kids, Briana was always in her head, thinking too much and unintentionally blocking out what was happening around her. It was how the wheels of her mind worked. Jax had teased that she wasn't situationally aware, that if it weren't for him, she'd walk into traffic or miss the world around her. She had to admit he was right. People thought she was standoffish at times, but really, she was figuring out a dilemma or puzzle in her head.

Once she became a police officer, she'd tried hard to keep her mind focused on the task at hand. She disciplined herself to be alert. But when it came down to investigating a crime, that's where her talent burned bright. She meticulously sifted through small details others might overlook or available facts she'd picked up to find answers. While Jax was always attentive and aware of his surroundings, she was more inclined to decipher clues. She hoped their different strengths would make them a good team.

When she'd been securing the cases in the vehicle locker last night, he'd been scanning the grounds for potential threats. When he suddenly grabbed her arm, it caught her off guard.

But what surprised her was not Jax warning her, but her reaction to his touch. The way her heart hitched, and her breath stalled in anticipation, made no sense. Until she gazed into those fathomless blue eyes, then all bets were off. She couldn't quite name the expression there, but she didn't think it was merely friendship. But that didn't make sense. This was Jax. She didn't get all starry-eyed when he was around. Her reaction had to be pure adrenaline due to the situation. Nothing more.

"Is that seat taken?"

Briana's thoughts evaporated as she glimpsed Jax's grandfather standing beside her.

"Not at all, Mr. Walker. Have a seat."

"We discussed this. I really wish you'd call me Alvin."

She hid a smile as she moved Cami's backpack to make room for the older man. "Alvin."

"You're out and about early," he commented as he lowered himself to the bench.

"Getting some playtime in with Cami before my shift starts."

"The joys of juggling motherhood?"

"Exactly."

"Mavis's favorite time with our kids was right here in this park. I'd duck out of the station to join them whenever possible."

Briana's gaze fell on Cami climbing the slide again. "I didn't know what to expect when I became a mother. I burn more energy running after Cami than I do at the gym."

A bittersweet expression crossed his face. "Enjoy these moments. They fly by too fast."

A reality she was living with on a daily basis.

Briana shifted in her seat. "And what brings you to the park this morning?"

He held up a cup from Sit A Spell. "Needed my morning kick."

"Is Jax still bothering you about keeping only decaf in the house?"

"Afraid so. That boy can be pretty bossy."

Didn't she know it.

She leaned over to bump his shoulder with hers. "But you love him."

A genuine grin curved the older man's lips. "Can't deny it."

"From what I understand, you have a deal with him. Or should I say, the Golden Watch Network."

Alvin's gray eyebrows rose over blue eyes similar to Jax's. "He told you?"

"We're partners. No secrets." She grinned. "And you made it pretty obvious something was going on at the resort yesterday. You might have thought you were cryptic—"

"But you had questions."

"Bingo." She grew serious. "I appreciate your help. Texting Jax with observations is actually a good idea."

"Glad you're onboard."

"As long as you guys don't go too far."

He held up a hand. "We know our limits."

"Got your phone with you?" she asked.

With a puzzled expression, Alvin pulled it from the chest pocket of his red-and-black plaid jacket. "Right here."

Briana held out her hand.

He dropped it into her palm.

"I'm going to add my contact number," she said as she tapped in the number. "If you can't get ahold of Jax, you can text me."

His face lit up.

"And when you're doing surveillance—"

Alvin opened his mouth to say something, but she stopped him. "Don't wear red. You stand out."

"This is my go-to-town and stand out jacket. Got a whole other wardrobe for clandestine activities."

Briana didn't doubt the man.

"Then I think you're set."

"Mommy," Cami yelled, "Holly is here!"

Briana glanced at the park entrance to see her sister Nicole walking hand in hand with her boyfriend's daughter. When Holly caught sight of Cami, she took off. Nicole veered Briana's way.

"Looks like you've got family joining you." Alvin rose.

"You can stay."

"No. It's good for sisters to visit." He paused. Grew serious. "But I do have a request."

"Sure."

"Patch things up with Jax. He doesn't say much, but I got the feeling things were off when he left town to join the military. He needs his good friend back."

She swallowed hard, something profound unfurling in her chest. "I want my friend back as well."

Alvin nodded, greeted Nicole, then sauntered away to spy on who knew who.

"Addie and Jacob will be here in a minute," Nicole said as she sat on the bench beside Briana. "What's up with Jax's grandfather?"

Briana shook her head, thrown off-kilter by the man's request.

"He and his buddies are unofficially assisting the PD while two major events are going on in town at the same time." She frowned. "Did you know they call themselves the Golden Watch Network?"

"First I'm hearing about it."

"Apparently, they haven't taken well to retirement."

"I know. Mom kicks them off the general store porch at least once a week."

"I get it. They were all so active when they were younger."

"Still, a watch group." Nicole grinned. "Where do I sign up?"

"Sign up for what?" Addie asked as she joined them, out of breath from sprinting across the park.

"The Golden Watch Network," Nicole answered to which Briana replied, "An unofficial group."

"Are they making the community safe?" Addie asked as she plopped down beside Briana.

"I suppose."

"Then I'm all for the network."

The fourth in the group, Taylor hurried across the grassy expanse. Nicole, Addie and Briana had the Connelly blond hair and different shades of blue eyes. Their half sister, Taylor, had her mother's coloring, thick auburn hair and hazel eyes.

"Sorry I'm late."

"It's okay," Nicole informed her. "We just got here now."

"And why, exactly, are we here?" Briana asked. After getting the phone call last night about the sisters' impromptu meeting this morning, she was more than curious.

"We feel bad that you're on duty tonight," Taylor said as she elegantly lowered herself to the bench. The sisters squeezed together in the limited space.

"Why? It's my job."

"It's been forever since you went out on the town," Nicole huffed. "How often do we get dressed up for a black-tie event in Golden?"

"You know I'm busy with Cami most of the time."

"That's an excuse. She's getting older, and Mom loves having her spend the night," Addie countered.

Briana read their faces and didn't like what she saw. "Is this an intervention of some kind?"

Addie bit her lip. "Not exactly."

"Then what?"

"It just occurred to us that you didn't get to have fun at the opening event yesterday," Nicole puffed out.

Briana gaped at her sister. "You weren't there."

"No, but Mom was. She said you and Jax were doing a great job."

"Then what's the problem?"

The sisters exchanged glances. "We were wondering, now that Jax is back, if you might start dating again."

She nearly choked on her response. "Date Jax?"

"Not Jax," Nicole replied with a frown. "I want to introduce you to a friend of Ethan's. He's coming to town next week."

"I'm… This is…"

Addie tilted her head. "Why would we suggest you date Jax?"

Briana's mind went to the exchange last night. The way Jax gently held her arm. How their gazes met and held with a potency she'd never experienced before. The swirling frenzy in the pit of her stomach.

"Because you mentioned him in the same sentence as dating," Briana answered, hoping her sisters were so focused on their mission that they missed her reaction.

"We only mean that he's always gotten you out of your comfort zone," Nicole continued. "If you say yes, we can recruit him to help us get you out there."

No way. She didn't need Jax involved in any dating scenarios, especially since she was confused enough by her reaction to him. She needed to call off her sisters. Now.

"Look, I appreciate you caring about me, but I'm too busy with work."

"You've been saying that forever," Addie groused.

Briana reined in her temper. "Why don't you all enjoy tonight's event and let me focus on my job."

Nicole had planned the party through her business, Events by Nicole, and was attending with Ethan. Addie's boyfriend Nolan, a retired pitcher, was invited to every event in baseball-crazy Golden. And Taylor had helped most of the guests select formal wear for tonight's party.

"But we can circle back?" Addie asked.

Briana rolled her eyes.

"That's not an answer," Nicole said.

"I think we've pushed her far enough," Taylor said, standing. "We didn't mean to offend."

"You didn't. And I'm happy we're all here." She swallowed. "Together."

There was a time none of them spoke to each other. Lately, they'd been dealing with the past in a positive way, but Briana always wondered if deep down, they still held grudges against her because of how she'd handled their father's betrayal.

Addie glanced at her watch. "I need to get to the fitness center for class." She jumped up. "Are you still okay with Jacob spending the morning with you?" she asked Nicole.

"Holly is looking forward to it."

"I need to open the store," Taylor said. "Several of the ladies going to the party tonight are picking up their dresses."

"I hope one day we won't all be rushing off in different directions," Nicole groused. "We never slow down long enough to visit."

Did her sisters want that? Time together? Nicole and Addie had become closer over the last couple of months. Addie and Taylor had mended fences. Yet Taylor still acted like the odd man out. Were there still unresolved issues among them? Until Briana faced her own issues, she'd probably never know.

Addie and Taylor waved then walked away together. Briana watched with something close to envy.

"They've worked out the complications in their relationship," Nicole said in a quiet tone.

"I know."

"And we don't blame you for sticking up for Dad. It was a long time ago and we're all moving on."

"I should have acted differently."

"You and Dad were inseparable. We understand why you initially stood up for him."

"But not at the cost of my sisters."

Nicole placed her arm around Briana's shoulder. "It's time to forgive. Him, and yourself."

"Easier said than done."

"Hey, you're my super smart older sister." Nicole squeezed her. "You'll figure it out."

Briana thought about the letter she'd received from her dad but hadn't yet opened. Was forgiveness possible?

Holly yelled for Nicole to join them.

"C'mon," she said to Briana. "Let's avoid adulting and go have fun with the kids."

"Sounds perfect."

LATER THAT EVENING Briana and Jax arrived at the resort prior to the transfer. The parking lot was full of cars.

"Seems the party hasn't broken up yet," he observed as they parked the SUV in the designated transfer spot.

Briana checked her watch. 8:00 p.m. "Brady wanted us to monitor the party as it winds down." She watched an elegantly dressed couple walk to their car. "I suppose if everyone is having a good time, it'll throw off our timeline."

"We should be fine as long as this doesn't go much later."

After exiting the SUV, Briana adjusted her ballistic vest as they walked to the main entrance and moved through the lobby. The doors of the multipurpose room were closed but judging by the voices leaking from inside, the guests were having a good time.

The Saturday night black-tie event for donors who had supported the movie collection tour was in full swing. It was a medium-sized crowd, but lively.

Apparently working with Mr. Franklin and his staff was causing major stress. Poor Heather was bearing the brunt of it. From what Briana had observed so far, Mr. Franklin was normally uptight, but as she and Jax entered the room, she noticed that he mingled and spoke to the donors with ease. He smiled a few times, which ratcheted down the tension. Perhaps the fact that the collection would be here longer than the prior stops on the tour had him on edge. All Briana could do was her job and make things easier for the team until they left.

Jax leaned close, his spicy cologne attracting her attention. She inhaled, losing herself in the scent, then remembered she was on the job.

"Why don't we move to separate areas of the room. We'll be less obtrusive."

"I'll stand by the kitchen."

Jax nodded. "I'll go over by the egress door."

Hoping no one would be concerned by their presence, Briana took her position. The caterers were in and out and a few of the spa staff hovered nearby. People were still admiring the collection, many stopping to chat about the pieces or the movie. The tiara, prominently displayed, was of high interest. Briana would have loved to study it more, but she had a job to do.

Once settled, her gaze moved to Jax, stationed across the room. Tall, carrying his vest as if it weighed nothing at all, his dark hair gleaming in the overhead light. Again, she was struck by how he'd matured. He was still Jax, still her old friend, but now he carried a cool confidence about him that hadn't yet developed when they were in high school. She'd always been attracted to confident men…

"Stop," she muttered to herself. Once the high

stakes from this detail were over, they'd fall into regular rhythms and this strange response to him would go away. She was sure of it.

Animated voices pulled her from her reverie.

As she scanned the crowd, she smiled. Her mother and Royce were chatting with one of the Heirloom Assets staff members. Her mom continued her role on the liaison committee and as a perk, was invited to the exclusive party. Since Linda Connelly loved Golden, it was the perfect job for her. The mayor and his wife, as well as Carrie and Adam and other friends were present, dressed in fancy evening clothing.

Nicole and Addie stood across the room, dressed to the nines with their handsome boyfriends. Taylor wasn't far away, speaking to another couple.

Briana blew out a sigh. She would love to get dressed up, which hadn't happened in quite a while. Her sisters were right, she did need to have more of a social life. After she adopted Cami, invitations to a lot of parties had dwindled. Mostly because her friends knew she didn't like to leave Cami for long and usually turned down their invitations. Her fault, for sure, but now that Cami was getting older and loved sleepovers at her grandmother's house, Briana admitted she should get out there again. It was October and the holidays were quickly approaching. She'd have to make sure she let her friends know she was ready to socialize again. Maybe attend a party or two with Jax.

*With Jax?*

She sighed. Yes. With Jax.

Fifteen minutes later, Mr. Franklin approached her. “I’m sorry for the delay. We’ll start winding down the party now.”

“It looks like a success.”

“Networking is a part of my job.” He sent her a wry glance. “Contrary to my behavior so far, I’m not always a hard taskmaster.”

“This is an unusual circumstance.”

“Indeed.” He nodded in Jax’s direction. “I’m pleased with the way the PD has been handling the transfer of the collection.”

This was only the second night, but she said, “Thank you.”

“Gil and Alec said that you and your partner are professional.”

“We take this responsibility very seriously.”

The man glanced around the room, then said, “I may not see you off tonight. I’ll be with the guests and then I have a meeting scheduled with the staff.”

“Understood.”

“I still need the phone call after the drop-off at the bank.”

“And it will happen, sir.”

Satisfied, Mr. Franklin made another circuit around the room, speaking with donors.

The caterers cleaned up while the party wound down. When the last server exited the kitchen, she stopped. “We’re all finished for the night. The kitchen is spotless.”

“Thanks,” Briana said. “I’ll let the staff know.”

A few donors left as well, but there was still a crowd. The Heirloom Assets team continued to mingle while the security guards discreetly walked the perimeter of the room. Jill and Kat began politely ushering people to the doorway so that they could pack up the collection for the night. Robert approached the women to say a few words before waving to Gil. She lost track of them when her mother approached, smiling from ear to ear.

"This party has been so much fun," she gushed.

Thrilled that her mom was so happy, Briana reached out and squeezed her arm.

"You look fabulous, Mom."

Her mom preened. "Taylor picked the perfect dress for me."

"She has taste, that's for sure."

Her mother blushed. "And Royce likes it too."

Briana chuckled. "Well, if Royce likes it…"

Her mother twirled in a circle. "It's all so magical."

Royce stepped into the twirl, taking her mother's hands in his. "I didn't know there'd be dancing."

The two laughed, in their own world, dancing to music only they heard. With a sigh, Briana glanced across the room. Her gaze collided with Jax's. His blue eyes were intense again, until he smiled and lifted his chin in the direction of her mother and date. Was he signaling that he wanted to dance? Or something else completely?

She returned his smile and went back to surveying the room.

About fifteen minutes later, her nose twitched. Briana breathed deeper, detecting a faint whiff of smoke. Scanning the room, she didn't identify anything suspicious. Could it be from the kitchen? From what she'd understood, the caterers were only using the space to unpack and serve food. The appliances weren't being used.

The smell grew stronger. She glanced at Jax, but he was speaking to Mr. Franklin. She couldn't wait to get his attention, so she slipped into the kitchen.

Most of the lights had been turned off since the caterers had left, except for the recessed light over the doorway. In the dim lighting of the large room, it took a moment for her eyes to adjust. She noticed a haziness on the far side of the room. Walking that way, she heard a click coming from the side door leading from the kitchen to the empty resort dining room. She stopped to check it out, but no one was there. Continuing her path, she noticed a large metal trash can situated near the back door. Smoke was drifting from the can and red glowed around the rim. She ran in that direction to peer inside, discovering a fire burning bright.

Taking a step back, she did a quick mental recall to visualize where the fire extinguisher was located. Remembering the large sign located near the stove, she sprinted over and unhooked the red canister from the wall. Returning to the fire, she pulled the pin at the top to break the seal, aimed the nozzle at the fire, then squeezed the handle to release the extinguishing agent into the flames. She swept it back and forth a few times, then let go of the handle. Edging forward, she could see that it wasn't completely out. She sprayed again. Thick smoke filled the air around her, but the flames were snuffed out.

Her throat grew tight as she inhaled. Coughing, she moved closer to make sure the fire was extinguished. A loud alarm blared, startling her. She jumped, the canister slipping from her hands. Juggling to hold on, the thick smoke disoriented her, and she tipped toward the can. Reaching out with her free hand to steady herself against the wall, her palm made contact with the side of the can instead.

"Ow," she yelped, pulling away, but not before her skin began to burn.

From the radio chatter, she heard Jax call in the fire alarm to dispatch and request backup.

Placing the extinguisher on the counter, she cradled her injured hand with the other and made her way toward the shouts coming from the multipurpose room. She used her back to push the door open, not wanting to use her injured hand, and stepped into a room of distressed voices. People were rushing for the door leading to the lobby. Someone bumped into her and she momentarily lost balance. She quickly regained her footing and attempted to get some control in the midst of the situation. Hearing Jax's voice asking for calm, she tried to make her way across the room. Before she could reach him or the main door, the overhead lights went out.

What was going on?

Voices rose over the alarm. She could barely make out people moving here and there. She'd already taken a few steps toward the door when she heard Jax's voice.

"I'm headed for the bank of switches," he yelled.

"Ten-four."

Before he moved, the lights flared overhead. Robert stood in the doorway, hands up. "It's okay now, folks," he shouted over the still blaring alarm.

Guests blinked and started asking questions among themselves.

Then she heard Jax's voice. "The collection."

Together, they weaved through the guests to get to the center of the room. The alarm suddenly quieted, making the voices louder. Briana first noticed that the pieces displayed on tables covered with blue velvet were untouched. She looked for the award, still on the pedestal, the gold dress on the mannequin, and then…

"The tiara," she said in an urgent tone. "It's gone."

# *CHAPTER SEVEN*

CHAOS ERUPTED IN the room.

"I'll check the lobby," Jax said then took off.

"Please, everyone, quiet down," Briana yelled as loud as she could. This seemed to capture the attention of most, except for the Heirloom Assets staff who now realized a showcase piece of their collection was gone.

Alec, the security guard, guided the guests to stand along the walls while the staff crowded by the collection. Mr. Franklin came to an abrupt stop as he took in the empty pedestal.

"Please tell me one of you have the tiara," he demanded.

"We don't," Jill answered, her face pale and lips trembling.

Mr. Franklin tunneled his hand through his immaculately styled hair. "Update."

No one answered him.

"Update!"

Briana inched near him. "It would appear that when the lights were momentarily off, someone took the tiara."

"Where is the other security guard?"

Gil was nowhere to be found.

Mr. Franklin pulled out his phone and sent a quick text.

He turned to her. "And where were you?"

"In the kitchen, sir. Extinguishing a fire."

His eyebrows rose to his hairline. "Fire?"

She lowered her now stinging hand to her side. "Yes, sir. It's completely out."

"How in…" He shook his head. "Never mind."

Jax walked up to them. "I didn't see anyone running either through the lobby or out in the parking lot." He addressed Mr. Franklin. "I called this in. The chief is coming."

"Find me when he gets here," Franklin barked then pulled his staff to the side.

When he walked away, Briana cradled her hand again.

Jax frowned. "Are you hurt?"

"I was in the kitchen putting out a fire."

"Fire?"

"I'll explain after we take care of this."

Briana read the concern in Jax's eyes, and knew he was about to get all protective of her. He gently took her hand, inhaling a sharp breath when he viewed the raw red skin.

"I'll be fine," she insisted.

Jax sent her a don't-kid-me look.

With a sigh she admitted, "It hurts."

Jax's face went rigid. "You need medical attention."

"After we've investigated," she insisted, ready to fight him on this.

He must have sensed her intent because he said, "Let Brady decide once he's here."

Briana rolled her neck, her head starting to pound, but she went about her duties questioning the guests. After each one answered, she sent them out to the lobby where Alec made sure they remained until further notice.

Once the excitement died down, Jax pulled her to a corner of the room. "Tell me what happened."

"I smelled smoke and went to investigate. A trash can in the kitchen contained flames."

Jax pressed his lips together in a hard line.

She opened her hand and stared. "Long story short, my palm landed on the hot metal."

Jax took her hand in his. "This looks bad."

"I'll have it examined but first..."

A commotion cut her off as Brady, wearing his cop face, approached them. "Report."

"The tiara is missing," Briana told him.

Mr. Franklin walked straight to Brady, his expression a dark thundercloud.

"Tell me your officers didn't allow a fortune in gold to disappear."

Briana wanted to correct him, but Brady shot her a don't-go-there look and answered.

"I just arrived. We're investigating and treating this as a crime scene."

"Of course it's a crime," Mr. Franklin yelled. "The tiara is gone!"

Jax stepped forward. “It had to have been taken during the time the fire alarm started, and the lights went out.”

“How doesn’t matter.” Mr. Franklin turned on him. “The tiara has vanished.”

Brady stepped in to intervene. “We will uncover what happened.”

Mr. Franklin ran a hand down his face, keeping his hand on his chin as he paced.

Briana took a deep breath. This was not good.

“We need time to investigate,” Brady announced. “I suggest you let us do our job.”

In an aggressive stance, Mr. Franklin moved back to Brady. “Not without an inventory.” He yelled at his staff to get started.

What they needed was to de-escalate the situation, Briana thought, but kept her mouth shut. Brady, correctly perceiving that Mr. Franklin was about to blow, said, “Ten-four.”

Briana bristled. Although they shouldn’t disturb anything right now because a thorough crime scene evaluation was necessary, Mr. Franklin and his staff were the people who would know for certain what was missing.

“I know it’s not protocol,” Brady said as if reading her mind. “We’ll need to do inventory at some point anyway. This will get us one step closer.”

Briana felt slightly nauseous as the reality of the night sank in.

Brady turned his attention to her. His eyes narrowed. “Are you okay, Connelly?”

When she didn't answer, Jax offered, "She was burned putting out a fire in the kitchen."

The chief's eyes went wide. "Why didn't you mention it? Do you need medical attention?"

"No, Chief. I'm fine."

Brady closed his eyes for a split second then stepped away to call EMS.

"Thanks," Briana muttered under her breath.

"You'd do the same if our positions were reversed," Jax disputed in a firm tone.

True, but she didn't want anyone to fuss over her. She wanted a bag of ice to cool her skin and to start investigating.

Jax paused and looked at her intently. "Are you dizzy? Lingering smoke inhalation?"

"No. Just angry."

She noted his small grin. "Not seeing double?"

"One of you is enough." She lightly pushed him away, annoyed by his hovering. What she needed was to take a deep breath and review in her mind what had just happened.

"Let's go to the lobby."

She followed him as the throbbing in her hand intensified.

Sirens sounded in the distance. Briana's nerves started to tingle in the aftermath of the excitement. Through the large lobby windows, she glanced at the parking lot. A backup squad car followed by an EMS truck and fire engine. She recognized fellow officer Hank Jones and Deputy Thompson. Two men jumped from the emergency vehicle, grabbed their gear and headed to the main entrance.

"Great," she muttered under her breath, walking their way to intercept the men.

Jax turned to her. "What?"

"You'll see."

A tall man with thick chestnut brown hair and brown eyes stopped in front of her. "Evan," she greeted him.

"We never had this much excitement when we were partners," he commented in a light tone.

"Good thing since rushing to medical emergencies is your specialty now."

His smile dimmed when she held up her hand. Her palm smarted like crazy.

"Burn?"

"Fire in the kitchen."

"Let's go over by the registration desk where the lighting is better."

With Jax on her heels, Briana went with Evan. Curious folks watched them pass but Briana tuned them out.

Evan pulled on a pair of disposable gloves, took her hand in his and examined the injury. "That burn looks pretty angry."

"It isn't bad."

"Not bad?" Evan said with a strangled voice. "Briana, you're white as a sheet."

"She won't admit she's hurting." Jax moved closer. "Jax Walker, new partner."

Evan nodded. "Evan Stiles, old partner."

"Isn't this just old home week," Briana muttered.

"Someone's grumpy." Evan offered a small grin.

She shifted the heavy vest which started to strain her shoulders. "You would be too if you put out a fire and got burned in the process."

Evan ignored her and assessed the issue. "The skin isn't broken, which is good. I'll place some salve with a numbing agent on it and you'll be good to go."

Briana puffed out a breath of relief.

Evan flicked a penlight back and forth to assess her pupils. "Does this bother you?"

"No. Why would it?"

He put the light away. "Because your body is under extreme stress." Then he glanced at Jax. "Pupils are fine."

She wanted to argue with the whole process but was quickly losing steam.

Evan went back to his gear, pulling out a square package. When he tore it open, Briana's nose wrinkled at the strong smell of medication.

"This is going to sting, isn't it."

"It should actually soothe your skin."

Holding her breath, she waited for the salve to sting. When it didn't, she relaxed until Ethan tightened his grasp on her wrist.

"Ow."

"Sorry."

Pain seared across her palm. The medication reduced the throbbing only a little. She bit the inside of her cheek when he applied a bandage, then wrapped her hand with gauze. After the final examination, he asked if she wanted to go to the hospital.

"No. I'm really okay, Evan."

He nodded. "I'll take you at your word, but if this looks worse tomorrow, you'll need to see a doctor."

"I promise."

He stored his gear then headed back to the emergency vehicle to meet up with his partner who had checked on other guests. Once Evan was out of sight, Briana tried to untangle the gauze. Jax saw what she was up to and stopped her.

"You need to keep that on," he said in a bossy tone.

"I don't want to scare Cami when I get home."

"The red skin will probably scare her more than the bandage."

She didn't want to admit it, but Jax was right. She must be rattled, that was the only conclusion.

The event room door swung open. Brady stuck his head out. "Please come inside," he told his officers.

Before moving, Jax held her gaze. "If there's any blame, it's on both of us. We were both in the room."

True, but she'd given up her post to check the kitchen. Later she'd inform him he was wrong, but for now, she'd take responsibility for her actions.

"It'll be okay, Brie."

This wasn't like when they were kids and could talk their way out of trouble.

"I don't think so, Jax."

Sure enough, when they entered the room, the tension was thick. Mr. Franklin was on his phone, pacing. Robert had removed his sports jacket which was lying across one of the velvet-covered tables. He called out the pieces to Jill and Kat, who held clipboards, checking off the inventory. At one point, the jacket slipped to the floor. With a huff, Robert kicked it halfway under the table, then continued. They soon learned that nothing else had been taken. Briana had to stop herself. *Stolen.* The tiara had been stolen.

"You." Mr. Franklin pointed at her.

Her stomach dropped.

"You left your position," he accused.

"I was putting out a fire, sir."

Mr. Franklin inhaled and dropped his head back to stare at the ceiling. "Any one of the fine people of Golden who attended this party could be the culprit."

The accusation sent a shiver over Briana.

Robert came up to Mr. Franklin. "What else can I do?"

Franklin's gaze narrowed. "Where were you?"

"Yes," Brady said. "I'll like to hear that answer."

Robert's throat moved as he swallowed. "The LA office called. I went to a quiet location to discuss business. When I heard the fire alarm I rushed back into the room and then the lights went out."

Mr. Franklin glanced around the room. "And Gil?"

Robert shrugged.

Brady looked over at Jax. "Go after—"

The door burst open. Gil rushed inside, his face red.

"Where have you been?" Mr. Franklin shouted.

Gil hurried closer. Before he could speak, Brady held up his hand. "Why weren't you with the other guard?"

"Ms. Baine asked me to check the lock on her office door before I brought the dress there later."

Briana didn't miss the sharp glance Gil sent in Robert's direction. Robert met his gaze with an expression she couldn't read, then Gil dropped his head.

Kat came forward, handing Franklin the clipboard. "Inventory complete. Only the tiara is missing."

Mr. Franklin scanned the list before shoving the clipboard back at Kat.

"This is a nightmare," he sputtered as his face turned bright red. "Our reputation is on the line."

"I'm afraid there is going to be a police investigation, Mr. Franklin," Brady said in a calm voice.

Mr. Franklin stared at him. His voice was shaky. "Nothing like this has ever happened before."

"We will get to the bottom of this," Brady pledged to the man.

Mr. Franklin checked his watch. "It's too late to call the insurance company. Tomorrow is Sunday. First thing Monday morning, I'll get their guidance on next steps."

Brady nodded. "And we'll be talking to the

guests from the party, as well as any resort staff who were on-site and the caterers who provided the food for the party. Once the firefighters finish their sweep of the kitchen to assure there are no other threats, we'll search in there."

"If it's okay," Robert said, "I'd like to check in with the firefighters and ask them to send a report to Heirloom Assets."

Brady nodded and the man took off.

Mr. Franklin straightened his tie as if trying to pull himself together. "I'll expect a meeting in this room first thing Monday morning. Nine a.m."

"We'll be here," Brady confirmed.

Giving them a terse nod, Mr. Franklin joined his staff who were huddled together, their faces lined with worry.

"Hank and Deputy Thompson are searching and interviewing the guests who haven't left yet," Brady informed Briana and Jax.

Sick with worry, it was all Briana could do not to clasp her bandaged hand to her chest. "What can we do?"

"Right now, you need to go home." Brady handed her the keys to his SUV. "Take my vehicle back to the station, go home and get some rest. Tomorrow we'll sort this all out."

"But what about transferring the remaining gold to the bank?"

"Jax and I will handle it tonight."

"But—"

"Take my vehicle, Officer Connelly," Brady commanded, his tone tight. "That's an order."

That's when Briana knew she was in deep trouble.

JAX TOOK A sip of the steaming coffee he'd just poured. He sighed at the hit of much desired caffeine. After a sleepless night, he needed an edge to keep him alert. It was eight o'clock on Sunday morning and all the officers had been notified about the mandatory meeting the chief had called.

Brady joined him at the coffee station. "Have you talked to Briana?"

"Not yet. I didn't want to disturb her last night."

"I'm sure she was up for hours going through events, coming at them from different angles."

Jax knew she'd take it personally. Take responsibility.

"Bottom line, she feels guilty."

"Which she shouldn't. If she hadn't smelled the smoke and investigated, the night would have ended with an additional disaster." Brady scrubbed a hand over his chin. "Besides, Franklin had his security team there as well and they didn't stop the theft."

Jax's gut felt as if a boulder was sitting at the bottom of his stomach. Pending an investigation, would Brie be sidelined? She wouldn't like that one bit.

Five minutes later she arrived, removing her sunglasses as she came indoors. She wouldn't meet his gaze, not good, and beelined straight to her desk to take a seat. Jax made his way over.

"How are you feeling?"

"Like I let the PD down."

"I meant your injury."

She held up a fresh bandage. "Nothing a few days won't cure."

He blew out an exasperated breath. "You don't need to downplay how you feel on my account."

She glared at him. "I'm not."

She was but he'd let it go.

He moved to another topic. "Last night was rough."

"I'm a professional. I'll take whatever discipline Brady hands out."

"He shouldn't be handing out anything. You did nothing wrong. Plus, you stopped a potential fire that could have destroyed the resort kitchen."

Brady walked out of his office and looked their way. "Conference room."

Brie jumped up to follow while Jax grabbed his notepad from his desk. Roan, Wes and Kelli brought up the rear. Hank was on patrol.

Was it just a few days ago that he'd sat in this very room, registering the surprise on Brie's face when she found out he'd be her partner? And what kind of partner was he when he let her get hurt?

After they'd all taken a seat, Brady spoke first.

"As Golden's chief of police, I need to inform you that there will be an internal investigation concerning last night's event."

Jax watched Brie's gaze cut away from Brady then move back again.

"First, I was out at the crime scene early this morning. Nothing new there, but the resort staff is gathering all security video for us to review."

Jax kept an eye on Brie. Her shoulders dropped a fraction at the news.

"Right now, there isn't enough physical evidence to guide our investigation."

She gnawed on her lower lip.

"Here's where we stand," Brady continued. "Hank and Deputy Thompson took statements last night from the guests who were on the premises for the party. No one saw anything out of the ordinary, nor did they see anyone take the tiara. They seemed to recall only confusion between the time the fire alarm sounded and after the lights came back on." He glanced down at his notebook. "No one knew anything about the fire until the alarm blared. I think it's safe to speculate that it was started as a diversion, but the Golden Fire Department is investigating. We'll have to wait for their final report."

He paused, ran a hand over his mouth before saying, "Franklin is blaming the city of Golden."

Questions and outrage came from all around the table. Brady held up his hand.

"It's ridiculous. Just because our citizens were at the party, he's convinced one of our own took the tiara."

"Which creates a problem," Jax said.

"Affirmative. We'll have to thoroughly investigate everyone who was at the party." Brady's gaze met and held each officer's gaze. "Someone took the tiara, that's where we stand."

"But how would the perp know to turn off the lights?" Brie asked. "Wouldn't the person expect the diversion from the fire alarm to cover their actions?"

"Chance?" Brady surmised. His intense gaze took in his officers. "I'll expect full reports on my desk immediately."

Brie's eyes were bleak. "I stayed up last night going over every movement minute by minute. I completed my report already."

When she should have been resting, Jax thought. He'd wanted to stop by her house but wasn't sure he'd be welcome.

Brady nodded, as if unsurprised by her proficiency. Jax still needed to go through his own memories of what had taken place.

Asking if Wes or Kelli had anything else to report about the resort, or with the morning transfer at the bank, they said no.

"As for the consortium," Brady continued, "I spoke with Franklin at length earlier. He actually managed to get ahold of someone at the insurance company. They'll be requesting witness statements and incident reports."

"What about the remainder of the tour?" Jax asked.

"Franklin still doesn't want to make a big deal about this. He insists that the displays be open to the public each day as scheduled as if nothing happened. He'll figure out a way to explain the tiara not being exhibited."

Jax frowned. "Is that wise?"

"He insists that they need to remain normal."

Jax jotted down another note. "And the insurance company is going along with this plan?"

"According to him, yes."

Brie frowned. "That seems risky."

"For Franklin, I think reputation comes before risk." Brady ran a hand over his mouth. "Wes and Kelli, you'll keep your assigned schedule. Stay alert."

"Yes, sir," they replied in unison.

"You can go."

Kelli sent Brie a sympathetic glance as she left the room.

Jax read the discomfort on Brady's face and knew there was more bad news. "Chief?"

Folding his hands atop the table, Brady said, "Franklin needs someone to blame for the theft and while blaming the guests is too wide, Briana is the most convenient target." He shifted to face her. "You were out of the room for a brief period of time, so he's grabbed hold of that excuse, even though you extinguished that fire. If you hadn't been there, the night could have ended in a much worse scenario."

"What does that mean for the transfer?" Brie asked. "Even during the investigation, the gold needs to be delivered to the bank each night."

"Yes. But not by you."

Jax caught her incredulous expression and inwardly grimaced.

"As of tomorrow, you're on regular duty until we clear this up," the chief informed her.

"But I can be useful."

"I know, Officer, but Franklin doesn't want you on the bank detail and as things stand right now, with your injury, I wouldn't let you. We'll go through proper channels with an internal review." He turned to Roan. "I'll have Hank take over your duty at Oktoberfest while you partner up with Jax."

"Chief," Brie said in a sharp tone at the same time Roan said, "Yes, sir."

Brady shot Brie a quelling glance. "Not now."

Jax's stomach clenched when she asked Brady, "You blame me?"

"No, but Franklin does. And he strikes me as the kind of man to threaten a lawsuit if he doesn't get his way."

"I can't just sit at my desk while you all investigate," Brie insisted.

"You won't, Officer. First, I want you to attend the events the Chamber of Commerce has going on in conjunction with the collection tour. Talk to the townspeople. They may know something but don't realize it."

Brie nodded.

"And then I want you to do what you do best."

Brie frowned. "Which is?"

"Dig."

At the one word, her expression lightened.

"What are you thinking, Chief?" Jax asked, his mind already focused on the big picture.

"That this was much too easy. No one knew what time the party was going to end. And to blame a roomful of people? A stretch."

Just what Jax was thinking. "So it's an inside job?"

"Possibly. What I need is a deep dive on the staff of Heirloom Assets."

Brie straightened. "I can do that."

"We don't have a lot of time, but I'm afraid Franklin's going to come after you personally, Briana. You need to be prepared."

She paled. It was all Jax could do not to express his concern. She wouldn't appreciate the gesture.

Brady looked right at her. "We have your back, Connelly."

"Thanks."

"In the meantime, we have our work cut out for us. Walker, get me your report from last night, then you and Roan go out to the resort and question the staff again. Tonight, you and I will transfer the collection to the bank."

Jax nodded.

"Briana, for now, I want you to go home and rest for the remainder of the day."

"Chief—"

"Department policy. You need to go home."

Brie looked like she wanted to argue but closed her mouth. She rose and said, "I'll see you tomorrow."

She slipped out the door, leaving a heaviness in the air. A troubled silence blanketed the room.

Jax spoke first. "Franklin's really going to go after her?"

Brady ran a hand over his chin. "Afraid so."

"She didn't have anything to do with the theft of the tiara," Roan insisted.

"You know that, and I know that, but Franklin isn't thinking straight."

"We need to clear her of any wrongdoing," Jax said.

Brady held his gaze. "Our first priority."

Jax's voice was steel when he said, "Copy that."

# CHAPTER EIGHT

"WE'RE ON DUTY, BOYS."

Alvin Walker stood in front of the fireplace, facing his oldest friends, who were seated around the living room. They varied in size and shape, many sported gray hair, but had shared love and laughter, grief and loss, along with happiness and disappointment, which, when added together, brought many years of expertise.

"What are you thinking, boss?" Gandy Spiers, also a retired police officer, asked with a hint of excitement in his voice.

"Our town is in trouble."

Four heads nodded, each man ready to do his part.

Besides Alvin and Gandy, his crew consisted of Monroe Miller, a semi-retired attorney, and Curt Smith, retired FBI. The years they'd spent in law enforcement had created a bond none of them would ever sever. Even if they squabbled over sports, trucks and the size of the fish they caught on the lake, they were loyal friends.

"When Jax came home last night," Alvin told

them, "he explained what went down at the resort. I read the worry on my grandson's face, so I peppered him with questions. That's when I decided to call in reinforcements."

"Did he tell you much?" Curt asked, his tanned face weathered by days spent outdoors.

"As much as he could. It won't take long for the rumor mill to get a headwind of the theft. Between what Jax could tell me and what I read between the lines, I picked up a few more details at Sit A Spell when I went downtown for my morning coffee."

Monroe folded his hands over his barrel chest. "The tiara is gone."

"Affirmative."

"And the folks who attended the fancy party are suspects," Curt surmised.

Alvin nodded.

"So where do we come in?" Monroe asked.

"Before this went down, Jax and I had a talk. I suggested that the Golden Watch Network do our part around town, what with Oktoberfest, and now the movie exhibit, happening. With this latest dustup, I need to include all y'all in more than our usual watch."

"Which makes what we observe more important now," Curt deduced.

Alvin nodded. "We have skills that retirement sure hasn't dulled. And Monroe, you've got the legal expertise to keep us on the right side of the law."

"You're right that we don't have legal standing,"

Monroe concurred as he pushed his glasses higher up the bridge of his nose, "but we are citizens of Golden. Our voice matters. Problem is, we don't have any idea of who we're looking for."

"Can Jax throw some intel in our direction?" Curt asked.

"Not as much as I'd like." Alvin rubbed his stubbled jaw. "Gandy, you still got those old walkie-talkies?"

"Somewhere at the house. I can dig 'em out. Put in new batteries."

"They aren't high-tech, but we can keep them nearby. If we see anything hinky, we'll let each other know, and then I'll contact Jax."

"Are you sure he won't mind?" Gandy asked. "He wasn't too happy with us the other day at Smitty's."

Alvin waved a hand. "He knows we didn't mean anything by the ruckus. But this is serious. We need to do our part. We can't have the good name of Golden besmirched."

The others nodded.

"I think we need lookout positions," Alvin said.

Curt rubbed a hand over his sparse hair. "As in?"

Alvin turned to the lawyer. "Monroe, you're still helping folks at the courthouse, right?"

"As often as I'm asked. All the staff knows me there."

"That can be your location."

"That works. No one will think it's strange that I'm hanging around."

"Gandy, you got Linda's General Store. Miss

Betty works there, and we all know you're sweet on her, so it makes sense you'd be hangin' around."

He shot up from the armchair. "Who said I'm sweet on Betty?"

Curt rolled his eyes. "We've all seen it, buddy."

Gandy crossed his arms and sat with a huff. "Fine."

"And Curt," Alvin continued. "Your grandson owns the T-shirt Depot and you work there from time to time. Good way to keep an eye on Main Street."

"Got it."

"What about you?" Monroe asked Alvin.

"Brady brings me in from time to time to consult. It's not strange for me to be around an investigation. Between the coffee shop and the PD, I can cover some ground."

"What are we on the outlook for exactly?" Gandy asked.

"Anything strange taking place. There are tourists in and out of town, but they are most likely not suspects of the theft at the resort since it was our people at that party. But we know our locals. We'll recognize anyone acting strange."

"Heard there was some pickpocketing going on at Oktoberfest," Curt said.

"Roan Donovan's on that. Doing a good job. We'll still show up there, but we also need to include the resort in our recon. The perp might have left a clue."

"We can do all that," Gandy said.

"There's more," Alvin said. He filled in the team about the fire, Briana putting it out and ultimately being the target of Franklin's ire. "While I have no doubt that girl is more than capable, she was rattled." Alvin shifted his stance. "Brady's on it, but from what I sensed from Jax, the head honcho from the consortium is putting pressure on the chief." He paused. "I've got a theory."

"Shoot," Gandy said as he moved to the edge of his seat.

"That tour hasn't had a lick of trouble while traveling across the country. Last stop, and someone decides to grab the goods? We gotta check out the team and make sure one of them isn't dirty."

"So what, we each pick a day and go see the display?" Monroe asked.

"Exactly. I'll go tomorrow, Curt the next and then Gandy, you invite Betty. Monroe, you and the missus can finish out the week."

Gandy blinked like an owl. "Invite Betty?"

Alvin shook his head. "You know you want to."

"And from what my wife says," Monroe added, "she's been waiting."

A slow smile curved the corners of Gandy's lips. "Perfect reason to ask her on a date."

"Finally," Curt deadpanned. "After all your hemming and hawing, you get to spy and impress Betty in one fell swoop."

Gandy's skinny chest puffed out. "I can do that."

The men fell into a thoughtful silence.

"This is the most important mission the Golden

Watch Network has ever undertaken," Monroe declared, his tone grave.

The others agreed.

"Okay, boys," Alvin said, wrangling them back on topic. "Are we in?"

"In," Gandy said.

"In," Curt echoed.

"I'm in," Monroe said with a decisive nod of his head.

Alvin smiled, satisfaction landing deep in his soul. He touched the side of his nose with his right index finger. The others followed suit. "Let the recon begin."

A CHILL RAN through him as Jax knocked on the door to Brie's house. The temperature had dipped significantly after the sun sank below the tree line and a nippy wind hurled between branches, knocking even more leaves to the hard ground. If his hands weren't full, he would have zipped up his jacket to ward against the cold.

The porch light came on and a face peered through the window. A second later, the locks turned, and Brie opened the door. Dressed in a sweatshirt, baggy lounge pants and slippers, she ran a hand through her damp hair.

"Jax. What're you doing here?"

"I didn't mean to bother you." He held up the bigger of the two bags. "Your mom sent dinner."

Her face brightened. "C'mon in."

He wiped his boots and stepped into the warm

interior. The air smelled like apple and cinnamon spice. Orange flames licked at a log in the fireplace. He'd only ever imagined how comfortable Brie's home would be, having never actually been inside.

She took the bags so he could remove the jacket zippered over his sweater. "How did you get all this?" she asked, peering into the bag.

"My grandfather's buddies are at the house, so I decided to stay clear after my shift before they cause trouble. I think it's card night and I assume there'll be yelling before too long."

"Even after the scene at Smitty's?"

"They're old buddies. They argue and then forget what the disagreement was all about before returning to being good friends. Especially if they band together for a cause."

"The Golden Watch Network?"

"So far they've colored within the lines."

"But you ducked out for your own peace of mind?"

"And went to the general store to get a sandwich from the deli. Your mom stopped me and asked me to make a delivery."

"Convenient." She peeked into the smaller bag. "A sandwich and dessert?" She pulled out a clear package. "Homemade brownies. I see you still have a sweet tooth."

"Some things never change."

Their gazes met and held until Brie looked away.

He cleared his throat. "I was going to come by

anyway. That conversation at the station this morning was rough."

A muscle bunched in her jaw at the reminder.

He motioned toward her. "How's your hand?"

"Fine. Tender, but I'll survive." She waved. "Let's get this food to the kitchen."

"You'd tell me otherwise, right? You're not covering up for my sake?"

Indignation filled her tone. "Jax, I've been taking care of myself for a long time. I'm also a mom now. I won't take unnecessary chances."

Fair enough, he thought. He'd be vigilant just to make sure, even if it meant they'd have a conversation neither of them would like.

Careful of her hand still wrapped in gauze, she led him through the cozy living room, carrying the larger bag to a small kitchen. The white cabinets and black granite countertop made a bold statement. Stainless steel appliances and a black-and-white patterned backsplash added a modern touch. She'd just placed the bag on the counter when Cami came running in.

"Jax. You're here."

He scooped her up. "I am."

She got right in his face. "Did you bring me anything?"

"How about dinner?"

"Yay. My belly is growling."

"You had a snack an hour ago," Brie reminded her.

"That was sooo long ago."

Brie shook her head. "Miss Drama Queen."

Jax smiled at the little girl. "I hate when that happens. Gotta fill the belly is what I say."

"See, Mama?" Cami rubbed her stomach. "Gotta feed the belly."

"Thanks," Brie said, shooting him a dubious expression.

Cami leaned forward, watching Brie unpack the bags. Jax held on tighter so she wouldn't tumble out of his arms.

"Let's see," Brie said as she pulled out the clear containers. "Looks like pot roast and vegetables, potatoes and coleslaw."

Jax leaned closer to the heavenly aroma. He and Cami sniffed at the same time.

Brie grinned at him. "How does that sandwich sound now?"

"Lacking," he answered as his stomach grumbled right on cue.

Cami giggled, shaking against his chest.

"That's the problem with being single. I never cook for myself."

Brie nodded toward the bag. "Good thing there's plenty. You can share our dinner."

"You don't mind?"

"You're standing in my kitchen after a delivery so I can't send you away."

He caught her gaze. "You'd send me away otherwise?"

She sighed. "Never. You know that."

In a way, she had, once before. Yes, she'd been the one to walk away that night in the park, sending him on his adventure in the military alone. After years of distance between them, it was good to hear her say the words.

Before long there were plates on the round black lacquer table, and they were tucking into the food. Cami kept up a running conversation, talking about her antics at the general store, the drawings she'd made and how she couldn't wait for Halloween.

"I'm going to be a princess," she informed Jax in a haughty tone.

He chuckled. "I can't imagine you being anyone else."

As he was taking a bite of the tender roast, something brushed his leg. He looked down to find a gray and white, well-fed cat staring up at him.

"You remember Mr. Darcy?" Brie asked.

"I remember his claws."

Brie frowned. "He's mellowed."

Jax's eyebrows rose. "Are you sure?"

"You'll see," she countered in a sure tone.

The cat meowed as if in agreement.

"Can I feed him?"

"Please don't." She pointed her fork at the cat. "I don't want him to get spoiled."

"Yeah, Mommy gave me talking-to about feeding him." Cami leaned close to Jax and whispered, "It's a no-no."

Jax held back a laugh and took a bite of the savory meat and vegetables. Mr. Darcy sniffed and walked away, gray tail in the air. "Not interested."

Brie shrugged. "He can be picky."

Jax scooped potatoes onto his fork. "From what I recall, he has you wrapped around his tiny paw."

"Hey, I can't help it if he's special. Besides, he's a sweetheart."

"He sleeps with me," Cami said.

"The narrow-eyed glance he's wielding my way is telling me to keep my distance from the pair of you."

Brie reached down to pick up the hefty cat and rubbed her cheek against his fur. "He's a sweetheart. I've had him since before I went to the police academy."

"Mama says he was her first child."

Jax watched Brie's face turn an appealing shade of pink.

"I'm glad you have him."

"Thanks." She lowered Mr. Darcy to the floor. "Dessert, anyone?"

Cami clapped her hands.

"I'll take that as a yes." Brie turned to Jax. "Mind clearing the table while I make coffee?"

"Sure thing."

"I'm going to my room to play," Cami announced.

"Have fun, sweetie."

As they went about their tasks, it was as if the same rhythms from the past kicked in. They sidestepped each other in a familiar dance, cleaning up in no time.

Brie removed a dish from the cabinet. "I talked

to your grandfather at the park yesterday. He seems excited to help the PD."

Jax leaned back against the counter. "We had a long discussion about his retirement. With Grams gone, he's having a hard time settling in."

"And Brady knows?"

"Full disclosure." He frowned. "What I didn't count on was the Golden Watch Network."

"Knowing that crew, they would have volunteered to be involved either way."

"True."

Brie placed the brownies on a pumpkin-shaped dish and removed autumn-themed mugs from the cabinet. Once the coffee was poured, she said, "Want to eat in the living room?"

"Wherever you want," he told her.

As they headed into the living room, mugs in hand, Jax noticed fall decorations everywhere. "You really get into the holidays," he commented.

Brie took a seat at one end of the couch and placed the plate and mug on the wooden coffee table. "I do it for Cami. She loves to decorate."

He took a seat at the opposite end. "I recall fall was your favorite season."

"It still is. I love the changing leaves. My mom always made a big deal about Halloween and Thanksgiving. Guess I inherited that trait."

He glanced around the room. The overstuffed blue-and-white-striped couch was situated under the front window, a solid navy chair angled beside it with an end table in between. A large area rug in shades of blue, mauve and tan covered the shiny wood floor. A television sat on a console in the corner, with the volume down, and the fireplace took up the opposite wall. The room was toasty, but he felt a draft coming through the window casing.

Before he turned his attention back to Brie, a book on the end table caught his attention. He picked the novel up and read the title. “I see you’re still reading historical romances.”

She reached over to grab the book from his hand to hide it behind her. “Tell anyone and I’ll deny it.”

“You always did have a mushy heart.”

“Take that back.”

“Brie, it’s a great quality to have. Love and compassion make you a great cop. You don’t always have to be tough as nails.”

She frowned. “I guess.”

Clearly uncomfortable about his observation, she said, “I need to get the windows replaced. Next on my to-do list.”

“Are there a lot of needed upgrades?”

She hooked one leg under herself and angled toward him. “This house was a fixer-upper when I moved in. I’ve managed to take care of many of the necessary fixes, like the kitchen, which was horrible, and I painted the entire inside. The windows are costly, so they’re the last project.” She patted the colorful crocheted throw on the back of the couch. “Thankfully we love to snuggle under the blankets.”

Sitting in the firelight, Brie never looked lovelier.

Her blond hair shone, having dried into a frenzy of waves. Her skin held a healthy glow despite the aftereffects from the previous night's events. She'd grown into a beautiful woman, not only in appearance, but in character. Being a mom added to the appeal. Even though they weren't as close as they once were, there was still a bond between them that Jax hoped would never be shaken.

He took a sip of his coffee, his gaze moving again, stopping on a whiteboard set up across the room. He leaned forward. "You keep a crime scene board in your living room?"

He could have sworn her cheeks colored. "Normally Cami and I practice numbers and letters, but I couldn't sleep last night so I started thinking. It's easier to keep track of information when I can see it."

He placed his mug on the coffee table and got up to study the board. The names of the rep and staff of Heirloom Assets were neatly written in black marker. A picture of the tiara took center space. Strands of red, black and yellow yarn were taped to the top of the board but hung free, not yet crisscrossed against the board.

Brie came up beside him. "This is how I process."

"You haven't connected the yarn to anything."

"Too early. Once I start investigating, the board will come together."

"Where'd you find the pictures?"

"Heirloom Assets website. Tomorrow, I plan on

going over the website and public records in more detail."

"You know you don't have to do this alone," he told her.

"You heard Brady. He wants me to dig." He felt her shift beside him. "Besides, I have the PD behind me."

Turning his head, he added, "And me. You always have me."

She pressed her lips together but continued staring at the board.

"You doubt that?"

"No, I… It's been a long time since we had each other's backs."

"This time is different. I'm home, Brie. I'm not going anywhere. And I'm not going to let you take the fall for the missing tiara."

Her expression softened. "Thanks."

"Mama, I put my jammies on," Cami announced as she ran into the room. Jax glimpsed the mismatched top and pants and bit the inside of his cheek.

Brie grinned. "Perfect."

Cami gracefully executed a pirouette like any professional ballerina.

"Let's sit," Brie suggested.

They resumed their seats and Cami climbed onto the couch to cuddle on Brie's lap. The picture made Jax speechless. And a little envious, something he'd have to ponder later.

"Mommy gots an owie," Cami said, her small

hand cupping Brie's hand. "I kissed it and made it better."

"That's the best medicine there is."

Cami snuggled deeper.

"So, the house," he said.

Brie glanced around the room with a smile. "Yeah, I bought it myself."

"Without any help?"

Shadows darkened her eyes. She knew what he was asking. "I insisted." Her expression turned hard. "My dad wanted to buy it for me, but I refused. After what he did, I couldn't take anything from him."

Jax was wise enough to refrain from continuing the topic of her father. "What about your mom?"

Brie slowly relaxed. "She was still getting the store up and running. I didn't want her to take any extra funds away from her dream."

"Your family is lucky to have you."

She shrugged. Cami wiggled onto the cushions, her head resting on Brie's lap. Her eyes drooped as they talked.

Curious about Brie's life now, he asked, "What do you and Cami like to do together?"

"Hiking. Going to the lake."

"That tracks." Anytime they could, he and Brie were outdoors.

Brie ran a finger over Cami's cheek. "Right now, any time I have off I spend with her. Our favorite is a walk to the park. Cami loves the swings."

"So did you."

She met his gaze. “We hung out in the park a lot.”

“Does she like to be pushed? Go high?”

Briana’s smile turned his heart. “She loves flying high.”

“Like you.”

She nodded. “We had so many good times when we were growing up. Golden was, and is, a terrific place for kids.”

“You’re right. We ran from one end of town to the other and got caught up in all kinds of shenanigans.”

They both grew quiet, lost in the past.

“I sent you pictures,” she said.

“You did. I was proud of you.”

A slight smile tipped Brie’s lips. Eyes on Cami, she stroked her daughter’s hair as Cami’s breathing evened out. “You never said anything.”

How did he explain that he was jealous at the time. She’d turned him down when he’d asked her to leave town with him, yet she’d continued on so effortlessly with her life. Finishing school. Joining the police academy. Buying a house. All while he still chose to live on base.

Instead of admitting that not so stellar envy, he nodded at Cami. “Is she asleep?”

Brie shifted her head to get a better look at her daughter’s face. “Yes.”

They were silent for a moment. The wind picked up outside while the logs snapped in the fireplace.

“Tell me about the adoption.”

Brie’s head came up, wariness in her eyes.

"I was out of line the other day at the station," he said. "I really want to know the full story. Not just the bits and pieces I've heard."

Brie tugged the blanket from the back of the couch and covered her slumbering daughter.

"I'd been with the PD for a few years when I caught a domestic call late one night. When we arrived, a girl, so scrawny she didn't look much older than sixteen, was outside a house on the outskirts of town. It was winter, she had no coat and was only wearing a thin T-shirt, threadbare jeans and socks. Her boyfriend was inside, ranting over some perceived slight from this poor girl. I was working with Brady then, before he was chief. While he questioned the male, I went to talk to the girl."

Gently running her fingers through Cami's hair, Brie's eyes got that faraway look, as if being transported back in time to the scene. Jax could relate. Some calls were more significant than others and left a mark.

"I found out her name was Katie. She was nearly hysterical because she had nowhere to go. I got a blanket out of the patrol car and as I placed it over her, I could see she was pregnant. I put her in the car and once she was warm, she started talking, telling me how she was only eighteen and her boyfriend was twenty. They hadn't been together long, but he'd taken her in because she was a runaway. Their relationship was contentious, as I'd confirm later when I saw the bruises on her arms."

She blinked, as if to wipe away the memory.

"Apparently the boyfriend had become belligerent. Scared, she called 911. When he found out, he kicked her out. She was worried about the baby, so eventually I took her to the clinic. Found out she was seven months along, although she didn't look it. Thankfully she and the baby were fine."

"What happened to the boyfriend?"

"He'd done some drugs earlier that night and was out of control, so we called for backup. They took him to the station while I looked after Katie. Later, I helped her find a safe place to stay while we handled the situation. The boyfriend was charged, Brady had found drugs and firearms in the house, so he went to jail. Katie wanted to get away from him but was afraid she'd give in and go back once he bailed out. I finally got her to talk about her family and found out she had a grandmother living near Atlanta. Over time, I convinced her to move there. She agreed on one condition. That I help her make arrangements to put the baby up for adoption."

"Probably wise under the circumstances."

"It was, but I couldn't get the idea of her baby going to a stranger out of my head. I guess I felt really invested." Brie ran a hand over Cami's back. "One night I couldn't sleep, and the idea came to me. I could adopt the child. Sure, I'm single, but there wasn't a good reason to stop me, especially if Katie was onboard. I had a good job, roots in the community, own my home. I ran the idea by Katie, and she started crying. I thought maybe she'd changed her mind, but she was happy that I wanted the baby. So, I went through the process and after Cami was born, I brought her home."

"Let me guess, you felt responsible for Katie."

"What if it had been one of my sisters? I would have done anything to help them."

"Which makes Katie a pretty lucky girl."

Brie tucked a few strands of Cami's hair behind one ear. "I never had a doubt. Not once."

"Why would you? You always stood up for the underdog and protected the weak. Even when we were kids."

She chuckled. "I'm not saying it was easy, but I wouldn't change a thing."

They sat in silence for a few moments, watching the fire crackle and burn.

"What happened to Katie?" Jax asked.

"Once she got to her grandmother's house, her life turned around. She finished high school, started taking classes at a local college. We've kept in touch with each other. I send her pictures of Cami and she keeps me up to date with her progress."

One of the success stories in a job where at times they had to deal with the worst side of humanity. Jax sipped the coffee that had grown cold, grimaced, and set it down.

"Can I ask why you didn't tell me?"

Regret simmered in her gaze.

"I'm sorry about that. Once I made the decision, things were kind of a blur. You'd been stationed at a new base with a new position. We didn't talk much during that time." She went quiet for a moment. "I also didn't think you'd approve."

He sat straight. "Why not?"

"You wanted me to go away with you when you entered the military, and I turned you down." She shrugged. "Now I was taking on this enormous responsibility with the adoption. I wanted to do this on my own."

"Why would I interfere? You'd always made decisions for yourself."

She shifted. "It wasn't you interfering so much as you wanting to protect me. I didn't need it."

He mulled over her reasoning, realizing that was a valid source of friction between them.

"I'm sorry I didn't tell you until after the fact."

"It was a shock."

Brie's forehead creased. "The first thing you asked me was how would I raise a child alone. I almost expected you to propose on the spot." Her voice grew tight. "Jax, taking care of me again."

He didn't reveal that he had wanted to propose on the spot, for those exact reasons, but she'd assured him that she didn't need a husband to raise her daughter. She was independent, which he knew, and with her mom's help, she would be fine.

To be honest, he was impressed with the life she'd built but felt a little left out.

"You made it clear that I was to be hands off," he said. "I respected your wishes."

"I didn't want not including you to come across as mean."

"It didn't." But the truth still hurt. She hadn't wanted or needed his help. Not when he left town or when she adopted Cami. Probably not now, either.

He watched the firelight shadow dance across her face. "And now?"

Her brows angled. "Now what?"

"If you meet the right guy, would you get married?"

Cami shifted in her sleep, a tiny moan puffing from her lips. Brie waited until she stilled, then stroked her back.

"Because of the way my parents' marriage ended, I've seen firsthand the damage one person can do to another." She tucked her daughter closer to her. "I'm afraid to take a chance."

Jax knew the history. Had let her cry on his shoulder when the truth about her father's affair had come to light. Brie had been hurt, angry and confused.

"His betrayal rocked me to my core. My father had always been bigger than life. He taught me so much. We shared so many interests. I…"

"I get it, Brie."

"I know you do. But after you left, life went on. I had to pick up the pieces, figure out how to deal with my dad." She shook her head. "Then later he moved back to Golden with his new wife and Taylor. Talk about awkward. Eventually they split up and…"

"You still carried the pain."

There was a shimmer in her eyes. "He'd always

wanted me to take over his business, even though I'd insisted I wasn't interested. Instead of supporting me when I went to the police academy, he pushed for me to go to business school. That wasn't going to happen. Over time, the strain between us grew."

"I didn't know."

"Because I didn't tell you." She blew out a gusty breath. "Near the end, Dad tried to get me involved in the things we used to do together. He loved history and legends around finding gold in the mountains. He asked me to join a local group with him, but I refused. We were still estranged when he died."

"I'm sorry, Brie."

She nodded. "Thanks for the flowers you sent for his memorial."

"I felt bad that I couldn't get back for the service."

"I didn't expect you to."

They went silent for a moment.

"He left you the building."

She stared at the fire. "That and a letter. All the sisters got one."

"Really? Do you mind telling me what he said?"

"I can't."

He backed off. "I understand. Too personal."

"No, I can't because I haven't read it."

Not what he'd expected, which caused a loss of words on his part.

"I don't know if I ever will." She shifted. "Back to marriage."

Okay, he'd play along.

"I have to imagine that if you meet your person, your perspective changes," he said.

"I suppose, but I haven't let my guard down long enough to find out." She sent him a sideways glance. "For you either?"

"No. Not for lack of trying."

"That right woman hasn't come into your life yet?"

The logs in the fire fell with a burst of sparks. Cami fidgeted in her sleep. Sitting here in Brie's cozy living room made it clear, he was ready for a serious relationship. "I want to get married, Brie."

Her shoulders sagged. "I wish I was so sure."

"You can't base a decision about a romantic relationship on your father's actions."

"I know, but it scares me. He adored my mom and loved us, until he didn't. It could happen to anyone."

"Don't you think love is worth taking the risk?"

His parents had. So had his siblings. He was the only holdout.

Brie shook her head, the edges of her bangs brushing her eyelashes. She blinked them from her eyes. "I don't know if I'm strong enough for that."

"You were fearless when we were kids."

"And then I grew up."

"We both did."

Without each other.

He hated the cynicism in her voice. Like life had taken any hope of falling in love away from her. He still had hope, even though he was thirty-four and not getting any younger. Brie was the same age. Had she adopted Cami because she thought her window for real love, for marriage and a family, was over?

And what about their friendship? Was it strong enough to weather what they would be facing in the days to come? Yes, being an adult was hard work, but there were lots of good moments he wanted to share with her. Could they help each other in the romance department or had the past ruined that chance?

Watching Brie stroke Cami's hair, he asked the question that had been plaguing him since he got home. "Brie, can we go back to the way things were?"

Her fingers went still. "I wish I knew."

# *CHAPTER NINE*

JAX'S QUESTION PERSISTED in Briana's head. His remark had put a damper on the rest of the night, so she'd put Cami to bed while he carried the mugs and plate to the kitchen. She'd been impressed that he'd rinsed them off before placing them in the dishwasher. After an awkward good-night, she'd locked up, then went to bed. Where she'd tossed and turned for hours.

*Can we go back to the way things were?*

She had no sure answers and trying to come up with any was futile. This was not the way she wanted to start her Monday morning.

"Mommy, I think Jax should come over for dinner again."

Distracted by her thoughts of the man, she said, "We can do that."

"Tonight."

Her hands tightened on the steering wheel. "He has to work tonight. Another time."

"No fair."

Moving her gaze to the rearview mirror, Briana glimpsed her daughter, strapped into a booster seat, her arms crossed and a major pout on her adorable face. She bit back a smile.

"I'll make sure it happens when Jax isn't on duty."

"Promise?"

"Promise."

"Good. I like him."

So did Briana. Again, she had to wonder, where was their relationship going?

Cami chattered away on the drive to Briana's mother's house, kicking her feet to the rhythm of the music on the radio. As she pulled into the driveway, there were no signs of her sisters' cars. After cutting the ignition, she got out and opened the back door to unstrap Cami from the seat. Once her tiny feet hit the ground, she ran to her grandmother who had just walked out to the front porch.

"Grammy!"

Briana's mother swept Cami into her arms as Briana grabbed Cami's backpack and shut the door. She strolled up the walkway just in time to hear, "Jax ate dinner with us last night."

Briana stopped. Met her mother's amused gaze.

"Did he?"

Briana rolled her eyes. "You know he did because you sent him over with food."

"But I didn't ask him to stay."

Good point, but Briana wasn't going there.

"He's going to come over again," Cami announced.

Her mother grinned.

"Where is everyone?" Briana asked, hoping to drop this line of conversation.

"Addie started a new fitness class, Jacob is in school, Nicole is meeting with a prospective client and Taylor has a shipment arriving this morning."

"Guess meeting for breakfast wasn't a good idea."

"Your current schedule won't last forever, and then we'll get back to our..." Her mother's gaze dropped to her hand. "What happened?"

She was surprised her mother hadn't heard the news, but Briana hadn't talked to her after the chaos Saturday night. "I put out a fire at the resort."

Her mother's face paled. "With your hand?"

"No. The extinguisher slid from my grasp. I tipped toward the metal trash can and burned myself."

"This happened at the party?"

Briana went into the details.

Panic filled her mom's voice. "Have you seen a doctor?"

"Evan took care of me. I'll be fine, Mom."

"I kissed it and made it better," Cami announced.

Her mother hugged Cami tightly and kissed her cheek. "Thank you."

"Everything will be okay. I—"

Briana was about to explain her job status when her cell phone rang. She pulled her phone from her pocket and read the screen. Seeing Jax's name, she felt a shiver of anticipation rush over her.

"It's work," she told her mom. "I need to take this."

"We'll be inside," her mother said, sending her a troubled look before the screen door slammed behind her.

Briana tapped the call button. "Jax. What's up?"

"Just calling to check on how you're feeling."

She gingerly flexed her fingers and thankfully her palm only smarted a little. "I'll survive."

"I know you will."

"Actually, I'm glad you called."

He paused. "Oh?"

"After you left last night, I scoured the Heirloom Assets website."

"Learn anything new?"

"I focused in on the staff bios. Franklin has been with the company since the beginning. I tried some additional avenues, but it took me down a rabbit hole."

Jax went silent. Briana could picture his furrowed brow as he thought the information through. "And the others?"

"Robert came onboard shortly after the company formed. He's an executive assistant. Not sure what that entails. And I couldn't find any other experience from him in this type of work."

"Maybe he took the job and learned as he went."

"Most likely. He was very well informed when we talked to him."

"What about the women?"

"Both Jill and Kat have been hired in recent

years, mainly to curate and do research. Nothing stands out. There are others who work at the LA office and are running things during the tour."

"So, it's a reputable company?"

"Seems so. I didn't have time to check out the security company that hired the guards. I'll do that when I get to the station."

"Okay. Keep me in the loop."

"I will." Strangely, she didn't want to hang up. After a few moments, Jax said, "Anything else?"

"No. I'll talk to you later."

"Until later," he said and ended the call.

She hung up and inhaled, missing the sound of Jax's voice. Mentally scolding herself for her outlandish reaction, she headed toward the front door.

The air was crisp, the kind of magical fall day where you wanted to play hooky and spend the time outdoors with your best friend.

*Stop.*

From a few doors down, she heard a car door slam. A deep voice carried in the wind. "Watch out."

At the command, her stomach tightened. She turned. It had sounded so much like…

Briana closed her eyes. It couldn't be her father. He was gone now.

She stared over the yard where she grew up, memories bombarding her.

*Briana, go farther out and I'll pitch the ball to you.*

*Watch out for the ice, you'll slip and fall.*

*Do you want to skip school so we can go to the exhibit?*

Briana blinked. She hadn't felt this close to her dad in years. Especially not after he left.

*"Is what they said true?"*

*"Briana, you have to understand."*

*"No, you have to tell me the truth."*

*Her father brushed a hand through his thick hair. The truth was written all over his face.*

*Outrage filled her. "How could you? I stood up for you."*

*"Things just...happened."*

*"Just happened? What about Mom?"*

*"Briana, you're old enough to know that people change."*

*"Not you," she whispered. "Why you?"*

*He couldn't answer.*

*"What happened to you telling me that your word is your bond? All that goes away because your feelings changed?" Panic welled up in her. "I defended you. Risked my relationship with my sisters for you. And it was all a lie!"*

*"Not all of it. I love you."*

*"But not enough to stay with Mom. To live at home. To be our dad."*

*"I'll always be your dad."*

*"Maybe I don't want you to be."*

*With that, Briana turned and ran. Ran as far and as fast as she could before a stitch in her side slowed her pace. Then she wandered the woods, her safe haven, until the sun began to sink. Know-*

*ing her mother was home alone, probably worried about her, Briana reversed direction and went back to the house that didn't feel like a home any longer.*

On the heels of the flashback, Briana placed a palm over her pounding heart. The searing pain of that day cut her like it was yesterday. She still didn't understand what had possessed her father to take up with Paula. Love wasn't supposed to work that way. Guess it didn't matter. The damage had been done and none of her sisters, or Briana, had ever been the same.

She dragged her feet as she entered the house. Reliving those memories was not the greatest way to start the day.

Once in the kitchen, she dropped Cami's backpack on a chair. Her daughter was at the table eating… "Are those scrambled eggs?"

Her mother was at the stove. "Yes."

"They're red."

"Because I wanted ketchup," Cami chimed in.

Her mother looked over her shoulder. "New phase."

Briana wrinkled her nose. "An unfortunate one."

"I don't know which is worse, smothering everything in ketchup or eating copious bags of potato chips."

"Hey, we each have our vices."

"Why couldn't yours be healthy?" she asked her daughter.

Briana sank down into a chair beside Cami.

"Please tell me you didn't give any ketchup to Mr. Darcy."

"No, I didn't think he'd like it."

"Good, because it would probably make him sick."

Worry gleamed in Cami's eyes. "I don't want to hurt him."

"I know, honey. That's why we need to be careful."

She nodded. "I'll tell Jax when he comes over. Maybe he knows what else a cat can't eat."

Briana puffed out a breath while her mother chuckled. "I can hear you, Mom."

"I'm not hiding anything." Her mother looked over her shoulder, humor written all over her face. "Are you?"

Not sure what that meant, and not eager to find out, Briana turned her attention back to Cami.

"I won't be working late so I'll pick you up for dinner."

"Okay. Grammy said she has plans for us today."

Her mother brought the pan of eggs over and spooned out a plateful for Briana. "Royce mentioned that there's a pumpkin patch at Crestview Farm. Do you mind if we take Cami?"

"Not at all. I've been meaning to get a pumpkin, but the time gets away from me."

"I want to make a face," Cami said. "Just like Jacob."

Briana covered a shiver. Her nephew's jack-o'-lantern had sharp teeth, a scar and creepy eyes.

"Maybe not quite like his but we'll have fun."

"Okay, Mommy." She wiggled out of her seat. "Grammy, can I watch my princess show on TV before we leave?"

Her mother glanced at Briana, who nodded. "Sure thing. Your mommy and I will eat and then we'll go to the store."

Cami stopped to give Briana a kiss, then danced into the living room. Briana's heart turned mushy at her daughter's affection. Then she frowned.

"You didn't like Cami's kiss?" Her mother asked as she took a seat with her plate.

"I did. I was thinking about something Jax said last night."

Her mother scooped a forkful of eggs. "Which was?"

"He said I have a mushy heart and that makes me a good cop."

"Compassion is a valuable trait in your profession."

Briana moved the eggs around her plate with her fork. "That's all well and good, but I want to be taken seriously."

"Briana, you never would have adopted Cami if you didn't have a soft heart."

"Okay, that's true, but the job is a different story."

Her mother's gaze moved to the gauze wrapped around her palm. "Like getting hurt on the job?"

Briana held up her hand. "It's just a precaution until the skin stops being tender."

"I don't like the idea of you being hurt, even if you were doing your job."

"Then you'll be thrilled to know I was put on regular duty."

Her mother's jaw dropped. "Why?"

"Because of the stolen tiara."

"But that wasn't your fault."

"No, but Mr. Franklin is upset. You saw how he reacted." Briana grimaced. "Can't say I blame him."

Her mother reached over to pat Briana's forearm.

"Brady took me off the transfer detail."

Her mother blinked, the only sign of her surprise. "Who will partner with Jax?"

"Roan."

She wasn't about to tell her mother that Mr. Franklin had basically blamed the town for the theft of the tiara and for the remainder of the tour, Briana would be mingling with folks at the chamber events to uncover anything they might have missed.

It was ludicrous. Briana couldn't even fathom the idea of anyone from Golden being guilty. She'd grown up with these people and couldn't think of one person at the party who would have committed this crime.

"You know I worry," her mother said.

They'd had this conversation multiple times since she'd gone to the police academy.

"After all we've been through as a family..."

Briana pushed her plate away. "Can I ask you something?"

"Of course." Her mother reached for her coffee.

"Were you upset with me when I defended Dad before I knew the truth?"

Mom's grip tightened on her mug. "What on earth brought up this bit of the past?"

"When I was outside, I heard a neighbor's voice. For a second, it reminded me of him."

Her mother placed the mug on the table.

"And last night, Jax and I touched on what happened. I guess it stirred things up."

Sitting back in her chair, a few moments passed until her mother spoke. "I understood. You and your father were inseparable when you were growing up. It was only natural that you'd see the best in him."

"Until I didn't." Briana exhaled. "I still can't wrap my mind around the fact that the man I spent so much time with could have hurt us all. Especially you." She met her mom's sympathetic gaze. "I didn't want to seem disloyal, even though Addie and Nicole interpreted it that way."

"You each had a different relationship with your father. Being the oldest, you were with him a lot and were much closer." Her expression was earnest when she spoke. "Let's face it, you were your dad's shadow. You two had so much in common. History. Music. Even those cop shows you watched together." Her mother chuckled. "Which is ironic because he was not happy when you decided to become a police officer."

"He tried to bribe me to go to business school."

Her mother rested her elbow on the table and dropped her chin into her palm. “I didn’t discover that until after the fact. He was furious when you turned him down.”

“You raised me to have my own thoughts. I shared them, popular or not.”

“Most definitely not.” She paused. “Your dad tried to convince me to talk you out of your decision. I reminded him that you were capable of making your own career plans and nothing could change your mind once it was set. It took a while, but he eventually stopped trying.”

“I couldn’t have done what he wanted. Fulfill his ultimate goal.”

Her mother’s voice was soft. “Take over his business?”

Briana ran a finger along the edge of the table. “Being the oldest, I guess he just assumed I would.”

“For a man who spent so much time with you, it was like he didn’t know you at all.”

And that’s what hurt the most.

“Since we’re having this conversation, I must say, I was always surprised that you hung around even though your sisters left.”

“I couldn’t leave you, Mom.”

They shared a glance that signaled they both knew this was why she didn’t go with Jax.

Her mother cleared her throat. “I may worry about you, but I know police work is your calling.”

“Thanks for understanding.”

Her mother pushed away from the table. "On that note, let's clean up and start the day."

Briana rose and collected her plate and fork. "Sounds like an order."

"Which I understand you're good at taking."

Briana bumped her shoulder into her mother's. "Have I told you lately that I love you?"

Her mother's expression turned gentle. "Yes, but I can't get enough of it."

"Ditto," Briana said then got to work cleaning up.

MIDMORNING, JAX WALKED into the Corner Café. The vibe was the same as he remembered, vintage furnishings, noisy customers and the scent of delicious food wafting from the bustling kitchen. His mother waved from a table in the back. Making his way toward her, he said hello to folks he knew, and others he didn't. Must have been the uniform.

Before he reached her, his grandfather rose from a table and stepped into his path. Weird. Gramps hadn't mentioned he'd be here.

His grandfather sidled up to him, leaned in and said in a low voice, "Run."

Jax's eyebrows rose. "What?"

"Trust me. You aren't going to like this conversation."

He glanced at his mom. "I can't leave now."

Gramps shrugged. "Don't say I didn't warn you." Then he ducked around Jax and left.

"Odd," he muttered under his breath and continued to the table. He leaned down to kiss his mother's cheek. "Hey, Mom."

"I'm glad you could stop by," she said, half joking. The other half was true indignation. Gloria Walker wasn't one to hold back. "I haven't seen you since you came home."

"Sorry. It wasn't intentional." He removed his Golden PD jacket and draped it over the back of his chair. "I intended to catch up with you and Dad, but things have been hectic at work," he told her as he took a seat.

"I heard about the theft."

Jax nodded.

A waitress stopped by the table. "Coffee?"

"Please."

His mother had invited him for a late breakfast before he went to the station. Since returning home, getting situated at his grandfather's place and being swept up in the current crime investigation, the days passed in a whirlwind. Considering everything that had happened in the short time span, he hadn't made time to sit down with his family.

She folded her hands beside her coffee cup. "There's so many rumors floating around, I wanted to talk to you directly."

"You know I can't discuss an active case."

"Fine." She nodded. "Then answer me this. Is Briana okay?"

"Her hand should heal just fine."

His mother relaxed. "That's good to hear."

He didn't mind his mother's interest; everyone

in Golden was caught off guard by the high-profile theft. And since this was a small town, various versions of the event and lots of suppositions were fodder for the rumor mill.

When he returned home from Brie's house last night, he'd reread the Heirloom Assets file of information she'd collected. Nothing stood out except for the fact that the tiara was the most valuable piece. He'd put the file aside, hoping for a good night's sleep, but instead, Brie's face filled his dreams. The way she'd tended to her daughter touched his heart and filled him with a deep longing to have a family.

The waitress interrupted his musings when she returned to fill his cup and top off his mother's coffee. He sat back to study his mom. She hadn't missed a beat raising a rowdy family. Sure, she'd been overwhelmed when they were younger, sometimes overlooking small things, but she had a big heart and loved them all. Her dark hair had started to gray, her face had a few more lines than he remembered, but all in all she was healthy and happy. That's all that mattered.

They placed their orders. His mother took a sip of her coffee, not directly meeting his gaze. Warning bells clanged in his head.

"What's up, Mom?"

She tried to act unconcerned. "Why does something have to be up?"

"Because you're acting kind of squirrely."

Her hand flew to her chest. "Me? Squirrely? That doesn't sound like me."

He laughed. "Really?" Any time his mother was digging for information, she acted this way.

"Since when?" she challenged.

"Since I was a kid. Remember when Joey broke his ankle? You tried to give us the third degree without being obvious." He grinned. "News flash, you were obvious."

"Okay, okay," she bristled. "Since you're such a smarty-pants, I'll get right down to it." She took a deep breath, then said, "It's time for you to get married."

He wasn't surprised but discovered he was a bit annoyed by her comment. Crossing his arms over his chest, he asked, "What brought you to that conclusion?"

He already knew but waited to see what she'd say.

Warming up to the topic now, she rested her arms on the table and folded her hands. "Your siblings are married, happily settled down, not gallivanting around the country. You're home now and it's a mother's right to make sure her son is settled in his life."

His lips quivered. "And how do you intend to make that happen?"

A crafty expression crossed her face, which made him nervous.

"It's very simple." She held her chin high. "I have connections."

"The Golden Matchmakers Club?"

Her face fell. "How did you know?"

"This is Golden, Mom. I've already had two people warn me about their antics."

"It had to be your grandfather," she groused, then changed tactics. "Honey, their ways work."

"And you've decided to sic them on me?"

"Please don't put it that way. They're very thoughtful in their matches." She reached over the table with her hand palm up. He uncrossed his arms and took her hand in his.

"I just want you to be happy," she said in a thick voice.

"Who says I'm not?"

"You'd be happier if you were married."

Jax let her hand go. "I'm not going to argue with you because you're right."

At first, she frowned, as if she needed to keep pushing the issue, then her face lit up when she realized what he said. "I'm right?"

He nodded.

"This was easier than I thought."

*What have I done?*

"Easier?"

"I had an entire list of reasons why you should marry."

He chuckled. "I'd probably agree with each of them."

In fact, after last night, he'd decided he wasn't going to oppose any help in his romantic quest. He wanted love and a family, full stop.

"But right now," he continued, "I have important things to focus on. I can't consider this until the collection leaves town."

"I understand. It's completely okay, but will you at least give permission for my friends to start selecting a possible match for you?"

He wasn't a fan of the method, but if he was being honest, he could admit that he hadn't gotten far in the romance department on his own. And by all accounts, the club had been successful.

"You've got my okay, Mom."

She clutched her hands to her chest. Were those tears in her eyes?

"I expected I was going to have to argue more vigorously."

"Am I that difficult?"

"No, you've just always been so sure of what you wanted. Like you didn't need my or your dad's help."

"The idea of marriage has been on my mind. I guess I might as well have your friends look into it." His voice was firm. "But I make the final decision and if I don't agree, you back down."

His mother held her hands up. "Fair."

The waitress brought their plates full of eggs, bacon and toast. The aroma made his stomach growl. With everything going on, Jax hadn't been eating well and realized he was hungry.

After they'd dug in, his mother wiped the corner of her mouth with a napkin. "And since you and Briana are working together, maybe you can talk her into letting the matchmakers club find her a husband. I know this idea is probably archaic to a woman who adopted a baby on her own, but it would be nice to see her happily settled down too."

Jax lowered his fork. "Excuse me?"

The sparkle in his mother's eyes indicated she was getting worked up. "Let the club find someone for Briana. Cami is such an adorable little girl and Briana is an excellent mother. Any man worth his salt would love to be part of a family like theirs."

His mind went to the evening he'd spent with Brie in her cozy living room, her daughter fast asleep on her lap, her cat prowling the room. He tried to picture a stranger in that house with her. Why didn't he like the idea that he wouldn't be that man?

"I'm not going to talk to Brie about this. If she wants help in that department, she can ask." He took a sip of his coffee and swallowed. "Please don't overstep, Mom. She has valid reasons why she's chosen to live her life the way she does."

"I know."

Like most of the folks in Golden, his mother knew about Brie's parents and their past problems.

"It's going to be a hard enough job trying to find someone for me."

His mother laughed. "True. You are picky."

"More like discerning." He pushed his plate away and motioned for the check. "Either way, don't include Brie."

"For now." She sent him a sly glance. "But if we

find the perfect woman for you, she might want our assistance."

"We?"

She threw her shoulders back. "I'm working with the matchmakers on this project."

"Oh, now I'm a project?"

"Don't be silly. You and Briana deserve the best."

The conversation changed direction and after they finished eating, he paid for the meal and escorted his mother outside. She reached up to pat his cheek. "Be safe."

"I will," he answered, then headed for the station. As he walked, the sunshine warmed his shoulders. His gaze moved about downtown, looking for anything out of the ordinary, but he saw only the residents of Golden going about their daily routines. Not tiara-stealing perps trying to get away with a heist.

He shook his head, wondering what he'd just done. Matchmakers? Really? But then he thought about his mom's suggestion that Brie get involved with them and his chest grew tight. If he wanted Brie to have a chance with anyone, he realized he wanted it to be him. He grudgingly admitted to himself that he was starting to have feelings for her that went beyond friendship. Could she ever feel the same? He wouldn't act on those feelings out of respect for their friendship, and the fear that she'd shut him down again, so he supposed that answered his own question.

# *CHAPTER TEN*

BRIANA LOOKED UP when the back door opened and Jax strolled into the station. His pensive expression made her stomach twist. Had he learned anything new about the case?

He met her gaze and crossed the room to his desk.

"Did you find something?" she asked.

"I haven't started working and Brady hasn't called me with any updates."

They had less than a week before the collection went back to LA. Brady and Roan had gone to the crime scene this morning to meet with Mr. Franklin while she spent the morning researching the security company that had hired the guards traveling with the collection team. The squad room had been quiet with the officers on patrol. Becky was in her office, occasionally checking in with Briana.

"You have a serious expression on your face," she said.

"Just thinking." Jax dropped his truck keys on his desk, removed his coat and ambled over. "What have you dug up?"

She nodded to an empty chair beside her desk. "I've been looking into the security company Alec and Gil work for."

He sat, resting his elbows on his knees as he leaned forward to view her computer screen.

"Safe Way Security Company, a reputable business located in LA. No legal troubles or problems with clients. No bankruptcy or financial issues."

"I can see Mr. Franklin only hiring a reputable company. Especially in light of the amount of travel they've done."

"That's what I thought. The guards are trained for every contingency. I called, posing as a possible client, and got their sales pitch. I mentioned Mr. Franklin and they told me he specifically asked for Alec. Seems he worked another event with Franklin and received good reviews."

She turned to the computer, clicked the mouse and pulled up another screen. "Alec Chambers. Been with the company for eight years. Good background check. Never written up for poor performance or conduct issues." She scrolled down. "Gil Summers, on the other hand, has been reprimanded, mostly for being tardy, but other than that, no personal complaints from clients."

Jax sat back. "Are you thinking either is good for the theft?"

"It doesn't appear that way." She swiveled in her seat. "Besides, the timing is off, for Alec at least. He was present in the room when the lights went out and didn't have the tiara on him. Gil, however, was missing during the incident."

Jax frowned. "Yeah, he showed up once everyone calmed down."

Briana moved her injured hand to a more comfortable position on the desktop. "Which is curious."

"I noticed guilt on his face when he finally came back to the room."

"Me too." She thought for a moment. "Maybe Gil left when he shouldn't have and stopped for something along the way, which kept him from returning before the commotion began. But like everyone else, he was searched and came up clean."

"I'll be at the resort later and will question him again."

"Sounds good." She tried to keep the disappointment of not being able to interrogate the guards with Jax from her face but must have failed.

"You did good getting this information, Brie."

"Too bad I can't do anything about it."

"Yeah, it stinks, but Brady has to do what's right for the PD."

The truth didn't make her feel any better.

The back door opened. Brady and Roan walked in.

"Good news?" Jax asked.

"No," Brady said. "We questioned the employees, but they're the day shift. Jax, you'll talk to the people who come in later."

"Got it."

"The security footage was inconclusive," Roan

told them, frustration lacing his tone. "There was no coverage when the lights went out and no one was seen removing the tiara afterward."

"So, no help," Briana presumed.

"None." Brady shook his head. "Wes and Kelli are on patrol, but why don't we go to the conference room."

Gathering the research she'd collected so far, Briana followed the men into the quiet room.

After they sat, Roan glanced her way. "What have you learned?"

She relayed the information she'd gleaned about the security company.

"Good job." Brady frowned. "The biggest concern we have right now is how the perp got away without anyone seeing him."

"Inside job?" Jax asked. "Either from Heirloom Assets, Mountain Spa Center or the caterers?"

"I'd hate to think it was anyone from the resort," Briana said. "I have friends who work there. And my sister was an employee at their fitness center."

"We can't rule out anyone, friend or not," Roan added, his tone tight. "Franklin has made Golden his target."

"Which is why we need to find something." Brady reached for a file. "Anything."

"Can I go to the resort and ask the manager questions? Find out about the employees?" Briana asked the chief. "I don't know if I can get all the intel we need from here."

"I asked Heather to gather that information. I'll

let you know when she calls me, and we'll go from there. To be honest, I don't see how the staff could factor in. They weren't given access to the collection and only a handful were at the party."

Brady then looked thoughtful. "A server from the catering company could have started the fire as a diversion. But why and what would be their connection?" He glanced across the table. "Jax, you take the lead there."

He nodded.

"How is the staff of Heirloom Assets explaining the tiara not being displayed?" Briana asked Brady.

"They're making the excuse that the tiara needed to go back to LA in advance of the movie premiere."

"It's plausible," Jax said. "No one viewing the collection would question the decision."

"Let's hope it holds up." Brady turned to Briana. "In the meantime, I need you to attend today's movie event at Sever House. The Golden Ladies Guild is hosting a tea commemorating the original *Riches of the Past* film. Some of the guests from the black-tie event will be there. See if you can jog some memories."

Not the assignment she'd hoped for, but she'd do her part.

Once the meeting ended, they walked out of the room. Jax stopped her. "Are you okay with this?"

"I'd really love to investigate at the resort, but talking to the townspeople is important."

"We need the intel, Brie."

"Then I'd better get going." When he didn't move, she tilted her head. "Was there something else?"

"You're good at what you do, Brie. You know that, right?"

His words made her heart race. The way he regarded her... Like she was the most important person in his life. It was humbling, exciting and scary at the same time.

"Thanks. I needed to hear that today."

His warm smile made her feel safe, and tingly, at the same time. If she didn't have to get moving, she might sit down and analyze these new reactions to Jax. Thankfully she had a full day and no time to question why she was suddenly aware of this unexpected attraction to her friend.

After changing from her uniform shirt into a pretty long-sleeved blouse, it took Briana ten minutes to walk from the station to the historic Victorian building located at the far end of Gold Dust Park. She entered, immediately enticed by the scent of sugary treats filling the air and the chatter from the women already gathered. The current president of the guild welcomed her to the tea party and soon Briana was mingling. Since the theft of the tiara was high on the minds of the townspeople, she was able to easily ask questions, especially of those who'd attended the party on Saturday night.

There was only one way to prove that nobody in Golden had stolen the tiara; find out who the real culprit was. Because there wasn't a chance that these lovely women were involved, Briana felt it in her bones. If there was any circumstance in which she needed her police skills to shine, it was proving that no one in Golden would steal the tiara.

She spoke to the mayor, but he didn't have any insight into what had happened at the resort. Volunteers working with the Chamber of Commerce had theories, but nothing that moved the needle in the investigation. Her sisters, who were also at the tea, couldn't add any details. Gayle Ann Masterson, head of the Golden Matchmakers Club and a woman who didn't miss a beat, had a different angle.

"It's a shame what happened. The party was so much fun and ended on a bad note."

"Did you notice anything strange?"

"Not especially. I had to take a call and went into the lobby so I could carry on a conversation given the loud voices in the room. One of the security guards was in the lobby."

"Was this before the theft of the tiara?"

"Definitely."

It had to be Gil because he was gone after the lights came back on. "What was the guard doing?"

Mrs. M. tapped her chin. "Let me think." Tap, tap, tap. "Oh, he was walking away from the reception desk."

"Was he with anyone?"

"Not that I could tell."

"That's good. I think—"

"And I spoke to Robert."

Briana's antenna perked up.

"He came from the resort's dining room. I stopped him to chat. Asked him if a nice man like him had a girlfriend. He got a silly smile on his face and said his girlfriend was back in LA and he couldn't wait to get home to see her. Then he leaned close and said, 'She's going to love me when I get back.'"

"Do you know what he meant by that?"

"He winked at me and said he was going to pop the question." Mrs. M. sighed. "Don't you just love couples falling in love?"

Since that wasn't generally on Briana's radar, she thanked Mrs. M. and made a mental note to call Jax as soon as possible.

Then Mrs. M. asked if Briana was seeing anyone. Not wanting to give the woman a reason to consider her a matchmaking candidate, she quickly disengaged from the conversation and moved on.

Once she'd made the rounds, Briana's next stop was the table set up with tea and pastries. She blinked when she spied Alvin and his buddy Gandy behind the long table, replacing goodies onto the festive platters.

"Do I even want to know?" she asked Alvin in a low voice as she picked out a treat and placed it on a dessert plate.

He handed her a cup of tea. "Just doing our civic duty."

"At a ladies' guild function?"

"Betty, from your mom's store, delivered the

bakery goods." Alvin nodded at Gandy. "Since he's sweet for her, we volunteered to help today."

She glanced over as Gandy's weathered face turned a cute shade of pink. "It's nothing."

Alvin rolled his eyes. "He won't admit his crush."

"I'm too old for a crush," Gandy insisted.

"I don't think age matters," Briana said. "If you're attracted, you're attracted."

*Listen to yourself,* a voice within her taunted. Hard as she tried, she couldn't brush the thought away.

A wide smile graced Gandy's face. "I like the way you think."

While he stared across the room, presumably at Betty, Briana focused on Alvin.

"Have you noticed anything useful?"

"No, but we're just getting started, like you." His easygoing smile disappeared, and his eyes went hard. "We've got trouble."

Briana turned in time to see Mr. Franklin coming through the front door of the old building, dressed in a dark suit. She should have expected he'd be here.

"Be careful," she heard Alvin say. "I don't trust him as far as I can throw him."

Briana turned back to him. "Why?"

"He's got that look about him. Too big for his britches."

"That's not a reason to suspect him."

"Just give me time to prove otherwise," Alvin promised.

"I do appreciate an extra set of eyes on the situation, but..."

"I know, keep it professional."

Taking a bracing breath, Briana rejoined the women. When Franklin finally noticed her, his eyebrows angled over his dark eyes. She made sure to keep her distance but couldn't ignore the dislike emanating from the man.

Thankfully the morning flew by. She waited until Franklin left before she slipped out to the wide wraparound veranda to text Jax about what Mrs. M. had seen before heading back to the station. Once she finished the text, her sisters ambushed her, concern radiating from each of them.

"Were you going to tell us what happened?" Nicole demanded as she nodded at Briana's bandaged hand. "Mom had to fill us in."

"I was going to explain at breakfast but none of you were there," Briana deadpanned. It was then she noticed that her sisters were all wearing dresses. "You sure got decked out."

"When a tea party is thrown by the Ladies Guild, you dress accordingly," Taylor said.

Briana glanced down at her blouse and slacks. "I missed the memo," she muttered, wishing she'd thought ahead before attending this shindig.

Addie rushed to her side. "Tell us the truth. Are you okay?"

"I'm fine," she insisted, overwhelmed by the genuine concern from her sisters. "Evan gave me the all-clear when the EMTs came to the scene."

The relief in her sisters' eyes touched her heart. They'd been growing closer in the past six months, but that guilt of how she'd stuck up for her dad when they were younger still overshadowed her. She'd been accused of being his favorite, which wasn't entirely off base. Putting the past behind her was becoming more essential every day.

"There have been fifty different rumors about what happened the other night," Addie said. "Can you fill us in?"

Waving her sisters away from the others leaving the building, Briana guided them to a far corner of the side porch.

"Is it true that the tiara was stolen?" Addie asked.

"You know I can't talk about an active investigation."

Nicole harrumphed, clearly not happy with Briana's answer. "I'll take that as a yes."

"But I can tell you that I'm back on regular duty. Not transferring the collection every night."

Taylor leaned over to pat her arm. "I'm sorry. That must be killing you."

She lifted one shoulder in a nonchalant shrug, but her sisters clearly weren't buying it.

"It was obvious Mr. Franklin was upset," Nicole said.

"Understandably," Addie added. "A lot of money just went up in smoke."

"And he was glaring at you," Taylor finished.

"I'm an easy scapegoat," Briana said.

"He's blaming you?" Nicole asked. "That's ridiculous."

"He thinks that because I left my post the culprit took the tiara. Really, he's just angry that the theft happened right under his nose."

Addie tilted her head. "Whoever took it has to be very comfortable with risk given the police and security that were there."

"Or desperate," Nicole said. "You must really need money if you'd steal a tiara that recognizable. Especially with the remake of *Riches of the Past* releasing soon. The collection has been all over the press and social media."

Addie met Briana's gaze. "Do you need our help?"

"I appreciate it but other than helping me out with Cami while we investigate, there's not much you can do." She noted the look on the face of each of her sisters and was surprised when tears stung her eyes. "Thanks for caring."

"We always have," Addie said, her eyes misty.

"When we were kids..." Briana began, her throat locking up.

"You don't need to say anything," Nicole told her.

She pushed through the emotion. Met Addie and Nicole's gazes. "You thought I put Dad over you. I didn't but I never tried hard enough to make things better between us."

Addie's expression was sympathetic. "You were hurting, like all of us."

She turned to Taylor, her voice raw. "And I didn't

take your feelings into consideration. You were caught up in what was happening as much as we were."

Taylor nodded, her expression tight. Briana could never get a handle on what her half sister was thinking.

"I'm sorry," she managed to get out. "To all of you."

"No apology necessary," Nicole said. She cleared her throat and straightened. "We're moving on, right, girls?"

"We are," Addie agreed.

Taylor smiled, but Briana could still see the old pain lingering in her eyes.

Nicole reached out a hand, palm down, into the empty space between them. Addie and Taylor added their hands on top. Nicole raised an eyebrow at Briana. "Well?"

Briana added her hand. "We're the Connelly sisters."

"And don't forget it," Nicole said.

After a round of hugs and "don't forget to call me," Briana stopped Taylor before she took off.

"Can I ask you something?"

Wariness flashed in Taylor's eyes. Briana hated that her sister kept her emotional walls intact.

"Sure. What's up?"

"You've worked on movie sets, right?"

"Yes. I had multiple duties depending on the project, but mostly I was a set dresser."

"Was it common practice to use expensive props on a project?"

Interest now replaced the wariness in Taylor's gaze.

"Depends on the movie. In most cases, the props are everyday items, costumes, jewelry, that sort of thing. Once in a while a high-profile piece might be used."

"And what happens after the movie wraps?"

"Everything goes back to the property department. The prop master would catalog the pieces and put them in storage."

"Were any props sold off?"

"If they weren't needed." She tucked her thick auburn hair behind one ear and twisted her earring. "Is this about the tiara?"

"I'm just trying to figure out why Heirloom Assets bought all the gold from the original production company."

"I'm not familiar with Heirloom Assets since I worked at several different Atlanta film studios, but I can make a few calls."

"I'd appreciate that."

Taylor hugged her purse closer to her torso. "Thanks."

Briana's eyebrows rose. "For what?"

"Including me."

Briana's heart squeezed. "Hey, what are sisters for?"

"We are." The shadows in Taylor's eyes dispersed. "Sisters."

Briana gave a quick hug before the two went in opposite directions. It wasn't until she was halfway to the station when Nicole's comment hit her. *"You must really need money if you'd steal a tiara that recognizable."*

Other than selfishly wanting the tiara, the only other reason to take it was the value of the gold. Which made Briana wonder, who desperately needed money?

LATER THAT NIGHT, Jax waited until the last group of tourists had viewed the collection before getting to work. Everyone was jumpy and on edge, as if waiting for another catastrophe to happen. Franklin could barely control his stormy mood, which didn't help matters. Even the tourists noticed the tension in the air.

When the staff started packing up the collection, Jax decided to use the lull to his advantage. Earlier, Roan had stated he would stay with the gold while Jax questioned Gil. Jax approached the security guard as he readied to roll the mannequin from the room.

"Do you have a minute?"

Gil blinked nervously. "Ah, sure. What do you need?"

"I wanted to ask about where you were the other night. You weren't in the room when the tiara went missing."

The security guard's throat moved as he swallowed hard. "I was in the lobby."

Jax pretended to check his notepad. "Because?"

Beads of sweat formed on Gil's forehead. "I had something to take care of."

"Something more important than guarding the collection?"

"I…ah…didn't want Mr. Franklin to know."

"Know what?"

He appeared to be having a mental debate on what to say. Finally, he spoke in a rush.

"There's this girl who works at the front desk. We've been getting friendly. Her shift was ending so I wanted to talk to her. That's why I left."

Jax made a note. "Her name?"

Gil hesitated.

"Name?" Jax echoed, infusing more authority in his tone.

He swallowed again. "Evie," Gil admitted.

"And when you were there, did you notice anyone leave the room in a hurry? Or act suspiciously?"

Gil's face clouded. "No. I…we were talking. I didn't notice."

"When did you realize something was wrong?"

"After I left Evie, I went to check the lock on Ms. Baine's office door like she requested. Afterward I made a quick stop in my room to check my text messages. We can't use our phone for personal reasons on the floor when we're on duty." His face flushed over his admission. "I didn't hear the fire alarm but once I got back to the lobby, I saw the police rushing in. They wouldn't allow me to reenter the room until I convinced them I was security for the collection."

Which explained why he showed up after the fact. If Gil was telling the truth, he wouldn't have had an opportunity to be the suspect. Jax would confirm the story with Evie.

"Was Robert with you?"

"I didn't see him. He must have been in the event room."

"Thanks, you can move the dress now."

Gil tugged on his shirt collar. "You aren't going to tell Mr. Franklin, are you?"

"The smart thing to do would be to fess up yourself."

Gil nodded, then on shaky legs pushed the mannequin forward.

"Wait." Jax stopped him. "Doesn't Robert go with you to the office?"

"I don't know where he is."

"Thanks."

Gil was nervous, but not about the stolen tiara. Flirting might cost him his job. He wouldn't be stopping at the front desk tonight, that was for sure. But where was Robert? Jax had wanted to question him before the transfer, especially after Brie had passed along the update of Mrs. M.'s interaction with him. When Roan waved him over, he knew he couldn't wait for the assistant.

The transfer went smoothly. After sending pictures to Mr. Franklin, Jax drove Roan back to the station so they could get their vehicles and go home.

Roan had been spending a lot of hours at work, so he was gone like a shot. Jax didn't blame him. If he had a family, he'd feel the same way.

After he typed up his report, an edgy energy buzzed through Jax. Without thinking, he drove to Brie's house. Before he knew it, he was knocking on her front door. The temperature had dropped, so he blew warm breath on his cold hands.

The door opened a slit. "Jax?"

"It's me."

She flung the door open. "What are you doing here?"

"I wasn't ready to go home so I thought I'd stop by and see how you're doing."

"I'm okay. I—"

Just then Cami danced into the living room. "Mommy, you said..." Her attention moved to Jax. She ran over. "You came to visit."

He crouched down to her level. "I did."

"See, Mommy. I told you he'd visit me."

Brie stepped back to let him in, the cold air following in his wake. "You didn't think I'd stop by?" he asked as he entered the house.

"Cami insisted I invite you over again."

He sent her a cocky grin.

She rolled her eyes. "Don't make a big deal out of it."

Cami grabbed Jax's hand after he shrugged out of his jacket. "Come dance."

"He just got here," Brie argued as she took his jacket and placed it over the back of the armchair.

"It's no problem."

Cami led Jax to the center of the room. It was then that he noticed the radio was playing an upbeat song.

The little girl took his other hand. "Like this," she instructed, and they danced for a full minute before Brie cut in.

"Okay, kiddo. It's time for bed," she told Cami as she turned off the radio.

"But Mommy, we have company."

Brie sent him a frown. "Who should have called."

Unrepentant, "My bad" was all he could come up with.

"Give me a minute."

While Brie went to help her daughter, Jax wandered around the living room, smiling at pictures of Brie and Cami, perusing her bookshelf and enjoying the hominess of the room. When his stomach growled, he scrounged through the kitchen pantry, coming up with a box of crackers and removing a block of cheese from the fridge. By the time he had the cheese sliced and plated, Brie came into the kitchen.

"Make yourself at home, why don't you."

"Thanks. I think I will."

Pushing past him, she removed a bag of chips from the pantry.

"Still your poison?" he asked.

"You know it." She took a big bite and crunched.

"How about a drink?"

A small smile tipped her lips. "Iced tea?"

"Sure."

Once poured, she waved, "Let's sit in the living room."

He followed, sinking into her comfortable couch.

"Didn't eat dinner?"

"No. I was busy." He related his conversation with Gil. "He wasn't where he was supposed to be, but I doubt he's the thief."

Brie walked to the crime board. Since Jax had been to her house, she'd taped pictures of her suspects, Franklin and his staff, as well as an empty silhouette with a question mark drawn in black marker inside. In the center was a picture of the Mountain Spa Center and a photo of the tiara. A red piece of yarn ran from Franklin to the item. She took an orange strand and connected it from Gil to the spa picture.

"It's not much, but it is a lead."

"I need to get Robert's take on what happened."

She turned to him. "He wasn't there tonight?"

"Not while I was on duty. Gil had no idea where he was. As we were leaving, Franklin said something about Robert working in his room."

She frowned. "Odd, since he's usually with Gil moving the dress once the viewing hours are over. And the other night at the party, he wouldn't let Kat or Jill close to the tables as he did inventory. He's always in the thick of things."

"I agree, but Heirloom Assets has more business going on than just this collection."

"True." She faced the board again. Jax could imagine the direction her thoughts were taking her.

"I keep staring at this puzzle, but a piece is missing. I can't quite put my finger on it."

"Probably because it's late. We can finish tomorrow."

He bit into a square of cheese when he noticed a shadow move in the corner of the room. Then Mr. Darcy slinked toward Jax, his nose twitching. Jax held out a small piece of cheddar. "Here you go, buddy."

Mr. Darcy sniffed, then licked Jax's fingers.

"What are you doing?" Brie demanded.

"Feeding my friend."

She placed her hands on her hips. "He doesn't eat table food."

"I could have sworn I saw Cami feeding him the other night."

Brie closed her eyes. He could read her lips counting to ten.

"I'm trying to teach her not to share our food."

Jax glanced toward the hallway Brie and Cami had gone to earlier, then back. "She's not listening?"

"Not to me," she groused. "My daughter thinks you have all the answers about cat feeding. Please, don't encourage her." Brie hurried over to pick up the gray-and-white cat. "I want him around for a long time."

With a sharp meow, the cat jumped from her arms onto the couch, then sniffed Jax.

"No way!"

"What?" Jax asked.

"He never sits with strangers."

"Maybe he doesn't think I'm a stranger."

Before he could reach out and pet Mr. Darcy, the cat took off.

"You scared him," he accused.

"Traitor," she called as the cat disappeared down the hallway.

"C'mon. He had to warm up to me sometime."

Her fisted hands returned to her hips. "You think you can come here and sweet-talk my daughter, tempt my cat, eat my food and lounge on my couch?"

He chuckled. "It's like old times."

And while the old times had been great, he was enjoying the new Jax and Brie. The laughter came easier the more they were together. They worked well as partners and still had the same outlook on life, with new opinions that made conversation interesting. Even her impressive frowns and wry responses were familiar yet held weight at the same time.

She tried to glare at him, but it didn't scare him off.

"What's with the lecture? You're acting all schoolmarmy," he said.

Her eyebrows rose and her lips quivered. "That's a picture."

He rose. "One I won't forget," he muttered under his breath.

"You're right. It's just..."

"Different now that we're older," he supplied.

"I suppose."

He carried the empty plate and glass to the kitchen then returned to grab his jacket. As he stopped at the front door, her discouraged expression tugged at his heart. He reached up to brush her bangs from her forehead. As he did so, her jasmine scent lifted. He took a deep breath before doing something unwise, like leaning down to kiss her. She was that close.

"We'll figure this out," he told her.

"Thanks."

She met his gaze, her blue-green eyes gentle. Until she seemed to realize how close they were and took a step back.

"Tomorrow, at the station, we'll dig deeper," he said.

"Thanks, Jax. It's nice having you around."

"Good thing it's permanent."

He didn't miss her shiver at his promise.

What would that permanence mean for them?

He opened the door, walked a few feet then stopped and turned to see her silhouetted in the doorway. She waved, then moved inside and closed the door.

As he continued to his truck parked at the curb, shoving his hands into his jacket pockets, the brisk air cleared his head. If he'd kissed Brie like he wanted to, that would have changed everything. He couldn't decide if he was a fool for not taking the chance.

# *CHAPTER ELEVEN*

"MONEY," BRIANA TOLD Jax the next morning when he arrived at the station. "It came to me after talking to my sisters yesterday. We need to focus on who needs money."

He dropped his keys and jacket at his desk and pulled up a chair beside her. "Have you found a connection?"

"I started taking a deeper look into the finances of the Heirloom Assets staff and the security guards."

Jax sat. He wore a navy Henley shirt that brought out the color of his eyes and a pair of worn jeans. She, on the other hand, wore her police uniform. "And hopefully answers to who gains by taking the tiara."

"I have a call into Carrie at the chamber asking if she or the event volunteers who oversee the daily events have heard anything worth pursuing. Especially from the consortium staff."

"Involving the community. I like it."

Briana felt her face flush. "Hey, if Franklin is

going to blame us, we need to prove our innocence."

"Don't forget, we still need to figure out what's happening at Oktoberfest." He pulled out his phone.

"What are you doing?" she asked.

"Texting Gramps. I'll ask him and his crew to be at Oktoberfest tonight."

While Jax texted with his grandfather, she studied his face. A face she was so familiar with. She enjoyed getting to know Jax again, maybe a little too much. They were gaining ground on their relationship, but it didn't feel like it was enough.

Briana thought back to the night before. She couldn't decide if Jax was about to kiss her. She thought so, then brushed it off. She'd been tired and frustrated by the case. Could she have imagined the heat in his eyes when he gazed at her? Or how she became dizzy over the way his cologne captured her senses? The way he leaned toward her…

"Okay, we're set."

She blinked. "What?"

"Gramps. He'll round up the guys." He tilted his head. "Are you okay?"

*When I'm not thinking about kissing you.*

"I'm just in my head," she said to cover her perplexing emotions. Lately, she wasn't on firm footing when it came to Jax.

"I'll follow up with the consortium staff today," Jax informed her. "There's something off there, too."

"Like Mr. Franklin eager to pin the theft on me

or the folks of Golden. I don't understand why he's so adamant, especially when he can't prove his claim."

"I get the feeling he's desperate. He's got to deal with explaining the theft to people back in LA. The movie production company will expect the tiara to be part of the collection at the film release. He seems worried about their reaction. Then there's the insurance company to deal with. And how does this crime affect the rest of the holdings of the consortium?"

"It's like a big circle."

"With Golden right in the center."

She turned in her chair to move the computer mouse and wake up her screen.

"It's been tricky getting a handle on the financials so far."

"Keep digging because any red flags might point us in the right direction of who to pursue next." His phone pinged. He glanced at the screen. "Gramps is at Sit A Spell. He's offered to buy me a cup of coffee."

"Tell him I said hi. And thanks."

Jax rose. "Will you be here when I clock in?"

"I'm not sure."

"Then I'll fill you in later." He grinned. "Maybe I'll stop by your place to dance with Cami."

"She'd love that."

"Would you?"

Her stomach dropped. Cami was the only one she danced with these days. She pretended to bristle at his comment. "As long as you bring your own food."

He chuckled. "Copy that."

Briana watched Jax cross the room, admiring his long-legged stride. He'd always been athletic while she'd preferred getting lost in a book. The only reason she'd stayed active as a kid was because she was always competing with him. Now, Brady made time at the gym a priority and since Addie opened the fitness center, Briana didn't have an excuse not to exercise. She made a fuss about not liking it, but secretly, Briana knew physical health affected her mental acuity and she needed a clear head to do her job. Lately, Jax had been messing with that clear head.

He stopped before walking out the door to slip on his sunglasses. The bright sunshine silhouetted him before he moved away. As the door closed with a thud, Briana exhaled a long breath.

"That is one fine-looking man," Becky said from beside Briana's desk.

Briana jumped. "Where did you come from?"

"My office. You didn't notice because you were too busy admiring Jax."

She frowned. "This isn't a very professional comment."

"No, but we both have eyes, don't we?"

Briana closed hers before getting back on track and asking, "Did you need something?"

Becky handed her a form. "Last injury report to fill out, I promise."

With a sigh Briana took the paper.

"Are you sure you're doing okay, hon?"

"My palm is still touchy but that won't keep me from doing the job."

"Glad to hear that." The concern on Becky's face melted away. "I'll expect that report by lunchtime."

"Yes, ma'am."

Between filling out the form and getting back to researching the financial accounts of Heirloom Holdings and its employees, the morning flew by. To her disappointment, Jax didn't return to the station. Not that he needed to, this was his time off until his shift started. But Briana liked the questions he posed when they were discussing the case. Liked how they worked through a problem together. His years in the military had honed skills that had already been developing under his grandfather's influence. The Golden PD was fortunate to have him.

*So are you.*

She shook off the thought. They had time to figure out their relationship once this case was resolved.

Picking up her cell phone from the top of her desk, she made a call to Taylor. No luck in learning anything new about Heirloom Assets, but Briana was glad she'd asked for her sister's assistance. Another step in repairing old wounds.

She then made phone calls to other holding companies to get more information on Mr. Franklin. He was a staple in the business and while no one had a bad word to say about him, most weren't big fans either. She then contacted the movie production office. Interestingly, when she mentioned the tiara, she learned that Mr. Franklin hadn't revealed to the production team that it had been stolen. The person she spoke to was surprised by her call. Briana quickly told them she was only doing a background check and learned that Franklin had promised to be at the movie premiere as planned. Was he hoping the PD would find the tiara by then? Jax was correct in thinking Mr. Franklin wanted to hide the truth, but why? It sure explained the pressure he was exerting on Brady.

Going through the financials was time-consuming. She still had to wait on some information, but at least she'd made a dent in the process.

Just before noon, Briana rubbed her eyes while stifling a yawn. Too much screen time. She lifted her arms overhead to stretch out the kinks, relieving the tension in her lower back. When her stomach growled, she decided to take a break and brought the medical form to Becky's office. "Here you go."

"Thanks." Becky took the form and placed it in a file with Briana's name on it. "Off to lunch?"

"Yes. I'll be back soon."

"Go outside. Enjoy the weather."

Which was exactly what she planned to do. She made a quick stop by the general store to grab a premade sandwich and bottle of iced tea. Her mother had finally taken Cami to Crestview Farm to select a pumpkin, so Briana drove to Bailey's

Trail for a hike and some downtime to enjoy nature and think.

Once she'd parked, she changed into a pair of hiking boots she always kept in her car. As she started the incline, Briana ate the sandwich and tried to come at the case from different angles, but returned to the same conclusion; they still didn't have any idea who would want the tiara. It wasn't like they could sell the piece. It was distinctive and any dealer worth their salt would figure out it belonged with the movie collection. Her gut was telling her that this was a spur-of-the-moment action, not a well-thought-out plan.

She reached Bailey's Point in no time, but instead of stopping to savor the view of Golden Lake, she kept climbing. Her heart rate increased with the incline. It felt good to stretch her legs and inhale fresh air to clear her mind. She turned off the main trail, opting for a less traveled path winding deeper into the woods, leading to her favorite spot.

The picturesque path was littered with fallen leaves that crunched under her boots. A light breeze lifted her bangs. She stopped to angle her head toward the sunlight that snuck through the branches overhead. This time of year always resonated in Briana. She loved the colors and the cooler temperatures, the way the ground had a distinctive earthy scent, especially here in the forest.

A smile lifted her lips as she heard the distant trickling of water before reaching the clearing. She picked up her pace.

Finally, she reached her destination. Her steps slowed as she took in the scene. Just ahead of her a narrow stream, water sparkling in the sunshine, rushed over a rocky bed. A small outcrop of rocks created a delightful waterfall that warmed Briana's heart. Colorful leaves scurried along with the quickly moving water. She knew from experience how slippery the rocks could be, having trooped down the mountain a time or two in wet shoes. Leaning down, she ran her fingers over the ripples, enjoying the chill.

When they were younger, she and Jax had been roaming in the woods when they happened upon this location. After that, it became their go-to when they wanted to get away from family drama, needed to think, or simply wanted to hang out together away from the curious eyes of Golden. Taking a deep breath, she drew strength from the peace she felt every time she came here—which was not often enough these days—then found a large boulder and took a seat, the rock warm to the touch. She replayed the conversation with Jax in her head. More and more she was leaning toward the tiara being taken for the money. Franklin moved into the prime suspect spot, but there was also Robert to consider. How had he happened to be in position to turn the lights back on? Mrs. M. said she'd talked to him in the lobby. And why wasn't he with Gil to move the dress last night? Hopefully Jax could uncover more on that front.

In the meantime, she had two more events in

town to attend. A charades game at the community center to act out scenes from the movie, and a lecture at the library by Kat and Jill, talking about the role of a curator or researcher for a company like Heirloom Holdings. She doubted Franklin would show up for the game, but she had noticed that he sent Robert to events he didn't want to attend. Perhaps she'd get a chance to observe and question Robert then. It wouldn't be the same as investigating at the resort, but she might gain different insight being away from the crime scene. And the Golden Watch Network would be at the same events, so she could compare notes later.

She'd just slid from the boulder wiping the seat of her pants, not ready to return to real life but needing to get back to the station, when she heard a branch snap. A shuffling of leaves. She froze. Listened. Only birds chirped overhead. She waited, but didn't hear anything out of place. Letting out a breath, she heard another crunch.

Easing down beside the boulder, but out of the way of the path, she withdrew her weapon. Waited as she followed a shadow moving through the trees. Soon, the figure moved closer, grew larger, then stopped.

"Brie?"

Briana jumped up at the sound of Jax's voice. "Why would you sneak up on me like that?"

JAX EYED THE FIREARM. "Mind putting that away?"

It seemed to take her a moment to relax and then she lowered the weapon into the holster.

"I didn't mean to scare you," he said. "I thought you heard me."

"Not until you were close." She leaned back against the boulder, her hand over her heart. "I guess my mind was elsewhere."

"I should have called out to you. Let you know I was approaching."

"It's okay."

He couldn't help himself; he moved in to read her expression. "Are you sure?"

She waved her hand. "I'm fine."

"You just admitted you're jumpy. That doesn't qualify as okay."

"Really, Jax, I'll be fine. There's no need to protect me," she said in a wry tone. "One of the reasons I came out here for my lunch hour was to recharge."

"Good to know."

She frowned at him. "How did you know I was here?"

"This was our place." A place he'd never forgotten in all his years away from Golden.

Brie didn't seem convinced. "And you knew for sure I'd be here?"

He shrugged. "I went back to the station and Becky mentioned that she'd told you to go enjoy the outdoors. Took a chance you might have come here. Saw your car parked in the lot and headed up this way."

She hoisted herself up to sit on the boulder. "I guess I'm predictable."

"Not to everyone. Despite everything that went on between us, I hoped coming here hadn't changed."

Thankfully he wasn't disappointed.

She narrowed her eyes. "So, you came to check up on me?"

"Partially." He held up his hand to stave off her argument. "But then it was about climbing up here. It's been too long since I made the trek."

He moved to rest his hip against the boulder. Her jasmine-scented perfume surrounded him. They were quiet, the life force of the forest; the wind rustling through leafy branches and the cascading waterfall, became their soundtrack.

"Do you remember the last time we were here?" she asked in a quiet tone.

The exact moment, in fact. "After you learned about your father."

Brie nodded, her eyes scanning the trees. "I defended him. Told my family that they were wrong. That he'd never betray us."

She let out a forlorn sigh that troubled his heart. "But I was wrong. He didn't love us as much as he claimed he did. All those adventures we went on, the bond we shared, all went up in smoke the minute he admitted his wrongdoing."

"I know it cut you deep."

"Before he died, he tried to reconnect with me."

Surprise knocked him off-kilter. "I didn't know."

"How would you have?"

Did she realize she'd inched closer to him? It

took everything in him not to place his arm around her in comfort.

"I couldn't risk his hurting me again, and especially not Cami, so I turned him down." She focused on him, her eyes misty. "Why would he try after so much time?"

"People change, Brie."

After a drawn-out moment, she asked, "Have you?"

He expelled a long sigh.

"Sorry, that wasn't fair."

"It was honest."

A leaf fluttered through the air from a branch above. Brie brushed it from her shirt. "I think that's the reason why I didn't go with you, Jax. I realize now that I was afraid things might blow up like they did with my dad."

"And I realize that I never expected you to say no."

"Your theory made sense, but it was like I was frozen in time. My mom needed me, but she also wouldn't have stopped me if I wanted to go with you. I think I used what happened with my dad as an excuse to stay put. There had been so much upheaval in my life. I guess I didn't want more."

Jax hadn't expected to have this discussion about the past as he'd hiked the path to Brie, but it was long overdue. Maybe talking now would do some healing.

"With everything that's going on right now, are you sure you want to get into this, Brie?"

Her expression was as serious as he'd ever seen it. "Yes. Ever since you showed up in the PD conference room, I knew that eventually we were going to have to talk about that night. Might as well yank off the bandage now."

Jax crossed his arms and thought about what to say. In his head, he'd had this conversation dozens of times. But here, in the woods, surrounded by nature and memories, standing beside this beautiful woman, he decided to be honest.

"I always understood why you didn't join me. You and your family were still reeling after your dad left." He met her gaze head-on. "I only came up with a solution to make the situation easier, just like you were trying to help your family."

"Deep down, I knew that."

"For me, it was the way the conversation ended that stung. You'd never refused me before. After all we'd shared for so many years, you were okay leaving me on my own." Emotion clogged his throat. It suddenly occurred to him that after that night, the crack in his heart had never healed. "In the park, when you walked away, it crushed me."

Brie glanced down and picked at a seam of her jeans. A similar gesture to that night. "I've had a long time to think about it," she finally said. When her gaze met his, tears swam in her eyes. "In retrospect, at that time, I figured you'd take my answer at face value, and we'd go on as normal. When that didn't happen, I didn't know how to fix it."

"It hurt, Brie." He swallowed hard. "But I shouldn't

have let the gulf between us grow deeper. Once I got on with my life, I should have talked to you instead of holding on to the painful memory so we could resolve the problem."

"Hurt has a way of confusing one's thinking."

It had. For both of them.

"After I left town, I allowed how I felt when you walked away to get bigger and bigger in my head."

"We both played a part in the distance that grew between us," she said.

There she was, taking responsibility again when his reaction fell on his shoulders alone.

"Probably, but I let the hurt expand unchecked and wouldn't come back to Golden. I wouldn't talk to you. I shouldn't have been surprised when you adopted Cami, a major event in your life, without telling me. I made it difficult. I'm just as guilty about what happened to us."

He stared at the pine trees soaring above them. Circumstances had brought him back to Golden, back to the place that was deeply ingrained in his heart. Just like Brie.

She asked in a small voice, "Are you saying we can get back to where we were?"

Her face, so dear and precious to him, was not only that of his best friend, but now, a woman he was attracted to. His feelings had morphed into more than just a friendship rekindled. Just when they'd gotten some solid footing concerning the past, would he blow up the future if he admitted how he felt?

Instead of going there, he said, "I think that after the case is solved, we sit down and evaluate what's going on between us."

She tilted her head, curiosity gleaming in her eyes. "What is going on?"

He ran a hand through his hair. "You do realize that I almost kissed you last night."

Her eyes grew wide. "I'm aware."

"And?"

"I think it's safe to assume that's not an aspect of our relationship that either of us had considered before now." She hesitated for a fraction of a moment. "Is it going to be a problem?"

Jax weighed the word carefully. "Kissing?"

"Is there going to be a kiss?"

His heart hammered in his chest. "How about we test that theory?"

Her lips parted. He leaned close, his eyes locked on hers. When he saw the smallest of nods, he slowly brushed his lips over hers. He stopped after a moment, gauged her reaction, and when he saw her small smile, kissed her again. This time he lingered, so caught up in the sensation he could have continued for hours.

"I'm…um…" Brie sputtered when they parted.

"Yeah. Me, too."

Brie pulled back and slid from the boulder. "I should probably get back to the station."

He moved out of the way. "Right. And I need to go over some notes before I head to the resort."

Both were caught up in their thoughts as they

walked through the woods to the main hiking path. The stroll was both too fast and strangely exhilarating. A place Jax had never found himself with a woman.

Kissing Brie had changed everything.

# *CHAPTER TWELVE*

THE NEXT MORNING, Briana arrived at the crowded community center amid a hubbub of activity. The good folks of Golden were out to prove themselves to the representative from Heirloom Assets. Just as she expected, Franklin wasn't there. It appeared that Robert would be the emcee.

While making her way around the room, greeting people she'd known her entire life, she watched Robert carefully. He spoke to people with ease. Did he suspect the thief to be a resident of Golden? Or was that just Mr. Franklin's theory? Robert didn't have a gruff personality like Franklin, instead seeming to adapt to every situation, which made him harder to read.

"Brady gave you time off?"

Briana started, so intently watching Robert, that she hadn't seen her mother approach. She pulled Briana into a hug, her floral perfume surrounding Briana, as constant and comforting as the woman she loved dearly. Her mother stepped back to check Briana from head to toe. "You look so pretty today."

Dressing for her assignment today, she'd opted to

wear a favorite blue-and-white-striped knit sweater, denim skirt and tall black boots. "Thanks."

Her mother wrinkled her nose. "You're investigating, aren't you?"

Briana placed a finger over her lips.

"I get it. Hush-hush."

Not that Briana expected the people gathered to think otherwise. Many of the guests who had been at the black-tie party were here today, knowing they were in the hot seat after the theft of the tiara. It seemed they wanted to prove their innocence with or without the PD's help.

"Your sister and I are putting charade teams together, so if you want to be involved, just let me know."

"It's best if I observe."

Her mother's happiness dimmed. "Do you really suspect someone from Golden of stealing the tiara?"

She couldn't go into details, so she smiled. "Mom, I'm just here in an official capacity."

"Which means you can't tell us anything," she griped.

Nicole walked over to join them. "We've lined up the teams," she explained. "I'm afraid you're an odd man out, so you'll have to watch."

"That's okay with me."

Nicole linked her arm with their mother's. "We have work to do and I think Briana is capable of being on her own."

*Thanks*, Briana mouthed.

Nicole winked as she walked away.

"Got a minute?"

She turned to find Alvin beside her. "What's up?"

For all intents and purposes, Alvin acted as though he was having an easygoing conversation with Briana. His tone belied that truth.

"Haven't had a chance to let Jax know, but just as we were arriving, I noticed Robert having an intense phone conversation."

Her investigative instincts ratcheted up. "Were you able to hear anything?"

"Gandy and I got as close as we could without seeming obvious when he started complaining about how his knees were hurting him, which is the truth. You'd think he'd use some ointment to ease the pain, but he just goes on about—"

"Mr. Walker—"

Alvin shook his head. She knew using his formal name would get him on the right path.

"Right. Anyway, while we were pretending to have a conversation about arthritis and old age, I leaned toward Robert. He was assuring whoever was on the other end that when he got back to LA, things were going to be different."

Hmm. Now that was interesting.

"The call ended soon after and he hustled inside." He paused, his expression turning pensive. "Gandy was out at the resort yesterday. Said the security guards seemed nervous."

"After the theft of the tiara, I'm not surprised."

"Monroe and the missus will be at the resort tomorrow to view the collection. He'll report back on their behavior."

"Thanks. I'll tell Jax."

"You two still working together?"

Was that a twinkle in Alvin's eyes?

"Some. The schedule has been changed a bit."

"Good. You both work well as a team. I expect you'll uncover what's going on."

If only he knew how true his words were and why it was making Briana question everything about her relationship with Jax. They did work well as a team, not just for the police department. But she still couldn't define the current state of their relationship.

Alvin regarded her with curiosity.

"That's the plan," she replied.

Alvin touched his nose with his right index finger and blended into the crowd.

As she scanned the room, Briana noticed Robert standing at a table set up in front of rows of folding chairs, flipping through index cards. Must be the scenes the teams would act out. Putting on her friendliest face, she approached him.

"Hi, Robert. You're leading today's charades game?"

He looked up. For a split second a dark cloud shadowed his eyes, but before she could decipher why, he smiled. "Good morning, Officer. And yes, being with the public is part of my job," he answered.

"I wanted to thank you for being so quick to get the lights on at the party the other night."

He shrugged but wouldn't meet her gaze. "Part of my job is fixing problems. Lights were out—I found a way to get them back on."

Briana chuckled. "Good thing, or who knows how much more chaos there might have been."

"The response was understandable under the circumstances."

"I'm sure the fire alarm made matters worse. I was wondering, did you happen to see anyone near the kitchen? Someone who looked out of place?"

He shifted. Was she adding too much pressure? Making him uncomfortable? "The only people I saw were the caterers."

"You checked on them?"

"From time to time upon Mr. Franklin's request." Concern shone in his eyes. "I heard you were burned putting out a fire."

Briana held up her palm. The redness was beginning to fade. "I'll be fine."

"That's a relief. We would never want anyone to get hurt at one of our events."

Now that they had established a bit of a rapport, she continued her line of questioning. "Can you think of anything that was odd the night of the party?"

His eyes narrowed. "Are you interrogating me?"

So much for using his concern to her advantage.

She sent him a rueful smile. "Sorry. Sometimes I can't put the job away."

His tone grew terse. “I told the other officers that I didn’t see anything worth mentioning.”

“Got it.”

Her mother chose that moment to interrupt. “I need to talk with Robert before we get started.”

Briana grinned at Robert. “Heads up, the folks of Golden are pretty competitive.”

Especially her sisters. Trivia night at Smitty’s Pub always turned into a rowdy affair when all her sisters were playing.

He smiled, not very enthusiastically she noted, before she walked away, searching for a place where she wouldn’t stand out. The large room echoed with the voices of the people gathered for today’s festivities. Briana inhaled the scent of coffee brewing in the kitchen. Edging toward the back of the room, she’d just found a spot to perch when the double doors opened, letting in bright sunshine.

Jax walked in.

She frowned as he took off his sunglasses and zeroed in on her.

What was he doing here? Brady hadn’t mentioned a change in assignment.

Her ridiculous heart picked up a beat when he walked into the room. He was dressed in a charcoal-colored sweater that accentuated his muscles. His indigo jeans and dark boots finished the casual look.

His blue eyes met hers. A shiver skittered down her spine.

Jax was becoming more than a friend, which surprised her. She had been wondering if she was beginning to have feelings for him, but after that kiss yesterday, the truth couldn't be denied. How had that happened?

When he stood beside her, his cologne enveloping her, she had to clear her throat before speaking. "Is anything wrong?"

"No, Brady wanted both of us here this morning."

Her back went up. She couldn't hide the edge to her voice.

"Why? I can handle it."

"He said something about keeping a lid on you and your competitive sisters."

"You're kidding, right?" she sputtered.

"Nope. Apparently he's been a victim of your family at trivia night."

Her frustration with Jax faded. "He's just mad because he doesn't like to lose." Which was totally true.

"Yeah? How often does that happen?"

She allowed a smug smile. "Regularly."

He chuckled. "Now I get why he sent me over." Then he gave her a once-over. "You look nice."

"You, too."

Could this be any more awkward? She felt her face warm, then rushed to say, "You don't have to worry about participating in this game. The teams have already been selected."

"Good. We can divide and conquer. Get more information from the people who attended the Saturday night party."

"Since you're here, does that mean you're off tonight?"

He scanned the room, answering distractedly, "Brady and Roan are handling the transfer."

"Any news concerning the tiara?"

He brought his gaze back to her. "I did another round of questioning at the resort. No one could add any pertinent information. I do want to speak to the woman Gil was flirting with at the reception desk during the party, but she's out of town until Friday." He glanced around the room. "What's going on here?"

"I talked to your grandfather." She relayed the information. "Then I talked to Robert. His reactions are all over the place. He was pleasant with the crowd, grew defensive when I asked him questions, then concerned that I was injured at their party. I can't get a handle on him."

Jax crossed his arms over his chest. "Then we can both observe him."

There was a tapping sound on the table up front. Mrs. M. stood beside Robert.

"Thank you for coming to the first *Riches of the Past* charades game," she greeted them.

The crowd clapped.

She waved away the applause. "Robert will be assisting me with the emcee duties. We're so happy Heirloom Assets is taking an interest in our little town."

"More so now that the tiara is missing," Jax said in a low tone that scraped her skin. She needed to focus on what was going on around her, not on how close Jax was standing next to her and the reactions he elicited.

Mrs. M. pointed to her right. "This side of the room will represent Golden. The other, Heirloom Assets."

"Let's hear it for our team," Robert said, getting his side pumped for the competition. They responded with a ruckus.

"Here are the rules." Mrs. M. held up a stack of cards. "One member of each opposing team will come up and select a clue. On each card, there is the title of a specific scene from the movie. That's the number of words you'll give the crowd so they can make their guesses. The round is over when one team is first to call out the correct answer. We'll tally up points and see which side wins."

"What's the prize?" someone yelled.

"Dinner at Roma's Italian Restaurant."

An excited buzz filled the room. In the pause, Nicole jogged toward Briana.

"Glad you two showed up."

"We're not here to play," Briana reminded her sister.

Nicole tilted her head. "What happened to blending in? If you two don't play, it'll be obvious."

"I..."

"Your sister has a point," Jax said. "How bad could it be?"

"Very," Briana muttered. "You have no idea."

"C'mon. Be a good sport."

She shrugged. "Don't say I didn't warn you."

He led her to two empty seats in the last row. Her unease grew at the sparkle in Mrs. M.'s eyes when she zeroed in on them.

Soon, the game was on. Briana enjoyed the high-spirited mood in the room. It was clear that everyone present had seen the movie. The scenes varied, one when the archaeologist and the historian first discovered the tomb of gold, another when they were fighting off the bad guys on the way back with the treasure, to another with the curator and historian explaining the treasures to the public when the collection went on display.

They were getting close to the end of the game when Mrs. M. sauntered their way, a knowing grin on her face. Briana went still. She recognized that smile and wanted to run.

The older woman handed Briana a card. "You're up."

Taking a deep breath, Briana read the scene. Her stomach dropped.

"Let's see," Jax said, hand out.

She handed over the card, her fingers brushing his, which didn't help her nerves. When her skin prickled, she felt him go as still as her.

"You've got to be kidding me," he muttered.

"I wish," she answered.

Of all the scenes in the movie to enact, Mrs. M. picked the kiss between the curator and the archaeologist.

"C'mon up," Mrs. M. beckoned. Briana was absolutely sure the woman had picked that scene for them on purpose. She did have a matchmaker reputation to uphold, didn't she?

"We can't do this," Jax said under his breath.

"Who was it that said it wouldn't be bad?" Briana puffed out a breath.

Like the rest of the group, they each took a minute to decide how they would portray the scene.

"If I recall," Jax said under his breath, "the couple are in the museum. It's late, the lights are low, and they are admiring the treasure they've finally gotten safely to New York City after all their misadventures."

Briana swallowed. "How do you want to play this?"

"I guess just like the movie."

Jax led the way up front. Briana squared her shoulders, faced the rows of people and held up two fingers.

Jax started the scene by pretending to take off a hat.

"The archaeologist," Nicole yelled.

Briana smoothed her skirt.

"The curator," someone else guessed.

Jax pretended to flip a switch.

"Lights," her mother said.

Briana stood beside Jax. They pretended to be entranced by whatever was in front of them.

"The treasure," Alvin shouted.

Then they turned to face each other.

Jax's eyes went dark. Briana breathed, waiting to

see what he'd do next. After that kiss in the woods, she'd be a liar if she said she didn't want it to happen again. She locked her gaze with his and suddenly no one else in the room mattered.

He moved a breath closer.

She leaned toward him.

He gently cupped her cheeks with his warm hands.

She fell into his spell.

Could everyone in the room feel the enchantment between them?

She was just going to close her eyes and kiss Jax for the greater good of the investigation—or so she convinced herself—when her sister called out. "The kiss!"

They continued to stare at each other until Briana vaguely heard clapping and Mrs. M. poked her head between them. "The scene is over, you two."

Jax slowly turned to face the room. Briana blinked, then prayed her face wasn't bright red.

"Go with me," Jax said as he took her hand and yanked her down into an overly dramatic bow. The crowd loved it and cheered as if the bow was all part of the game.

"Remind me to always be on the same team as you," he said as they rose.

She met his serious gaze. There was so much to read in those blue depths. She didn't know where to start. All she knew for certain was that things were not the same as when they were kids.

After a taut moment, Jax said in a husky voice, "Time to get back to work."

Right. Work.

How in the world was that possible?

JAX HADN'T BEEN PLAYING. He'd wanted to kiss Brie in front of the entire room.

With her lovely face tipped toward him, he couldn't resist. Unlike most of the times he'd spent with her since returning home, she wasn't in uniform. Her outfit made her more lovely and, well, Brie. He didn't need any more reasons to kiss her besides the growing list in his head, so he'd tried to keep his cool while they acted out the scene. Now, all bets were off.

"How do you think that went?" Mrs. M. asked as she edged next to him.

He reluctantly shook off thoughts of Briana. "Excuse me?"

"You and Briana?" She elbowed him in the side. "Do you think there's a spark?"

Spark? As far as Jax was concerned, there was an entire bonfire.

Mrs. M.'s smile dipped. "Your mother said she told you about our club. That you're onboard."

That explained her question. "She did. I asked her to wait until the tiara case is over before finding my…"

"True love?" She laughed. "I'm sorry. I saw an opportunity and took it upon myself to get started."

"I'm not sure this was the right place."

Her smile spread, making his nerves clang in alarm. “I promise to do a better job next time.”

As far as Jax was concerned there wouldn’t be a second attempt. He needed to figure out where this attraction to Brie was going, because he swore that Brie had drifted toward him during the playacting, waiting for his lips to touch hers.

He shook off his musing. “While I have you here, can I ask a question?”

Mrs. M.’s eyebrows angled over perceptive eyes. “About the case?”

His mother was right. The woman didn’t miss a thing. “Have you had a chance to think more clearly about the party?”

“Now that you mention it, I have. I recall that Robert was very…nervous…when I caught him coming from the dining room into the lobby. I didn’t put two and two together at first because he was gushing over his girlfriend. He said he had big news when he got home. I assumed it was a marriage proposal, but maybe he’s concerned about their future?”

“In what way?”

“He covered it well, but the way his forehead wrinkled, I think now that he was distressed.” She paused. “He had his sports jacket draped over his arm and his tie was crooked. He looked sweaty, almost like he’d been outside and had walked a great distance. There was even a smudge on his shirt sleeve.” She waved that idea off. “But he couldn’t have been outside. He had to be at the party until that point."

"But you're not sure?"

"It's not like I kept an eagle eye on him, but I remember Mr. Franklin asking someone where Robert was before I stepped into the lobby."

"So there's no telling how long he was out of the room."

Mrs. M. frowned. "Or when he came back."

Jax remembered that after the lights came on and the alarm was silenced, the tiara was discovered missing. But had Robert entered the room before the lights had gone off? After talking to Mrs. M.? If he was in the room, did that give him enough time to snatch the tiara and remove it right under everyone's nose while they were socializing? Then turn off the lights to cause additional confusion? And if so, where did he hide it? They'd done a complete search of the room and had come up empty. "And later? After the tiara was taken?" he asked Mrs. M.

"He seemed fine." Mrs. M. leaned close. "Although if his mood had anything to do with the man he works for, I can see why he'd be nervous. Mr. Franklin is not very nice."

Jax silently agreed.

He asked a few more people who were at the party if they recalled anything. Most remembered Robert turning on the lights, but no one could recall him leaving or returning to the multipurpose room. He continued questioning until he noticed Robert hightail it from the community center.

His grandfather stood on the opposite side of the room, as if on high alert. Jax knew the man would have information.

His grandfather's face lit up when Jax approached him.

"Fun game," Gramps said. "If I didn't know better, I'd have thought you were gonna kiss Briana."

Jax didn't take the bait.

"Brie brought me up to speed on your conversation."

Gramps's demeanor changed. "There's been a development."

Jax raised an eyebrow.

"Just overhead Robert on the phone again. He was in the kitchen away from folks so I went in to gather up the garbage bag."

"And?"

"It was pretty clear he was talking to Franklin. Asked what the big hurry was about returning to the resort. Whatever Franklin said made his face go white as a sheet."

"That's why he hurried out of here."

"Could be big." His grandfather grinned. "I've got Curt on resort duty today. I'll ask him to observe the dynamics between those two."

Jax squeezed his grandfather's shoulder. "Thanks, Gramps. I need to get Brie up to speed."

Gramps got a cagey smile on his face. "Because you're partners and all."

Jax shot his grandfather a puzzled look.

"Go on now," Gramps instructed.

Bewildered at his grandfather's meaning, Jax met Brie near the door.

"We should go to the caterers'," Brie said at the same time Jax said, "Robert got a call from Franklin."

Her eyebrow rose. "Do we need to go to the resort?"

"No, that's covered. You're right, let's drop in on the caterer."

It wasn't far to walk to Delicious Tidbits, located a few blocks away. The storefront featured a main room with a tasting table and wine area, a small office and an industrial kitchen in the back. When they entered, Marie, the owner, greeted them. She was a friend of Brie's mother, with big blond hair and bright green eyes.

"I heard the charades game was fun," she said.

"That was fast," Jax said under his breath.

Brie hid her smile. "Do you have a minute?" she asked the owner.

"Take a seat at the tasting table. You arrived at a good time. I'm getting ready to remove a new appetizer from the oven and you can be my testers."

"Food and an interrogation," Brie said. "My kind of gig."

This was why he loved hanging around with her.

The woman returned moments later, her hands in oven mitts, holding a tray with what resembled puff pastries.

"That smells amazing," Jax said as he sniffed the air.

"A new creation for an upcoming wedding. They wanted all new dishes, so I had to come up with different options." She set the tray down to reveal a light pastry hugging colorful mini peppers stuffed with…

"Is that spinach and cheese?" Brie asked.

"And chicken. Try it."

Brie dug in and hummed her satisfaction. Jax picked up a yellow pepper and couldn't deny the zap of flavor on his tongue.

Marie watched their faces. "What do you think?"

"Amazing," Brie said around a mouthful. Jax waited until he'd devoured the entire thing before giving Marie a thumbs-up.

"I'm glad you like it," Marie beamed. "I'll add this to the menu."

Jax grabbed some napkins and wiped his fingers. "Were you with your servers the night of the party?"

Marie shook her head. "No. The party was a last-minute gig. I had to be at a wedding, but I had my best servers there."

"Are any of them here?"

She nodded and called in a loud voice, "Liza."

A twenty-something woman with jet-black hair who Jax recognized from the party came into the room. Her eyes went wide when she saw Jax and Brie.

"Is everything okay?" she asked, twisting the dish towel in her hands.

"We just wanted to ask you a few questions since

you worked the party at the resort Saturday night," Brie said in a soothing tone.

"We left the kitchen in order," Liza rushed to say.

"There are no complaints," Brie assured her. "I was curious, did you take out all the trash?"

"Yes, we do that after every event."

"Did you see any guests or resort staff in the kitchen?"

"No. We were the only people allowed in there." She frowned. "But the boss… Mr. Franklin?"

"That's correct," Jax said.

"He kept asking when we were leaving. I told him about thirty minutes before the party was scheduled to end. I assured him we would be serving guests until then and he seemed satisfied." Her face colored to a soft pink. "About fifteen minutes until the party was to end, we all gathered in the kitchen to make sure we left it spotless."

"And the metal trash can near the back door. Was it empty when you left?" Brie asked.

"We didn't use that can," Liza said. "The smaller plastic bins were sufficient. We took all the bags out to the dumpster."

"And no guests ever entered the kitchen," Jax asked again.

"Not that I'm aware of." Her forehead wrinkled in thought. "At one point I heard a voice coming from the direction of the empty dining room, but didn't think anything of it since the party was still in full swing."

And Mrs. M. had talked to Robert, who was coming from the dining room.

Jax thanked Liza and she hurried back to the kitchen.

"I hope that was helpful," Marie said.

"It was," Brie assured her, her expression lighting up when she met Jax's gaze. "We'll check in if we need any more details."

"We'll be here. And if you need a caterer for any event—" Marie winked at them "—you know who to call."

Brie took hold of Jax's arm and dragged him outside. "Why do you look like you discovered something big?"

He told her about Mrs. M. seeing Robert coming from the dining room and their subsequent conversation.

"Just after the caterers left is when I smelled the fire. They were running late, so whoever started the fire had a brief opportunity to start it *and* get back to the room full of guests." She squeezed his arm. "It had to be in the window of time that Robert was missing." She brushed her bangs from her animated face. "Do you think it was Robert who started the fire?"

Jax thought back to what Mrs. M. said. "I can't imagine why he'd go to the trouble, but I'll let Brady know. Someone needs to keep an eye on him until we receive the report from the fire department determining if the fire was intentional."

"And we don't want to spook him any further with questions until we have the answer."

Briana's phone made a sound like wind chimes. She pulled it from her skirt pocket. "It's my mom. I need to pick up Cami and the pumpkin she bought so we can carve it tonight."

Jax grinned. "Cami did say she wanted to carve one just like Jacob's."

Brie shook her head. "No. Ours will be princess style."

"Interesting."

She took a moment to replace her phone in her pocket. Then in an offhand tone asked, "You said you aren't on duty tonight, but are you busy?"

His chest went tight. "No plans."

"Would you like to carve the pumpkin with us? It's getting close to Halloween and Cami is in the spirit."

He did. More than anything he'd done in a long time.

"I'll be there."

# CHAPTER THIRTEEN

"OKAY, LET'S SCOOP the guts out," Jax said, hands on his hips as he scrutinized the bright orange pumpkin on the kitchen table. After dinner, Brie spread newspaper over the tabletop and placed the pumpkin at the center.

"Guts," Cami said with a giggle. She was dressed in a sparkly yellow princess dress. When Jax had asked her if it was going to be her Halloween costume, she informed him that her trick-or-treating dress was a secret. The one she had on was for play.

Boy, did he have a lot to learn about little girls.

Brie glowered at him. "I prefer to call it pulp."

"That's not what we called it when we were kids," he reminded her. He'd forgotten how much fun it was to tease her.

"Yeah, well, maybe I'm going in a different direction with my daughter."

With that declaration she handed him a knife. Cami climbed atop a chair to see better. He sliced into the meaty skin to remove the lid. Then Brie used a large spoon to remove the insides.

Cami placed her palms on the table and leaned

in to watch. "I can't wait to tell Jacob that we took out the guts."

Brie scowled at Jax. "Thanks."

After each scoop, Brie dropped the stringy pulp into a large bowl. "Cami, why don't you pick out the seeds and place them in the empty bowl."

The little girl wrinkled her nose. "It smells funny."

Jax was about to say it was because of the guts, but Brie's warning frown cut him off.

"It's just how a pumpkin smells. Kind of like a watery vegetable," Brie said.

Cami nodded and started her task of picking out the seeds. "Mommy, what are we going to do with these?"

"We'll rinse them off then put them in the oven to crisp up so we can eat them."

"Can we eat the guts?"

"The pulp," Jax corrected before he landed in the doghouse. "And you can, but I don't know anyone who does."

Cami seemed satisfied with his answer.

Brie continued scooping until the spoon slipped in her wet fingers, flew up and a blob of pulp landed on her cheek. Cami laughed like it was the funniest thing she'd ever seen.

"Ew. Ick," Brie muttered as she brushed her hand over her face.

"Let me," he said, using his thumb to remove the last bit of pulp. Her skin was soft under his touch.

He met her gaze. She didn't blink. He didn't think he breathed. The tension between them rose.

"You got it," Cami said, breaking the silent connection.

Jax pulled his hand back. "Better."

"Right. Better."

Everything was better with Brie.

Once Brie cleaned out the cavity of the pumpkin, she washed her hands and returned with a black marker and paper.

"What design do you want for the face?" she asked Cami.

"A princess!"

"I don't think I've ever seen a princess pumpkin face," Jax said.

Cami's smile wavered. "Should it be something else?"

His heart dropped at her disappointed expression. "I think it can be anything you want it to be," he answered quickly.

Cami's smile returned. "How about a funny face?"

"We can do that." Brie made a big circle on the paper and asked, "What about the mouth?"

"Big with lots of teeth."

Brie drew a big, curved smile and square teeth. "Now, how about the eyes?"

Thinking about it for a moment, Cami answered, "Round."

Brie sketched two round eyes.

"The nose?" Jax asked.

Cami puckered her lip then said, "A triangle."

Brie grinned at him. "She aced shapes when I taught her."

"Smart girl," he said, taking in Brie's profile as she drew. "Just like her mother."

Brie didn't respond, but he was positive he saw her lips twitch. When she stepped back to view her portrait, Jax grabbed the marker and flipped the page over.

"Hey!"

He proceeded to draw googly eyes and an even wider mouth.

Cami giggled. "You're silly."

Jax could confidently say that no one had ever accused him of that.

After a lively debate, they finally settled on Jax's eyes and mouth and Brie's nose. Cami clapped her hands as Brie traced the shapes onto the pumpkin shell.

"She's going to be so pretty," Cami gushed. "I already named her Princess Pumpkin."

Jax chuckled. "I sense a theme here."

After setting the marker down, Brie took the knife from the counter. Before the tip sliced into the pumpkin, Cami stopped her.

"No, Mommy. Let Jax do it."

Surprise welled up in him at her request. He tried to gauge Brie's reaction, but she covered it well.

After a brief hesitation, Brie handed him the knife.

He met her gaze. "Are you sure? I don't want to mess with your traditions."

"I'm sure." She smiled and when it reached her eyes, he breathed in relief. "And as far as traditions go, this is only the second year Cami has watched the process, so I'm good with the change."

Without hesitation, Jax went to work, carving out the shapes.

"What's tradition?" Cami asked as she watched Jax work.

"Special things that families do together," Brie explained while removing more seeds from the pulp. "Like you going trick-or-treating with Jacob or going to Grammy's on Christmas morning."

"I like those."

Jax handed a chunk of the shape he'd cut to Cami. As she inspected it, she asked, "How about you? Do you got traditions?"

His fingers tightened around the knife handle. "I haven't done anything special in a lot of years."

"Why not?"

He certainly couldn't explain that he'd stayed away from Golden and all its traditions because Brie had wounded his heart. Cami wouldn't understand and he was tired of blaming his decisions on that night she'd walked away. He could have come home any time he wanted. He chose not to.

"Well, I suppose it's because of your mom."

Brie's eyes widened. "Me?"

"Sure. You and I had plenty of traditions. Remember how we used to sneak out of our houses the night before Halloween to toilet paper the neighborhood on prank night?"

"I almost forgot." She laughed. "Especially now that I'm an upstanding police officer."

He glanced up from carving the mouth. "That you are."

Their gazes met and held. He could have frozen this moment forever, drinking her in. Here, in Brie's kitchen, with her daughter, he'd never been happier.

"What else did you do?" Cami demanded.

"We would go to your grammy's house and dump our bag of Halloween loot on the floor. Your mom would put the candy or treats in different categories and then we'd trade."

Cami's face lit up. "Can I do that with Jacob?"

"If Aunt Addie says okay," Brie said, then chuckled. "She used to hide her candy so we wouldn't take any."

"You shouldn't take other people's candy," Cami sternly instructed her mother.

Jax smiled as he added curlicue shapes on the top and side of the face to resemble hair.

"We didn't. Turns out the year Addie thought we were stealing from her she had a hole in her bag." Brie smiled at him. "Jax retraced her steps to find the wrapped candy that dropped into the grass and brought it back to her."

Jax had forgotten all about that.

"You're a hero," Cami breathed. "Just like in my princess movies."

He hoped Brie wasn't watching him because he swore his face was heating.

After a few more stories, Brie picked up the pumpkin and turned it to face Cami. "What do you think?"

Her mouth dropped open. "I think she's bootiful." She looked up at Brie. "Now what?"

"Princess Pumpkin goes on the front porch so everyone can see her. I'll put a candle inside so she glows when it's dark out."

"She can glow!"

"She can."

Cami jumped down from the chair and wrapped her arms around Brie's waist. Jax reached out to grab the pumpkin to keep it from spilling from her hands. When he took it, Brie folded Cami into a hug.

Jax had just placed the pumpkin down when Cami flung herself at him. "Thank you," she said, squeezing as hard as a four-year-old could manage. For a second, he was at a loss. His heart melted, and he crouched down to envelop her.

When Brie cleared her throat, he stood. "It's time to get ready for bed," she announced.

"Oh, Mommy. Do I have to?"

"You do. Go get in your jammies and I'll be in to tell you a story."

"Can Jax read to me tonight?"

If his heart hadn't already been lost to this little girl, her invitation finished the job.

Brie seemed taken off guard by the question. "Um…sure. I'll clean up while you're reading."

He watched Cami race from the room. "Brie, I've never read to a child."

She laughed. "It's not rocket science."

The gravity of Cami's request shook him. "But it's important."

Brie slipped her hand in his. "Just use funny voices. And read the bunny book. It's her favorite."

He nodded.

"I'm ready," came Cami's muffled voice from the other side of the house.

Brie nodded her head in the direction of her daughter's bedroom. "You can do this, hero."

He'd worked in military intelligence. Had gone after some really bad guys. Was now a cop working on an active investigation. Why was the thought of reading to Cami so daunting?

He nodded then walked to her room, silently building up his confidence as he went. He entered the room with pink walls, princess décor and a slight bubblegum scent to find Cami standing in front of a small bookshelf. She removed a slim volume and jumped up on the bed, handing the book to Jax.

"Read this one."

"Is this about the bunny?"

"No." Cami climbed under the covers. "It's a book about mommies and daddies. But Mommy doesn't got a daddy anymore. I don't want her to be sad, so I hid it."

He swallowed at the emotion clogging his throat. When Cami patted the mattress, he sank down beside her.

He opened the book and soon they were enjoying the antics of a bear family. He tried different voices which had Cami laughing. As he got near the end of the story, he felt her inch closer to him. When he finished, she handed him the bunny book, which he dutifully read while Cami burrowed into his side. As he closed the cover, he glanced over to see her eyelids drooping.

"How'd I do?"

She gave him a thumbs-up before her breathing evened out and she was fast asleep.

It took him several moments to pull himself together. Could this be what a family would look like? Tonight was wonderful. It was everything he wanted. To read stories to his children. To come home at night and find his family waiting for him. To have a wife to love and laugh with.

This was what he'd been searching for, why he'd agreed to allow his mother to join the matchmaking bandwagon. But could they find anything better than what he felt right here?

Feeling hollow, he eased himself away from the slumbering girl. Her steady breathing sounded loud in the quiet room. Placing the books on top of the bookshelf, he turned out the light before stepping from the room.

Straightening his shoulders, he marched into the kitchen, wanting to tell Brie how he felt. "I think we should talk about—" He stopped short when he found her holding an envelope in her hands, staring at it. "Brie?"

She glanced up, such misery in her eyes that it took his breath away.

"This is from my dad."

ONLY A MINUTE before Jax returned to the kitchen, Briana had been rummaging in a drawer, looking for a small candle to place inside the pumpkin. Her fingers had brushed up against the envelope and she'd pulled it out. When she read the distinctive handwriting, she froze.

"Brie?"

She glanced up, blinking rapidly as tears filled her eyes. "This is from my dad."

He walked over and placed his hands on her shoulders. "Are you okay?"

"I… I don't know."

"Is this the letter you received with the inheritance?"

"Yes." She shuddered. "I stuffed it in the drawer and intentionally made myself forget about it."

Jax moved closer. "You don't have to read it if you're not ready."

She glanced up at his face, glad he was here, otherwise she would have crammed it back into its hiding place. And what good would that do if she never faced up to her fear?

She blew out a trembling breath. "I don't think I'll ever be ready, but I have to face it."

Jax squeezed her shoulder. "Do you want to sit down?"

Yes. She needed to sit. "Can we go into the living room?"

"Wherever you want."

The envelope was still crumpled in her hand as they moved to the other room. She shivered, grabbing the blanket from the back of the couch to wrap around her trembling body.

Jax hovered. "Are you cold?"

She was numb, but chilly at the same time.

When she didn't answer, he offered, "How about I start a fire?"

"Please."

While Jax placed logs in the fireplace, she settled onto the couch. Was this how her sisters had felt when faced with the gravity of their father's words? Stressed, emotional and unsure? She currently suffered from all three.

The flames soon began to flicker and grow. The burning wood scent filled the room. It took a moment for the warmth to reach her. From his place beside the fireplace, Jax asked, "I'll take off now if you're okay."

She realized she didn't want him to go. She didn't want to be alone when she finally opened the letter.

Her voice reedy, she asked, "Would you mind staying?"

"Of course."

In a few steps, Jax crossed the room and sat beside her, leaving a small space between them. As if he didn't want to intrude but wanted to be near her at the same time.

She pressed out the wrinkles in the envelope. "Is it cowardly of me to have put this off for so long?"

He leaned into her. "Brie, your relationship with your dad was complicated. It stands to reason you'd hesitate."

She dropped the envelope into her lap and rubbed her hands up and down her face. When she was a bit calmer, she said, "Thanks for starting the fire."

"Anything to help."

She tried to grin at him but was sure she failed. "Always looking out for me."

"And I always will."

For once she appreciated his protective streak.

She took a deep breath. Except for the snap and pop of the burning logs, the room was strangely silent. Picking up the envelope, she ran her fingernail under the flap to tear it open. Then, with shaky fingers, she removed the letter. As she did, a frayed friendship bracelet made with green, blue and tan string tumbled into her lap. She picked it up to stare at it.

"What's that?"

Swallowing past the lump in her throat, she remembered.

"I made this in the arts and crafts summer program at the community center." She ran the soft material through her fingers. "Actually, two. One for Dad and one for me."

Jax nodded toward the bracelet. "He kept it."

If she had to guess where her bracelet was, she'd come up empty. The thought pierced her heart.

Taking a bracing breath, she set the bracelet aside. This process of confronting the past was heavier than she'd imagined.

She turned to Jax. "Will you read it with me?"

Surprise shone in his eyes. "If you want me to."

"You were there through it all, Jax, so yes, I want you with me now."

He leaned over and kissed her forehead. "You can do anything you put your mind to, Brie."

She wasn't so sure about this.

Glancing up at his soft smile calmed the tempest storming in her. Once she unfolded the letter, she took hold of Jax's hand. He squeezed tight.

She started to read out loud.

"My dearest Briana."

She paused. Swallowed hard. Did she want to do this? *It's time*, came a voice from inside, sounding just like her sister Nicole. If Nicole and Addie could read their letters, then she could too.

She started over.

"My dearest Briana,

"I think this is the hardest letter I've ever written. There is so much to say, so many ways to tell you I'm sorry. I don't blame you for turning your back on me. You were right. I turned my back on the family. I deserve your resentment. But know that for all my bad decisions, I never stopped loving you.

"I realized all these years later that the bond we

shared when you were a child was special. I broke it. No one else understood our quest for mountain gold. Or how we could sit for hours watching police shows. You even enjoyed coming to the warehouse, sitting at my desk and pretending to be the CEO. I should have savored those precious moments but to my everlasting regret, I squandered them.

"We are so alike, you and I. Focused. Curious. Stubborn. But unlike me, you have an added layer of compassion that has made you a beautiful person. You care, Briana. I wish I'd had an ounce of your strength. Maybe I wouldn't have walked away from our family."

Briana blinked back tears as she imagined her father's face. Had there been tears in his eyes when he wrote this? Had his throat been heavy with emotion?

She swallowed through the thickness and continued. "Through the years I've had time to reflect. I see now that police work is the right profession for you. I never got to tell you this, but I'm glad you didn't let me talk you into taking over my business. You stood up for the path you wanted for your future. You've succeeded in ways I never did. And for that, I proudly call you daughter."

She paused. Hitched a breath.

"I only met Cami a few times, but I was touched that you named her after my mother Camilla. Proud that you loved her enough to raise her on your own. It gave me hope that although we were estranged, perhaps that dear child would be the bridge to us reconnecting again. You are going to have your hands full with that one. She is full of life, just as you were at her age.

"I left a picture of my mother with your mom. Maybe Cami would like to see and hear about her namesake."

Briana's lips trembled. How could the man who'd caused such pain end up so sweet?

*Because somewhere along the way he changed.*

"I'm also sorry that your relationship with your sisters suffered because of me. You all need each other. There is strength in knowing that you have sisters in your life. It's selfish of me to make this request, but I ask that you reconcile with them. I left the Sinclair building so you would all be in each other's lives. As the oldest child in the family, I'm sure you can appreciate my tactics. I only hope you can tuck away your animosity toward me and take the lead. You grasped early on what an honor it is to take responsibility for a family, but you were never meant to do it alone. I hope that the four of you share that task going forward.

"You are all strong, special women who will have wonderful lives. If you do life together, there will be many moments of joy and happiness. I don't want you to miss out on those memories. Embrace them. Not on my behalf, but your own.

"I love you, Briana. Raise your daughter to be strong, just like you, your mother and your sisters. Make this world a better place with your love and compassion. And know that you are always in my heart.

"Dad."

As she spoke the final word, Briana began to shake. Jax wrapped his arms around her, sharing his warmth and strength. She buried her face in his chest, her tears dampening his shirt. She couldn't stop the torrent of long overdue emotions. Knowing that Jax was here to protect her, she held on as if he was the only safe haven in a storm. Her storm. Which he was willing to share with her. That he'd stayed made her hug him more fiercely.

She didn't know how long she'd cried, but she finally moved from Jax's embrace, wiping her wet cheeks. She wasn't sure what she'd feel after reading the letter, but it was as though a missing piece had snapped back into place. Her father had made mistakes, but in the end, he'd taken responsibility for them and made amends. She'd hold onto that for the rest of her life.

Suddenly all the good memories she'd locked away flooded her mind. All the stored-up anger and hurt receded until she could breathe more easily.

"You okay?" Jax whispered against her hair.

"I will be." She glanced at the paper. "I just wish I hadn't held onto the hurt for so long. We might have been able to rebuild our relationship if I hadn't been so stubborn."

He gently brushed her bangs from her eyes. "You can't change the past, Brie. But after reading what your father poured out from his heart, maybe you can begin to heal."

And heal she would. Just like her sisters, she could accept her father's apology. Nicole was right, she had to stop blaming herself for the estrangement with her sisters. They'd all acted badly, but they were now trying to correct those mistakes. It was time to act like the older sister and make sure the peace between them continued. "It's a place to start."

For a long time, they sat watching the fire. Wrapped in the blanket and nestled in Jax's arms, she was able to accept that while her father wouldn't physically be in her future, he'd live on in her heart and she was good with that.

Jax kissed her temple. "What now?"

The kiss was innocent, unlike the one they'd shared in the forest. While that kiss had made her toes curl, this one promised comfort and stability. Strength and hope. Something she realized had been missing from her life.

Gathering up the letter and bracelet, she placed them back in the envelope and set it on the coffee table. "First, thank you for not running for the hills after seeing me get all emotional."

"Never gonna happen."

"Next, I tell my sisters that I read the letter. If they know, it will make our relationship deeper and maybe encourage Taylor to read hers."

"A solid plan."

"And last, I move on. It's time, Jax." She twisted

to face him. "You came back into my life for a reason, I'm sure of it."

"I never should have stayed away as long as I did."

She reached a hand out to place against his stubbled cheek. "If I learned anything since my sisters moved back to town, and especially after tonight, it's that we have to let go of the past. There's a big wonderful future waiting for us and I can't wait to embrace it."

His eyes blazed and he leaned forward—to kiss her?—when Cami wandered into the room, rubbing her eyes.

"Mommy, I had a bad dream."

Briana swung around and opened her arms. "Oh, sweetie, come here."

Cami ran to her and Briana scooped her daughter into her embrace, settling her on her lap. Jax remained by her side.

"There was a pumpkin with a scary face chasing me."

Briana kissed the top of her head, her lips brushing the soft hair that smelled like strawberry shampoo.

"I don't think I like Jacob's pumpkin anymore."

"It's okay," Briana crooned. "We're here and we won't let anything happen to you."

After Briana said the words, she went still. Is this what she wanted? For Jax to be part of her family? She'd had a huge emotional upheaval after reading the letter. She'd have to seriously consider what she wanted with Jax, a friendship or a family, before she broached the subject with him.

Briana could feel Cami relax in her arms. "I'll have to get her back to bed," she whispered to Jax.

He nodded. "I should probably take off."

She rose, hauling Cami up with her as her daughter wrapped her arms around Briana's neck and cuddled close. Jax took the blanket that had slipped from her shoulders, folded it and placed it on a cushion.

"Thanks, Jax."

He nodded then went to retrieve his jacket. Before he walked out the door, she remembered what he'd said after reading Cami's bedtime story.

"Wait. You said we need to talk."

He shoved his arms into the jacket sleeves. "It can wait."

"Are you sure?"

"Positive."

Still holding Cami, she joined him as he opened the door, wondering why she didn't believe him. He pulled the collar up around his ears before going out into the cold, blustery night. "I'll see you tomorrow."

The wind blew as Jax jogged to his truck. The moon winked in and out of scuttling clouds. She waited until the engine started and Jax pulled away from the curb before closing the door behind him, feeling oddly empty.

## *CHAPTER FOURTEEN*

AFTER PLAYING CHARADES at the community center yesterday, Alvin had called the crew to the resort today for another look around. All of them, except for Monroe, had forgone the lecture by the two women traveling with Heirloom Assets at the library this morning. So far, attending the Chamber of Commerce events hadn't generated any clues on who had stolen the tiara. Since Curt hadn't learned anything useful yesterday, Alvin wanted another chance to gather intel for Jax. The clock was ticking down. It was Thursday and the collection would be on its way back to LA on Saturday. Alvin didn't like the fact that he was letting Jax, and Golden, down.

"You said Monroe is already here?" Gandy asked as they strolled inside. Their footsteps echoed in the open lobby space.

"He and the missus came to view the collection after the lecture this morning." He pulled back his cuff to check his watch. "Told him to meet us here at 2:00 p.m."

At this point Curt walked in and joined them. "Got a plan?" he asked in way of greeting.

"Hold on until Monroe gets here."

Five minutes later Monroe left the multipurpose room with his wife on his arm. He said something to her and her face lit up. She hugged him and hurried off to the reception desk.

"What was that all about?" Gandy asked as Monroe came their way.

"Treated Lenore to a manicure so we can confab and figure out our next steps."

Alvin waved them over to a quiet area in the lobby.

"Here's the update," Monroe said. "I saw Mr. Franklin and Robert having a heated discussion when we arrived. Noticed them right off the bat when I parked the car. They were standing a few feet away from the main entrance. I got a text from you, pretty good timing, and stopped to read it. Lenore went inside and as I texted back, I observed the two."

Excitement coursed through Alvin. It was like the old days when he served on the PD. "What do you think they were up to?"

"Couldn't hear much, but their body language said it all. They were really having it out."

Curt smiled. "Yeah, that's not suspicious at all."

"There's more," Monroe went on. "Franklin was doing all the talking. At first, Robert's face got real pale and then the longer Franklin talked, Robert's face started to turn red. Franklin must have said something to set Robert off because he started raising his hands and got real animated."

Gandy scratched his head. "There's something up between the two of them."

"Once we went to see the display, the two of them were throwing dirty looks at each other. Tension was high even though they stayed on opposite sides of the room."

Alvin rubbed his chin. What was going on between those two? Then he asked Monroe, "Besides that, how was your time during the viewing of the collection?"

"The women working for Heirloom Assets are friendly enough. I started up a conversation about their lecture this morning. Their work is quite fascinating."

"What work?" Gandy asked.

"Researching and curating a collection like this one."

Gandy's eyes glazed over. "Not my thing."

"Let's get back on topic," Alvin said.

"The girls were very chatty, seemed like they were making up for the men not being too welcoming. Franklin stopped by one of the tables and stared at it for a long time."

Perplexed, Alvin asked, "To what end?"

"Beats me." Monroe shrugged. "I need to get back to Lenore. Good luck." As Monroe ambled off, Alvin, Gandy and Curt entered the multipurpose room. The crowd was thin. Alvin immediately noticed that Franklin wasn't there. His gaze landed on Robert, who was in a corner, texting.

"Let's spread out," he said under his breath, his eyes narrowing on the table covered in blue velvet closest to him. He jutted his chin toward the women. "Maybe engage with them. And Robert."

"I just said I'm not interested in the research stuff," Gandy complained.

"I got a plan, so keep them busy."

Curt pushed Gandy's shoulder. "Go talk to Robert. I got the girls."

As they dispersed, Alvin moved to the table closest to where the tiara pedestal had originally been located. He examined the rings and doodads that probably cost a pretty penny, but not enough to go to the trouble to steal. A single item, like the tiara, would be easier to remove from the room. But how?

He remembered Jax telling him that Robert had dropped his jacket by the table and kicked it away. Under the table? A good way to throw off suspicion if you'd taken something, like the tiara, in the dark. Place it under the table and come back to get it later.

Intrigued by this line of thought, Alvin pulled his phone from his pocket and pretended to start texting, then bumbling with the device, let it slip to the floor, uttering, "infernal thing" loud enough for anyone nearby to hear.

Getting down on one knee, he pushed the phone under the table. He made a show of searching for it, then lifted the hem of the velvet table covering. Underneath the table was a metal case. The same as the ones used to transfer the collection each night? Or store the tiara in, right under everyone's nose? If only he could reach it…

The other side of the velvet flipped up. Robert's face appeared. "Can I help you, sir?"

Busted.

"These old fingers just aren't the same with this darn arthritis. My phone fell plum out of my hand. I got to check in with my grandson. You know, heart issues and all."

Robert didn't move away. Since he was caught, Alvin decided to throw caution to the wind.

"What's that?" he asked, pointing to the case.

"We use it to store the collection when not on display."

Alvin tilted his head. The case would easily fit a tiara.

Robert pushed the case toward Alvin. "Go ahead, open it."

This was way too easy.

To Alvin's chagrin, the case was empty. He sent Robert a clueless look. "Pretty nice traveling case."

Robert's smile went cold when he asked, "Just trying to help your grandson, the officer? The officer who searched but did not find the tiara?"

"That's what family does." Alvin retrieved his phone and rose. So much for his theory. "Sorry for the inconvenience," he told Robert then rounded up his buddies. They filed out into the lobby in silence. No one spoke until they were outside of the building.

The wind had picked up, carrying a distinctive nip of autumn in the air.

"Robert got away from me," Gandy said. "I tried to waylay him, but he saw you snooping around and took off."

"Are you saying I wasn't very stealthy?"

"You were on the floor," Curt pointed out.

"Because I had a thought."

"Care to share?" Gandy asked.

"Not worth it now. I thought Robert might have found a hiding place, but it wouldn't have worked. The police would have searched the cases along with everything else."

Curt nodded. "So we're back to square one."

"I'd really hoped to have a theory to run by Jax." Alvin exhaled. "Let's get going."

On the way to the car, he asked, "You boys going to Oktoberfest tonight?" Maybe they'd have more luck there finding the pickpocketing culprit than they had here finding the tiara thief.

"I asked Betty to come with me," Gandy said with a grin.

He felt Curt nudge him with his elbow. "Told ya."

"Guess I didn't think I had it in me after all these years," Gandy said.

"You always were a ladies' man," Curt reminded him.

"Yeah, but after we all retired, I just figured on being alone."

"Does this mean you're going to bow out of the watch network?" He'd hate for his buddy to leave, but if it meant moving on, Alvin wouldn't say a thing.

"No way," Gandy said. "In fact, that's one of the many things Betty admires about me."

Curt threw his arm over Alvin's shoulder in camaraderie. "That leaves just the two of us representing the single guys."

"We don't have time for that," Alvin countered. "We're getting close, I can smell it."

To that, each man touched their nose with their right index finger.

THE SUN WAS starting to set. The evening had turned downright chilly even though the wind had tapered off. Briana was glad she'd dressed Cami in warm outer clothing as they walked into the park to meet their friends and family. They both sported knit hats and gloves, along with heavy jackets to ward against the cold snap.

The annual Oktoberfest festivities were winding down. There was still an air of excitement, especially from the beer hall. The scent of sausage, roasted chicken and sauerkraut drifted from the food tent. This weekend was the final hurrah before the folks of Golden had a week to slow down and get ready for Halloween. In lieu of family dinner, Briana's mother had suggested they all gather at the park to spend some outdoor time together.

As she approached, holding Cami's hand, she saw Nicole with Ethan and Holly. Standing beside them were Addie, Jacob and Nolan, along with her mother and Royce. That strange sense of loneliness she'd felt after Jax left her house last night struck her again. She'd tried not to dwell on it and had done a pretty good job of it, until now. Since there were only a few days left to apprehend the Oktoberfest pickpocket, Brady was hyper focused on catching the culprit. He'd recruited Jax to work at the park tonight, even though Brady would only be onsite until he and Roan went to transfer the collection. Which meant Briana would see Jax here. She kept scanning the crowd, looking for him, which was silly. It wasn't like they were attending the festival as a couple. Why was she making such a big deal out it?

Between reading her father's letter and sharing it with Jax, Briana found herself on shaky footing. She couldn't explain what was happening to her relationship with Jax and for a person who researched all the facts and dug deeply to understand the whys of things, she was feeling out of sorts.

"You made it," Addie said, her cheeks pink from the cold. Or from Nolan holding her hand? Could have easily been both.

Cami pulled from Briana's grasp and rushed over to see her friend Holly. It wasn't long before Jacob joined them. Then the Donovan family arrived with their five children and the energy level rose.

"Cami's been excited ever since I picked her up from the babysitter. No way could we miss meeting you."

"I like it when the kids are together," Nicole said,

her eyes on the children. "Holly really feels like a part of the family."

Briana studied her. "So, when are you going to make it official?"

Nicole's face went pink. "We aren't rushing things."

"But there's a possibility?" Addie prodded.

Nicole's grin said it all.

"I'll take that as more than a good chance," Briana said, ignoring a funny pinch in the vicinity of her heart. Was that envy?

"Where is Jax tonight?" her mother asked as she joined the group, leaving the men to visit.

"He'll be here to patrol the park."

Her mother frowned. "That's no fun."

Briana shrugged. "That's what happens when you have a small police department. Roan and Brady are taking care of the transfer."

"I had hoped he'd join our party."

Before Briana could answer, Taylor walked their way, a long plaid coat wrapped around her.

"We're all here," Briana's mother said, clearly basking in the joy of her family.

Before long the conversation shifted from the kids, to work, to what they were going to eat tonight. Briana kept her eyes moving over the crowd. She didn't find Jax, but she did notice Alvin. When he returned her gaze, he gave her the signal that he too was on duty.

"Hey." Addie nudged her. "Why are you so distracted?"

"This is the first time I've been at the park since the movie collection arrived. I guess I was hoping we would have apprehended the person who's been pickpocketing."

"You can't seriously be thinking about work," her mother scolded.

"Actually, with everything going on, it's about all I can focus on."

They still hadn't discovered who'd stolen the tiara and the reputation of Golden was on the line.

"Can't you put being an officer on hold for a few hours?"

At her mother's request, Briana nodded.

"Oh, I forgot to tell you," Addie said. "I had a business owner come into the fitness center asking about one of the offices for rent. We might have the second floor full soon."

As usual, the mention of the building their father had left them brought about different responses. Briana looked away.

"Are you okay?" Nicole asked.

She had to tell them sometime. Why not now, when there was a lot going on and they wouldn't spend much time analyzing Briana's feelings.

"I read Dad's letter."

All eyes zoomed to her. No one spoke, but it was clear they wanted details.

"I'd been trying to forget about it but came across it in a kitchen drawer last night."

"And?" Nicole queried.

"I'll be honest, what he had to say lifted a lot of

guilt from my shoulders." She met each of her sister's gazes before continuing. "I always thought you resented me because of the relationship I had with him. And then I took on too much responsibility for the family when I didn't need to. The way Dad spoke about all of us made me see that I was putting up walls. Made excuses to pull away from all of you." She intentionally met Taylor's gaze. "He loved us all in his own way. I think that was the part that really stood out to me."

Taylor nodded. Whenever she decided to read her letter would have to be when she was emotionally ready. Briana hadn't realized that until she found the letter in her hands and knew she had to find out what her father wanted her to know.

"I'm so happy you finally read it." Nicole grabbed her hand. "You could have called afterward so we could talk about it."

"Jax was with me, so I wasn't alone."

"You read it with Jax?" Addie asked, her eyes wide.

"He was at the house. I was emotional and…" She shrugged. What more could she say? If Jax hadn't been there, she might have chickened out altogether.

Her mother cupped her cheeks. "I'm glad he was with you."

"Me too," she said, truly meaning it. "Dad mentioned a picture of Grandma. You knew?"

"I did." With a smile, her mother brushed her

bangs from Briana's forehead. "It's waiting for you."

Thankfully, the children chose that moment to run around them. As much as Briana wanted her sisters to know she'd read the letter, she still had some healing to do.

"Let's eat," her mother suggested. As they were rounding up the group, Cami started running in the opposite direction.

"Wait," Briana called, only to see Jax scoop her daughter into his arms and walk their way.

"I caught a runner," he said, a twinkle in his blue eyes. His cheeks were red and the wind had tousled his dark hair.

She stared at him, happy to see him, her heart pounding as his eyes settled only on her. It occurred to her that she might have made a step forward by reading her dad's letter, but she still hadn't sorted out her new feelings for Jax.

"Are you okay?" he asked.

Shaking off her physical reaction to him, she said, "Thanks for wrangling Cami. I was afraid I'd have a chase on my hands."

"No chase, Mommy. I saw Jax and ran to him."

"She likes me," he said as if to rub it in.

"Everyone likes you," Briana countered.

A dark eyebrow rose. "Yeah? Including you?"

"Of course."

"More than just as a friend?"

She thought about the kiss in the woods. "What do you think?"

"Good. I was beginning to wonder if you'd admit it."

His words created a shiver. He saw the movement and winked at her.

Cami wiggled to be let down and soon she and Jax were at the tail end of the group.

"How long have you been here?" she asked.

"About an hour."

"Any leads?"

"No one has reported any unusual activity so it might be a quiet night."

"Can you get a bite to eat with us?"

"Sure. Brady is walking through the crowd so I can take five."

As they moved, his hand brushed hers. Her head jerked in his direction. He met her surprised gaze before intertwining his fingers in hers. At the slow smile spreading over his lips, her stomach did cartwheels.

He leaned down, close enough to her ear that she felt his breath and shivered again.

"I'd really like to kiss you right now."

"While you're on duty, Officer?"

"Yeah, not great timing."

"No, but it might make you feel better to know I'm thinking the same?"

He stopped.

She released his hand. "I'm not sure what's happening with us."

"We should really talk."

"I agree. How about when you finish your shift?"

He nodded. "I'd like that. If we don't run into any problems, that is."

"I'll be awake," she told him, knowing that whether she spoke to Jax tonight, tomorrow or the next day, he was going to keep her tossing and turning.

They moved ahead in the food line when a shout came from their right.

"I've got to go," Jax said, sprinting after the commotion taking place.

Roan stepped out of line and followed Jax.

Briana started to move, then realized she couldn't leave Cami behind. Thankfully Nicole took Cami's hand and told Briana, "Go."

"Thanks."

She took off and soon saw Brady running to the less busy outer rim of the park. As she grew closer, she noticed a figure ahead of the chief, veering off the path into a secluded woodsy area. The next thing she knew, Jax came around from a different angle and tackled the person. She and Roan arrived to find Jax yanking up a young man who looked no older than sixteen. The boy struggled while Jax held on.

"Mickey?" Brady asked as soon as he realized who the kid was.

The boy clamped his mouth shut.

"What are you doing?" Brady asked.

Briana's heart sank. Brady had started a program dear to his heart to keep at-risk boys from getting into trouble. She recognized Mickey as one of the boys Brady had taken under his wing.

When the boy refused to answer, an impressive pout on his lips, Brady's expression closed up. He glanced at Jax. "Take him to the station."

This got the boy's attention.

"Wait. I didn't do anything," Mickey insisted.

"Then how do you explain someone pointing you out as a pickpocket?"

Mickey's gaze shifted to his sneakers.

"Take him, Officer Walker."

"You can't take me," Mickey argued. "There's nothing on me."

"Maybe so, but I have an eyewitness who claims to have seen a young man about your shape and height stealing."

"It's a mistake. It wasn't me."

"Then be cooperative and tell me who the thief is."

The boy refused to speak.

Brady looked at Jax with a hard gaze. "Take him to the station."

"C'mon," Jax said, turning the boy in the direction of the park exit. Before leaving, he met Briana's gaze. She could tell he felt bad about who the culprit turned out to be.

Brady paced as he watched them go, running a hand through his hair.

"Are you okay, Chief?" she chanced asking.

"I can't believe this."

"Do you want to go to the station and handle this?" Roan asked. "Jax can do the transfer with me."

"No, I need time to cool down." His frustration was evident, but as Briana looked closer, she noted a distinct sadness in his eyes. "I never expected Mickey to be involved."

"There has to be a story," Briana said.

"One I most likely don't want to hear." He shook off his anger and said, "Let Jax handle the kid. I'll hear the details tomorrow."

Briana was at a loss. She'd never seen Brady this upset. She realized this was personal to him. Not only did Brady and the PD work together to protect Golden, they also needed to find out who took the tiara so that no one in Golden was blamed. Dealing with Mickey was adding another level to his stress.

"It's getting dark now, but would you two mind searching the area?"

"We can do that," Briana answered after meeting Roan's nod.

Their search didn't yield a wallet or any other missing valuables, and then it became too dark to complete the process.

"The man who shouted the alarm told me his wallet was gone. Mickey claims he doesn't have it, but that doesn't mean he didn't chuck it in the woods when he took off running. We'll need to come back tomorrow to finish the job," Roan said, hands on his hips. "Might as well get something to eat."

They returned to their families, who were happy

to have them in their midst. Since word had spread through the park like wildfire, they didn't have to explain the chase. When Briana took a seat, not hungry after what had just transpired, Cami ran over and climbed onto her lap.

"Did you catch the bad guy?"

"Jax did."

Cami rested her head on Briana's chest. "Good."

Briana hugged her daughter for a long time before Cami became animated again.

Her phone chimed. Briana pulled it from her pocket to find a text from Jax telling her they'd talk tomorrow. She tucked the phone away, on one hand disappointed, on the other relieved.

# *CHAPTER FIFTEEN*

THE NEXT MORNING, Jax stood at the kitchen window sipping a mug of freshly brewed coffee. The day was bright. Leaves were falling from branches more frequently now, making his grandfather's backyard a kaleidoscope of color. Once again, he wondered how he'd ever left Golden. Left Brie.

Yet at the same time the change had been good for him. He'd grown and matured while away from his hometown. It had been lonely at times, but he'd persevered. Proved to himself he could handle adversity. And then he'd been able to come home.

*But to what?*

Brie had her life, her daughter. His siblings were married and had kids, busy with their own lives. His mother was working with a matchmaking group on his behalf. He had a new career. He found he liked protecting Golden, more than he'd imagined. And while he should be content, he wanted… more.

Gramps shuffled into the kitchen, pouring himself a steaming cup and joining Jax to stare out the window.

After a sip he said, "Contemplating life?"

Jax grinned. "How'd you guess?"

"Stood here many a time pondering what I have, what I need."

For Jax it was the opposite. He didn't have what he wanted or needed.

"Saw you capture that kid last night. Is he the perp?"

Jax shook his head. "He wasn't forthcoming. At the station, he stuck by the story of wrong place, wrong time." Jax took a swallow of coffee. "Plus, he didn't have any physical evidence on him. While we might suspect he had a hand in events, we didn't have anything to hold him."

"How's Brady taking it."

"Like you'd expect. Apparently, Mickey has been a part of Brady's program to keep young men out of trouble. Sorta blindsided him."

"It's not easy when you put your time and energy into a project and it falls apart."

Jax turned his head. "You think the program failed?"

"No, the kid."

Gramp's attention went back to the window. Jax followed his grandfather's gaze to see a deer foraging in the far perimeter of the yard. A sound must have spooked it because its head reared up and it raced into the woods.

"Sometimes dealing with folks, gaining their trust, makes them skittish."

"Sounds like you speak from experience?"

Gramps shrugged. “Had a project or two when I was on the PD. Some were a success. Others weren’t.”

They went silent for a long moment.

“Heard you gave your mother the thumbs-up on the whole matchmaking thing. Gotta say, I never thought you’d fall for her tricks.”

“It was just easier than fighting about it.”

“You ask me, the entire notion is futile.”

Jax shifted, resting his hip against the counter to face his grandfather. “Oh, why is that?”

Gramps met his gaze. “What’s most important to you?”

“Keeping everyone I love safe.”

“Noble. Part of your DNA.”

“But?”

His grandfather pointed to the table with his mug. “Let’s sit.”

Jax had time before he needed to be at the station. And he was curious about the wisdom Gramps was about to lay on him.

After they took scats at opposite sides of the table, his grandfather spoke. “Before I met your grandmother, I wasn’t in a hurry to settle down. Thought I needed to live large, as you young people like to say.”

Jax’s lips quivered in amusement.

“But then I saw Mavis standing outside the general store with some of her friends and everything changed. Once I worked up the nerve to pursue her, the idea of giving up being single made a world of sense."

"Your point?"

"What's going on with you and Briana?"

Jax stared at his splayed hands on the worn tabletop. "I'm not sure."

"C'mon, you're a lot brighter than that."

Sighing, Jax decided to confide in his grandfather.

"Something changed when I came back to Golden. I'm…attracted to Brie. I think it's mutual, but we haven't fully analyzed it."

"Son, that's your first problem."

Jax sat back in his chair. "Pardon?"

His grandfather locked gazes with him. "You can't analyze love. You either love Brie or you don't."

"I do love Brie. We're best friends."

Gramps frowned at him.

"Our lives are different, Gramps. Could it even work?"

"Let me ask you something."

In a wary tone, Jax said, "Okay."

"You never got serious with a woman all the years you were away from Golden. Why do you think that is?"

Because he'd always been in love with Brie. Now, there was no denying that they were growing closer. The shifting feelings for his best friend were changing into something more profound and he found himself wanting to win her heart. He'd loved her since first grade when they shared a seat at the lunch table. He'd come back to Golden wanting to fall in love, to have a family, but he only had eyes for Brie.

The only way to find out what she was feeling was to lay it all on the line.

"Wow," he muttered under his breath.

Gramps chuckled. "Took you long enough."

"It's always been Brie."

"Sure has." Gramps shot Jax a smug smile. "Now go tell the girl how you feel."

THE MOOD IN the station was downcast. Briana sat at her desk, reading the report Jax had filed last night. There hadn't been an arrest. Brady was quiet, holed up in his office. And the worst thing was, they didn't have the pickpocket who'd been plaguing Oktoberfest or the person who had stolen the tiara. Not a stellar moment for the Golden PD.

Once Jax arrived she hoped to go with him to the resort to question the woman who'd worked at the reception desk the night the tiara disappeared. Jax was sure the security guard, Gil, had nothing to do with the theft. Nor did they suspect any of the Golden residents who'd been at the party that night. But Robert and Mr. Franklin still loomed large on the suspect list. They were all leaving tomorrow and if she and Jax didn't come up with answers, they might never solve the case.

She'd been working on another angle, checking more deeply into the finances of Franklin and Robert. Robert didn't have much to hide, there were no red flags in any of his accounts. But Franklin? Following his finances was like a twisty rabbit trail. The more Briana dug, the more dead ends she encountered.

The door to Brady's office opened. Briana went still as he marched in her direction.

"Did you call in the insurance company regarding the tiara?"

"I was waiting until you'd heard from Mr. Franklin."

"He hasn't called me about the matter." Brady frowned. "In fact, he's put me off every time I inquire about the insurance. Said the agent was going to call us."

She checked her log. "There's no record of them calling."

Brady placed his hands on his hips. "Go ahead and get them on the phone. They'll want the police report."

"On it."

She pulled up the information log stored on her computer that she'd created for the case and found the number Mr. Franklin had given the chief.

"Good morning," she said, then introduced herself as an officer of the Golden PD. "I'm calling about a claim filed this week by Heirloom Assets."

"Do you have a contact agent?" the woman on the other end asked.

"No, Mr. Franklin, with Heirloom Assets, called

you about the stolen tiara. I'm following up with the police report."

"Stolen tiara?" The woman sounded confused. "Hold on."

While Briana was on hold, Jax walked through the back door. After removing his sunglasses he met her gaze. As he crossed the room, she noticed something different in his eyes. She couldn't put her finger on what it was but responded with a twirling in her stomach. Her childhood friend had recently become so much more important in her life.

"Officer Connelly?"

Briana pulled her gaze from Jax and focused on the call.

"Yes, I'm here."

The agent gave his name, which Briana typed into the open document. "I'm afraid there's been a misunderstanding."

A warning clanged through Briana. "In what way?"

"I handle the policy for Heirloom Assets. Mr. Franklin put in a claim for stolen pieces from the movie collection, but this is the first I'm hearing of a tiara being stolen. It's not on the list."

How could that be? And why would Franklin lie? *Because he's involved.*

"You said stolen pieces?" Briana verified.

"Yes. Some smaller gold pieces."

This was news to Briana. No one had mentioned any missing pieces.

"Specifically?"

"Rings, I believe. Mr. Franklin said he'd send a detailed list later."

Of course he would.

"I'm sorry for the confusion," Briana quickly said. "We'll speak to Mr. Franklin immediately and get this straightened out. If you would, please don't call Mr. Franklin until we get back to you."

"Of course."

Curious, she called Heirloom Assets' main office and asked to speak to an administrator. When a woman answered, Briana identified herself and asked about the current insurance information.

"Which company?"

Surprise nearly made her speechless. "There is more than one policy?"

"Yes, general liability and a policy that protects specific items that we own."

"One policy doesn't cover both?"

"Mr. Franklin insisted on more than one policy."

Briana digested that information.

"Mr. Franklin says we can never have too much coverage."

Convenient. "Can I have the names, please?"

The woman listed off two more insurance companies, in addition to the one Briana had just called. She wrote the names down, asked for the contact info and thanked the woman on the other end.

Wanting to find out if Mr. Franklin had filed a claim for the stolen tiara with a different company, she called each one. One call went to voice mail. Briana left a brief message and asked for a call back. The next was an automated message, so she sent an email, following the same procedure.

Finished, Briana signed off her computer and jumped up from her seat. Jax was beside his desk rummaging through paperwork, so she grabbed his arm and tugged him to Brady's office. She knocked once then barged in.

"Franklin lied to the insurance company."

Brady's brows angled over his eyes.

"And get this. He has more than one policy."

"Does that matter?"

"Depends on how many claims he files."

Brady considered this as he crossed his arms over his chest. "What do you mean?"

"Having multiple policies doesn't mean you can file a claim for a particular item more than once. He filed a claim for pieces missing from the collection with one, but not specifically the missing tiara."

"Wait." Jax held up his hand. "What pieces?"

"That's what I asked." She explained that Franklin had notified another company of items from the collection being missing, items that hadn't been reported to the Golden PD.

Brady's eyes narrowed. "Unbelievable."

"I have calls in to the other companies to ask about the tiara. I'm waiting for a call back."

"I have a meeting," Brady said with a shake of his head, "but I want you two to head to the resort. Talk to Franklin and clear this up. Now."

"Ten-four," Briana responded, hurrying to her

desk to gather her tablet, which had the same info on it as her computer. She slipped it into a bag and followed Jax to the SUV.

"How did we miss this?" Jax asked as he started the engine and pulled out to Main Street.

"We didn't. Brady's been asking for the information all week. Franklin was never honest with him."

"So who do we suspect? Franklin or Robert?"

Briana twisted in her seat to face him. "Both?"

He grinned at her, making her heart squeeze. "I like the way you think."

And she also liked him, more than she should. She couldn't deny how deep her feelings for Jax were buried in her heart. When, exactly, had she fallen in love with him?

Now was not the time to figure it out.

They made good time and before she knew it, they were exiting the car and walking to the resort entrance at a fast clip. As soon as they were inside, they went directly to the multipurpose room. Neither Franklin nor Robert was there.

Briana approached Jill. "Where is Mr. Franklin?"

Jill placed an item from the collection on the blue velvet table covering. "He's leaving this morning."

"To go where?" Jax asked.

"Back to LA."

Briana glanced around the room. "Why not wait and return with all of you?"

By now Kat and the two security guards moved closer.

Jill started to look nervous. "I'm not sure, exactly." She sent her co-worker a frown.

"He said he needed to return early to take some of the collection with him," Kat answered.

"Some of the collection?" Briana asked. "Rings?"

Kat frowned. "That's right."

Briana exchanged glances with Jax. "Why didn't he tell us?"

"He said we had the last day of the tour under control," Jill said. "And also said something about the movie company needing an early peek at the pieces to be featured at the release party."

"And Robert?"

"He hasn't shown up yet." Alec pulled out his phone. "I can call him."

"No," Jax commanded. "We need to speak to him first."

Gil swallowed hard. "Is everything okay?"

"Just go about the viewing as usual," Briana said. She nodded to the guards. "Keep your positions."

"You know something," Alec said.

"Once we finish investigating, we'll come back," Jax said as he jerked his chin toward the door. Briana followed him into the lobby, heading straight for reception. When they stopped to ask the woman on duty questions, Briana noticed her name tag read Evie. The woman Jax had wanted to talk to.

"We're with the Golden PD," Briana said, identifying them. "Can you please tell us if Mr. Franklin is in his room?"

The woman hesitated. "I'm not sure—"

"This is a police investigation." When the woman didn't type the request into her computer, Jax added, "You're also part of the investigation."

Her eyes went wide. "What?"

"On the night the tiara was stolen, you were on duty?"

The woman paled. "I was."

"And you spent time talking to Gil, one of the security guards with Heirloom Assets."

"Yes. We were just flirting. It wasn't anything serious."

"Can you confirm he was with you when the commotion started in the multipurpose room?"

Flustered now, she stuttered, "Yes, I ah… I mean no. He was here but then he left."

"Did you see anyone else out here that should have been in the event room?"

"Um, I wasn't really paying… Oh, wait. Gil was concerned when he saw Robert near the dining area. He was afraid he might get into trouble by talking to me. But Robert didn't see him since he was talking to one of the party guests."

"Were you still on duty after the party ended?"

"I was here until the police let all the guests leave and the Heirloom Assets staff went to their rooms."

"Together?"

The woman closed her eyes, then after a moment, they opened. "Come to think of it, Robert left while the police were questioning the other staff."

Briana's stomach tightened. "Did he seem like himself?"

"I guess." She frowned. "He was adjusting his jacket. I said hello as he walked past but he ignored me and hurried to the guest wing."

Jax pointed to the computer screen. "We need to know about Franklin and Robert. Are they in their rooms?"

With nimble fingers, Evie pulled up the information. "Franklin checked out." She tapped the keys. "Robert is still here."

"Room number?" Briana asked.

"One ten."

"Let's go," Jax said.

Together they ran to the guest wing. As they drew closer to the room, Briana noticed the door was partially open. She met Jax's gaze. They both withdrew their service weapons as they approached the door. Hearing voices inside the room, Briana held up a closed fist to stop their progress.

"You aren't taking anything," Robert said, his voice tight.

Franklin's voice was smug when he said, "Unless you want the police to learn the truth, you'll hand it over."

"This was my plan, not yours."

"A very good one, but I'm afraid I've worked too hard over the years to not take advantage of your actions. This tour cost a fortune I don't have. No one has found the tiara, nor will they, which means once I get back to LA I'll complete the report to the insurance company and then sell it privately. I also stashed away a few smaller items from the tour to file an additional claim and add a future sale. Win, win."

"But the tiara is right here."

Briana locked gazes with Jax.

"Look, I've already got a buyer for the tiara, so we'll have plenty of money to share."

"I don't trust you," Robert said.

"Wise, since I hold the cards. I discovered you took the tiara, I can either turn you over to the police or give you a cut. It's up to you."

At the confession, Briana nodded to Jax. They moved in tandem to the door. She pushed it open and with her weapon raised, she shouted, "Freeze."

# *CHAPTER SIXTEEN*

JAX ENTERED THE ROOM, moving one way, while Brie moved the other. The surprise on both men's faces gave them the time they needed to establish control. But Franklin snapped out of it sooner than Robert and grabbed the tiara, sitting on the end of the bed, plain as day. He backed toward the sliding doors on the far side of the room, placing the tiara in a travel bag, and then withdrew his own gun.

Jax tightened his grip on the weapon. He didn't like the arrogant expression on Franklin's face, or the fact he was within reach of Brie. He couldn't snag her attention to motion for her to move away. Franklin must have noticed Jax's concern because he turned the gun on Brie and said, "Drop your weapons."

Brie didn't waver, making Jax even more nervous.

Franklin's smile was anything but humorous. "You can do as I ask or regret the consequences."

Jax slowly lowered his gun. When Brie realized that Franklin had her in his sights, she too lowered her gun.

"Drop it."

He did. Brie followed suit. The instant the gun left her fingers Franklin grabbed her and moved to the door. Jax thought his heart would stop beating.

"Pick up the bag," he hissed in her ear.

She did, her eyes never leaving Jax. She held her head high, but he could read the glimmer of fear in her eyes. How was he going to protect her without getting them hurt or worse?

His heart in his throat, he said, "Brie, you can't."

"It'll be okay," she assured him.

He took a step forward, but Franklin pushed the gun into Brie's side.

"We're going to leave now. Don't follow unless you want harm to come to your partner."

He dragged her to the door. Before she disappeared, he blurted, "Brie, I—" and then she was gone.

"YOUR PARTNER IS worried about you," Franklin mocked as he opened the wrought iron gate at the waist-high fence surrounding the patio and pushed her along the grassy side of the hotel toward the parking lot. "But ill advised. Now I have leverage."

She forced the moment of fear to pass. Briana's mind switched to thinking strategically like she'd been trained.

She was going to make sure he was wrong. Franklin was more concerned about her hold on the bag than he really was about hurting her. After all, he needed the tiara to carry out the sale and the insurance scam. If he didn't have access to his prize…

She hated seeing the alarmed expression on Jax's face when she left the room, hated not fighting Franklin, but she knew there would come a time Franklin would let his guard down. He was too focused on the tiara and thought he had the upper hand.

When they rounded the building to the parking lot, he pushed her to a sedan, fumbling with the key fob. This was her chance. The moment his grip eased on her arm, she twisted and swung the bag directly at the hand holding the firearm. It slipped from his grasp. Then she tossed the bag as hard as she could into the hedges bordering the parking lot. Franklin screeched and pushed her away to go after the bag. She followed, grabbing one arm to hold him back.

He struggled, and then another pair of hands grabbed him. Jax. Franklin went to the ground. Sirens sounded in the distance as Briana pulled out her handcuffs to subdue Franklin.

"Robert?" she asked Jax as she took a minute to catch her breath. He was in the process of kicking Franklin's gun out of reach.

"Cuffed him to the fence outside his room then called for backup."

Jax tugged Franklin up, the man twisting, turning and yelling. "Stop resisting."

Briana fished the bag out of the shrubs. When

Franklin finally realized he was caught, his shoulders slumped. Jax started to lead him to the SUV.

The chief's car skidded to a halt and Brady jumped out, Roan exiting the passenger seat. "Report."

"Franklin was trying to get away with the tiara," Jax told him. "He took Brie at gunpoint. She managed to subdue him before he could flee."

Brady's gaze moved to her. "Are you okay?"

"Fine, Chief."

SHE MAY SAY she was okay, but Jax noticed the slight tremor in her hand holding the bag with the tiara inside.

Jax leveled his gaze on Roan. "Room one ten. The real thief is cuffed to the patio railing."

Roan grinned. "On it."

"What went down?" Brady asked.

Jax went over the big picture until he could update the chief with step-by-step details.

Brady took ahold of Franklin. "What have you got to say for yourself?"

"Lawyer," Franklin spat, then went silent.

"That can be arranged."

As Brady dragged Franklin to his vehicle, Roan came out the front door of the resort, Robert in cuffs. The women from Heirloom Assets and the security guards followed, shock written on their faces.

Roan jerked his chin to the SUV. "You'll take him in."

"With pleasure," Jax answered.

After getting Robert secured in the back seat, Jax sent Brie a long glance.

"I'm okay," she insisted.

He opened his mouth to say more but she held up a hand. "Later."

Right. This wasn't the place to discuss his feelings for her. Or how his heart had nearly stopped beating when Franklin dragged her away.

Once back at the station, they were too busy to talk. There was processing to take care of, as well as questioning. Franklin didn't talk, but Robert freely answered any question asked. He'd admitted to stealing the tiara, explaining that he needed the money the tiara would bring to impress his current girlfriend. Not exactly a master heist, but instead it had been a spur-of-the-moment decision. One he clearly regretted.

He confessed that he'd been the one to start the fire in the kitchen to cause a distraction. Taking advantage of the confusion in the multipurpose room when the alarm sounded, he hurried to the tiara, lifted it, moved swiftly into the kitchen to hide it, then returned to the group still in chaos, with no one noticing his actions. On impulse he switched off the lights to further throw off the people in the room. Then he turned them back on, acting like he'd just happened to stumble onto the scene. Under the guise of going into the kitchen to ask the fire chief for a report, he retrieved the tiara while the team was focused on determining the origin of the fire. Before the officers got in there to execute a search, he took the tiara to his room.

If Franklin hadn't had his suspicions and confronted Robert, no one would have figured it out. At least that was Robert's reasoning. Jax would argue that they had been closing in on him and it would have been a matter of time before they picked him up anyway. And the way Robert quickly folded when confronted with the truth? The guy never would have held out in an interrogation.

They'd found the additional pieces of the collection in the bag with the tiara. Franklin fumed when faced with the truth, that they knew about his insurance scam. He wouldn't get an insurance payment or money from a private sale.

When things finally slowed down, Jax noticed that Brie had been busy at her desk for a while. He went over to see what she was working on.

She turned in her seat and rose, nearly bumping into him. He caught her by the shoulders to keep her from tumbling.

"Hold on there."

His grip tightened. *She's safe*, he assured himself, never wanting to find them in that situation again.

"Thanks." She brushed her bangs from her eyes. "I have new information."

Jax reluctantly let go and she headed to Brady's office.

"Come on." She motioned for Roan to join them.

They all walked into Brady's office. "I have an update."

Brady waved his hand. "Go ahead."

"I got a voice message and email from the additional companies Heirloom Assets uses. One received a request for a claim concerning the tiara. Franklin said he'd contact them when he returned to LA."

"And eventually sell it, like we heard him say in the hotel room," Jax concluded.

Brady nodded. "Before we were called to the resort for backup, I called a contact at the LAPD. Seems Franklin has come up on their radar."

"For fraud," Brie deduced.

Jax ran a hand over his chin. "He's done this before?"

"There was a string of small thefts of the consortium's property. Unbeknownst to Franklin, the insurance companies had discovered some discrepancies and were working with the police to uncover his actions," the chief said. "If it hadn't been for Robert, he most likely would have gone with the original scam of taking a few small items that wouldn't stand out. Somehow discovering Robert had the tiara was too much of a temptation."

"Now he'll pay for his actions," Roan said.

"Confirmed by LAPD," Brady added.

"The tiara and rings?" Brie asked.

"We'll hold onto them for the time being." Brady grinned. "Thanks for all your work."

"It was a group effort," Jax said.

"And now we can breathe easier knowing the people of Golden won't be suspects any longer." Brie smiled.

"Or you," Jax said, also smiling.

"Not that they ever were," Roan said.

Brie nodded. "True, but Franklin sure had us worried about what he'd do."

Jax thought about his grandfather. "Like the Golden Watch Network would have allowed him to get away with it." He smiled more. "I need to call Gramps and get him up to speed."

Brady shooed them from his office. The afternoon flew by and when it was time to leave, Jax walked out with Brie. When they were close to their personal vehicles, he pulled her into his arms.

"You scared the life out of me," he said.

"Why? I was doing my job."

"You just went with him."

She moved back a fraction to see his face. "Because I knew he'd mess up eventually. He couldn't hold the gun on me, worry about the bag and get into his car, all at the same time."

"But he could have hurt you."

"He didn't." She frowned at him. "I had it under control, Jax."

He couldn't stop the turmoil inside him when Franklin took off with her. "You didn't see the arrogance in Franklin's eyes."

"So what, you wanted us to switch places?"

"If it meant you were safe."

She stepped out of his embrace, her eyebrows

angling over her eyes. "You didn't think I could handle him, did you?"

He went silent.

"I'm a trained officer, just like you."

His tortured gaze met hers.

She crossed her arms over her chest. "Oh my gosh, you don't think I can take care of myself."

"I do but..."

"Either you do, or you don't, Jax."

"You always need to be responsible for everyone at the expense of yourself."

"Franklin blamed me. Blamed Golden. I had to prove him wrong." She dropped her arms. "I can take care of myself. I have since you left town and that's not going to change."

"But things are different now," he said. "We're different with each other." He paused for a moment then said what was in his heart. "I love you, Brie. I tried to tell you before Franklin took you out of that room."

Her eyes went wide.

"I realize that I've always loved you."

She placed a hand over her heart. "I... I love you too," she said in a hushed voice.

His heart squeezed tight at her confession. He'd hoped she felt the same way, but to hear her say so was everything to him.

"Then you can understand why I would have done anything to protect you."

She took a step back, the love shining in her eyes fading.

"We're equals, Jax. I would never question your skills, no matter how much I love you." Her voice broke. "You doubting my ability as an officer makes me question how we can move forward. And if I can't believe in us..."

She backed away. "I need to get Cami and go home."

Then she turned on her heel and walked away just like that night in the park all those years ago, taking his heart with her. Only this time, he wasn't sure if he'd recover from the pain.

"You look pretty, Mommy."

Briana stood in front of the full-length mirror in her bedroom, admiring the beautiful black lace dress her mother had dropped off a few days ago. Now that the case had been wrapped up and the movie collection was safely back in LA, Briana could concentrate on Cami and Halloween.

Her daughter loved her aqua-colored chiffon princess dress. She even had a sparkly tiara, significantly less valuable than the tiara Robert had stolen, but priceless in Cami's eyes. She twirled around the room while Briana fastened vintage pearl barrettes to keep her bangs from falling in her face.

"Are you ready?" she asked Cami, picking up the small black bag and heavy wool coat from her bed.

"Mommy, do you think Jax will be there? He never told me how he was going to dress up on Halloween."

"I don't know, sweetie. I haven't spoken to him."

Her chest squeezed tight. After their parting words in the PD parking lot, she figured they'd apologize and move on. At first, she couldn't bring herself to call him, not after her doubts took control. But she hadn't heard from him in a week. Brady had placed them on opposite shifts, so they missed each other at the station. And unsure of what to do, she hadn't sought him out.

It wasn't lost on her that she'd walked away from him, for a second time, after they'd poured their hearts out. Admitted they loved each other. Now what did she do? She'd fallen hard for Jax and had no clue where they stood.

"Do you think he'll be trick-or-treating?"

She had no idea what his plans were, and she hated disappointing her daughter. "I suppose we'll find out when we get there."

She got Cami into the booster seat and drove to Main Street, her nerves on edge. Parking behind a row of shops, she took her daughter's hand as they navigated the crowd to rendezvous with her sisters at the designated meeting location. Weaving between adults and children holding goody bags, she found the group, dressed up in costumes ranging from Jacob as a superhero, Holly as an explorer and her sisters, Nicole a pirate and Addie a queen. Ethan rocked a cowboy hat, with a red and black bandanna around his neck. Nolan wore a top hat and red clown nose. Even Tayor got in on the fun, dressed in a full-length ball gown.

"Auntie Taylor," Cami gasped. "You look bootiful!"

"What about me?" Addie asked.

"You're bootiful too."

Briana grinned when she joined them. "Apparently you're all beautiful while I get merely pretty."

"I'm unique," Nicole said with a laugh. "Didn't go for the princess vibe."

"Neither did I." Briana removed her coat. The night air was chilly and a steady wind whistled through the tree branches, but she couldn't resist showing off the gorgeous dress. It had been forever since she'd put on a fancy outfit.

"Where's Mom?" she asked, searching around them. "I wanted her to see my finished look."

"She's at the general store giving out goodies," Addie informed her as she handed Jacob his candy bag. "We'll end up there at the end."

And so they went, stopping at the shops along Main Street so the children could show off their costumes and receive candy and compliments in return. She still hadn't seen Jax, wondering if Brady had given him a shift since Roan was here with his family. It made sense. Brady always tried to work the schedule to keep families together whenever possible for special events.

In front of Sit A Spell, she ran into Alvin.

"You look very nice, Briana."

"Thank you, *Alvin*."

He smiled over her emphasis on his name. "Glad we settled that once and for all."

Alvin regarded her with a twinkle in his eyes

and she was glad she could do a small thing to make him happy.

She grinned, even though seeing him made her wonder about Jax. She knew she'd messed up when she walked away, letting her pride get the better of her. But not hearing from him had her worried that she'd crossed a line. And made her uncertain of what to do next.

"Run into my grandson yet?"

Her heart raced. "He's here?"

Alvin peered into the crowd. "Somewhere."

"Then I suppose I'll see him eventually."

With a cagey grin, Alvin tapped his nose with his right index finger before he wandered off to hang with his buddies.

She caught up with Cami, who was having a ball. Briana should be experiencing the same fun, but her feet hurt in the high-heeled pumps, she was getting cold and couldn't get her mind off Jax. If her actions ruined what she hoped they could have together, a life filled with love and happiness, she'd never forgive herself.

She'd just started to put one arm in the sleeve of her coat when Cami stopped her.

"No, Mommy. Grammy wants pictures."

"Of course she does."

With a sigh she followed the group, which included Roan, his wife, Faith, and children, to the general store. The group seemed to part just as they reached the building, Briana in the middle.

The lights were off inside.

"What's going on?" Briana asked. "I thought Mom was handing out candy?"

"Actually," Nicole said. "She's doing something better."

Suddenly, tiny twinkling white lights outlining the trees around the store lit up. She noticed a tall figure standing before the porch steps to the store, and her heart started to pound.

Her mother came out of nowhere, taking Briana's coat and said, "Someone would like to talk to you."

She glanced at those around her in surprise. "Is this real?"

"As real as it gets," Taylor said, pushing her forward.

She didn't feel the cold or her pinched toes as she walked to Jax. He was dressed in a boxy suit, a long black overcoat and fedora.

"Let me guess," she said, taking him in. "The Fed working the stolen antiquity case from *Riches in the Past*?"

"And you're the historian with the killer wardrobe."

She nodded, her throat tightening up.

"You look amazing," he said.

"You're not so shabby yourself."

He took hold of her cold hands, warming her with his touch. "I'm sorry for the other day. I was off base."

"And I was overly touchy." She swallowed hard. "So why haven't I heard from you?"

"I had some soul searching to do."

"Me too," she admitted.

"Oh yeah? What did you come up with?"

"I'm sorry for walking away from you. Again. It's a pattern I don't like, and I promise never to do it again." She bit her lip then said, "I overreacted. I know you'll always protect me. I love that about you, even if I do get prickly."

"Prickly." She heard the humor in his tone.

"Yeah, that sums it up."

His face turned serious. She didn't like the uncertainty on his handsome face.

"Instead of upsetting you, I should have told you that you're a strong woman. That I'm proud of you."

Her heart lifted and she grinned. "You still can."

His chuckle calmed her nerves.

"I have other plans."

"Oh?"

"I needed a few days to pull this together. I knew if I saw you, I'd have given it away." He squeezed her hands. "You know me better than anyone, Brie. You'd have read right off the bat that I was up to something and I wanted to surprise you."

"You certainly have. What's going on?"

Under the twinkling white lights, he got down on one knee, the grip on her hands tighter. She could barely breathe.

"Jax…?"

"A man should go to any length to win a woman's heart." He gazed up at her. "I love you, Brie. Always have. Always will. Our long friendship just makes this better."

Tears misted in her eyes. "I love you too, Jax. Maybe a little slower discovering the truth of my heart, but it's there all the same."

"Then what do you say? Should we make it official?"

When he reached into his coat pocket, her mouth dropped open. Had he gotten her a ring? Oh my. This was so fast, yet after all the years together, it felt so right.

He withdrew his hand and placed…a bag of potato chips in her palm. Just like he'd done all those years ago when they'd first met.

She burst out laughing. Of course he'd go this route. One thing was for sure, life with Jax would never be boring.

"Isn't this kind of sudden?" she quipped.

"Not when we've loved each other our entire lives."

She tugged him to stand up, cupped his face and soundly kissed him. When she heard her family cheering in the background, she broke away, grinning from ear to ear.

"We have an audience."

"Who were in on the entire plan."

Turning to face the people she most loved in the world, she saw the happy faces of Cami, her mother and Royce, her sisters, their children and the men they loved. Roan and his family and Alvin, too.

Music began to flow from somewhere. Cami popped up beside her, tugging on her sleeve. "Dance with Jax and me, Mommy."

Briana tossed the chip bag in Nicole's direction. The three held hands and danced to an upbeat song until Cami ran off to dance with the other children. Jax opened his arms, letting her choose if she would step into his embrace. She didn't hesitate, wanting to spend the rest of her life dancing with him.

Soon they were swaying to a love song, their friends and family joining in around them.

"Just so you know, I do have a real ring," Jax said as they drifted away from the others, "but I figure we can cross that bridge once we sit down and talk. Really talk, Brie. About everything. Like we did when we were kids. No holding back."

"I want that too." She blinked away the happy tears. "For right now, this is perfect. Just like you."

He pulled her into his arms and sealed their love with a kiss.

* * * * *

*For more great romances set in Golden by acclaimed author Tara Randel, visit www.Harlequin.com today!*